RAVEN BORN

Wings of Rebellion Book 1

BREE MOORE

Raven Born by Bree Moore

Published by Innate Ink Publishing

www.AuthorBreeMoore.com

© 2020 Bree Moore

Fourth Edition © 2025

Ebook ISBN: 978-0-9600087-3-5

Paperback ISBN: 978-0-9600087-5-9

PREQUEL NOVELLA

BOOK ONE

BOOK TWO

BOOK THREE

BONUS NOVELLA
BECCA + AVAAN

BONUS NOVELLA
IAN + KAMRI

BOOK FOUR

To Vall.

Without you, these characters, this book, and this entire series wouldn't exist.

CHAPTER ONE

HARPER

WINGED-WOMAN SIGHTED: EXPERTS ARGUE—SUCCUBUS OR WERE-EAGLE?

Harper squinted at the grainy black and white photograph on the cover of *Supernaturals Monthly*. It wasn't likely to be anyone she knew. The figure could have easily been photoshopped, or maybe it was a distant airplane at just the right angle.

"Miss??"

The cashier's voice startled Harper, and she nearly dropped everything in her arms.

Harper drew her hand back and resisted adding the magazine to the pile in her arms. Her brother, Quinn, would agree the photo was a fake. And gossip magazine wasn't a reliable source, even if the picture did turn out to be real.

She slid several cookie packages, two wrapped sandwiches, a bottle of Fanta, and a handful of jerky sticks across to the cashier, then snatched a Milky Way from the display by the counter and slapped it on the pile.

The cashier raised her penciled eyebrows and reached for the first item to ring up.

"Road trip?" she asked.

Harper nodded absently, her fingers lingering on a single lint-covered bill in her pocket while she watched the gas station windows.

The woman cleared her throat. "That'll be $13.07." She popped her gum.

Harper handed over the twenty. She needed to get more money somehow, but there weren't many job opportunities for someone like her anymore. People were too scared.

A sleek silver Camry pulled up outside, parking in a stall near the front. A man in a suit emerged from the driver side, auburn hair flashing in Harper's peripheral.

She tugged down on the ball cap covering her short-cropped hair as the woman behind the counter tried to grasp a bag for the items, but her false nails seemed to get in the way. She licked her fingers and tried again.

Harper breathed in through her nose, then out again slowly to calm her itch to run. The door chimed and the man stepped in. Harper's breathing hitched.

He passed behind her, moving toward the coolers lining the back wall. The cashier extended the bag and change. Harper snatched them up and pivoted toward the door.

"Have a nice day," the cashier said, snapping her gum.

A crash and a shriek came from the back of the station. Harper turned, seeing the contents of a display of canned tuna salad rolling on the tiled floor while the suited men pinned down a struggling girl with dirty blonde hair. Her eyes caught Harper's, pleading.

Harper gave a slight shrug and took several shuffling steps toward the door, wishing she could explain. She couldn't do anything to save her without getting caught.

The girl grimaced, and her eyes flared with determination. Her skin began to shift, to transform. Fur grew, her arms shrank and moved forward, sliding out of the cuffs the man had put on her.

He yelped in surprise—an amateur hunter if Harper ever saw one. The cashier snapped her gum and pulled the phone receiver off her wall, so calm she must have done this a hundred times.

A wolf with mottled gray fur squirmed out from beneath the auburn-haired man, snapping and snarling. He yelled and scrambled back.

"We have a 6-1-1. I repeat, a 6-1-1," The cashier's nasally voice announced. Stiffs would arrive any minute. That was Harper's cue.

The glass door swung shut as she released it, obscuring the chaos within.

Outside, Harper froze. There was a second man getting out of the car, slicked-back blond hair and sunglasses.

Act natural. She angled her head down, hat visor obscuring her face. Her stride lengthened as she passed the car. The blonde man dashed inside to help his partner. Harper stuffed down the urge to sprint. Halfway across the parking lot, she let out her breath.

Then came the sirens.

Stiffs.

Harper broke into a run, tightening her grip on the bag in her fist so it didn't bounce. Stiffs were always bad news. They'd infest the entire place, their detection equipment picking up all traces of paranormal presence. Including Harper's.

She veered toward a black truck, running around the back side, her fingers fumbling against the door latch before it gave way. She dove onto the dirty seat. A wave of fresh cigarette smoke wafted into her nose as she sucked air and slapped the dashboard. "Go, go!"

The beard-faced driver grabbed the stick and shifted, pulling out fast. The sirens wailed and he looked at Harper, his human ears finally picking up on the sound.

"Is that for you? I hope you have another cenote for me. What'd you do, steal that?" He nods at the bag clutched in her hand.

"Not exactly. Turn right." The truck halted at a stop sign. Harper could almost see the man's brain working. It was slow and painful to watch. The green lights flashed out the driver's side window. The driver noticed and squinted at her.

"Those ain't cops. You ain't one of them paranormal freaks, are you?"

Three cars pulled into the gas station, bearing the insignia of the S.T.F, or Supernatural Task Force. More would be coming. Their response time was reported as being three minutes or less in populated areas, and once they locked a target, their pursuit was relentless.

The driver grabbed his door handle, but Harper moved first.

She swung her fist, catching the side of his head in a hard right hook, putting more power behind the blow than she intended.

He slammed into the driver side window, cracking the glass. The truck sputtered and died, thrown out of gear as the clutch released.

The guy put a hand to his head in a daze. It came away red. His eyes widened. Harper leaned between his bulk and the wheel to open the driver side door, then shoved the stunned man out onto the road. Idiot never put on his seat belt.

Sliding into the now-vacant driver's seat, Harper started the car and shifted the truck into gear. Her foot jammed down on the gas and clutch. The truck jolted, then died.

Out the rearview she saw the task force swarming the gas station. Several looked her way. *Damn.* She rotated the key again. The truck rumbled to life.

"Yes!" Harper tore out of there with tires squealing, sweaty hands adjusting on the wheel. She pulled too wide into traffic and forced an oncoming car to swerve. They struck the median and spun out in Harper's rearview, hitting another oncoming car and blocking the path of pursuit.

"Take that, Stiffs!" She gave a whoop and stepped on the gas, relief and adrenaline flooding her system. She kept her hands clasped tightly to the wheel, stilling the tremors in her arms while she surveyed the damage in the rearview. No one would die, at least.

She couldn't believe she had pulled off a move like that in a truck. She did feel a little guilty about the guy who owned the truck. Her punch probably didn't cause permanent damage, but she had to be more careful. Incidents like that were what made paranormals illegal in the first place.

Harper's victory was short-lived. From the corner of her eye, a green light flashed on the dashboard. The Stiff insignia. She cursed. Because the truck was old, she hadn't bothered checking for the call button. They were only installed in newer vehicles, or so she assumed. And this guy had been willing enough to give a hitchhiker a ride, as long as he got paid. He hadn't seemed like the paranoid type.

Harper pushed the button again, hoping it might turn the signal off, but no such luck. Likely it wouldn't turn off until the Supernatural Task Force answered the panic signal.

"6-1-1, describe what you see." The call came through the dashboard, like one of those roadside assistance features.

Harper cleared her throat. Should she answer and say everything was fine? That she had hit the button on accident?

"Sir?"

Damn it. They were expecting a man. It made sense; a man owned this truck after all. Harper stayed silent, focusing on the road. Might as well get as far as she could.

"Sir, if you can hear me, help is on the way. Stay where you are."

Like hell.

The truck was being tracked. She would get caught. Getting caught meant her current mission would fail, and her butt would get sacked into a Naturalization camp. And that was the last place she wanted to end up.

Harper's stomach pinched, more out of hunger than fear, but the fear was definitely there. She couldn't think with an empty stomach. She rummaged through the bag on the passenger seat, grabbing a sandwich and unwrapping it.

Chewing, she washed down mouthfuls with the crisp citrus drink. Her body relaxed as the food hit her stomach. She opened a cookie package with her teeth.

Stomach satisfied, her mind moved on to tackle the problem at hand.

Once the Stiffs got a handle on that werewolf at the gas station, they would be after her in a second. How far could she get on one tank of gas? There was no way she could outpace their cars without starting a high-speed chase, and they would catch her for sure.

Unless she flew.

Woods surrounded the road on both sides. She didn't have the lung stamina to fly above the clouds for long, but they could cover her long enough for her to get out of reach.

Harper veered to the shoulder and parked, truck idling while she took inventory of the truck. She needed a map. Nothing in the glove compartment.

Unbuckling, she checked the space behind the seat. Nothing. She frowned, brushing uneven bangs from her eyes, then leaned over the passenger side again, feeling underneath.

There, tucked under the seat, her fingers found the hard edge of a vinyl cover. Two tugs and it slid out. She grinned at the warped and dusty maroon plastic before throwing it open against the wheel.

A book of maps spread out before her. Its surface, wrinkled and yellowed with brown water stains and dirt, showed a map of Oregon. Exactly what she needed.

Harper's finger darted along the yellow highway line marked 97 to where it connected with highway 20. She pulled a scrap of paper from her back pocket. The words "Eastern Oregon Youth Correctional Facility" scrawled above an address and several lines of directions.

The facility didn't exist; she already knew that. She knew it from the moment they told her that her brother had been sent there for "minor infractions of violence." Someone was covering up.

She had never understood why they didn't drag her off at the same time, but she'd always be grateful. It gave her time to formulate her escape from the foster system, and she'd been running ever since.

Three years on the streets. Three years looking for her brother. Harper's latest lead would take her to him. It had to. Anticipation buzzed in her bones. That twitchy Salem vampire better not have faked her, not for the price she paid him to give her directions to the secret location of the nearest paranormal Naturalization facility.

Harper rubbed the pinprick marks on her wrist. The spot still felt sore, though the fatigue of losing a significant amount of blood had faded days ago. *The things I do for you, Quinn.*

She took a final bite of the cookie and chewed furiously, then rolled the last sandwich up as tight as she could and shoved it in her hoodie pocket, briefly mourning the loss of the other items. She couldn't take them with her, not if she wanted to go fast.

Harper shut the truck off and jumped out onto the side of the road. Sure enough, sirens sounded behind her. She had to get into the sky.

There were cars on the road, but they were moving fast. By the time the Stiffs got here, there wouldn't be any witnesses to tell them where she went. Hopefully.

She gave in to the burn between her shoulder blades, breathing deeply when the familiar fire consumed her back and her black feathered wings flared. Cars honked. Tires skidded.

Harper pumped her wings, lifting slightly, then coming back down and running a few steps before leaping off the ground.

Air rushed past her face as she beat against the pull of gravity and thrust up past the trees and toward the clouds. Sirens and flashing green lights sped down the road. They were still two miles away, but no doubt they could see her. Time to hide.

Wings and lungs burning, Harper soared up as fast as she could, flying faster than any bird, faster than a plane could take off. It wasn't sustainable, but she only had to hold it for a moment longer to get up to those low-hanging clouds.

Harper heard a twang and glanced down in time to see a net gun in the hands of two Stiffs. How did they get there so fast?

She dodged to the left. The net whistled past, the edge flicking her right wingtip. She wobbled and corrected her flight. The clouds were only a couple hundred feet away. If they couldn't see her, they couldn't hit her.

Another twang. Harper closed her eyes and strained her wings, everything on fire, air pushing past her face.

It was a perfect shot. She had no time to dodge and just enough time to wonder how bad it would hurt to hit the pavement as it rushed toward her.

CHAPTER TWO

TYSON

Tyson rubbed his eyes against the brightness of the LED screen as he read the text message, sitting up on his bed in the dark bedroom. It was after 1:00 a.m., and Dr. Hartford had texted him.

Tom. He said to call him Tom, but Tyson was still building the habit. He blinked at the text message. It was significant, but he couldn't quite wrap his head around why.

New resident coming in.

His thumb hovered over the keys to type a reply, when another text blinked in below the first.

I'm headed to Chicago. Batter up!

Crap.

Tyson ran his hand through his hair. His mentor, Dr. Thomas Hartford, was presenting at a seminar in Chicago. That meant the only paranormal counselor available to check in this new resident was Tyson.

Tyson swiped across the screen. *When?* He asked.

Any minute. Tom responded.

I have a two-hour drive. I'll get there as soon as I can.

Call Violet. Came the swift reply.

No. There had to be another way into the camp beside relying on that...that...*witch.*

Tyson stood, leaving his phone on the bed while he paced. The policies that governed the Naturalization camp he worked at required that a certified human counselor be in place when a new resident was brought in.

Tyson had done check-ins before, but never without Tom. Usually, Tyson had weekends off so he could afford to live close to Nana. His grandmother didn't have anyone else. He was paying the price for that now.

Tyson let out an exasperated half-growl and lunged for his phone. He dialed Violet's number.

"Miller? What a surprise. Did Tom get a hold of you?"

"Yes," Tyson snapped, grimacing at the knowing gloat in Violet's voice.

"And what can I do for you?"

Tyson clenched his teeth, sucking air in and blowing it out slowly. "Get a 209c permit and meet me at my place in half an hour."

"A portal? Well, imagine that. The human needs me to do magic for him."

"Don't be condescending, Violet. It's not flattering."

"It's just that I didn't expect a purist like you to ever need the services of a witch like me. A portal is a big deal, Miller. A 209c is no small bit of paperwork."

Tyson ground his teeth at her simpering. "There's a time and place. They wouldn't have licenses for this sort of thing otherwise." He rubbed a hand along his jaw, trying to convince the muscles to relax.

"Half an hour, then."

He cut the call off before she could, then tossed the phone back on his bed.

Not all witches were as obnoxious as Violet, he reminded himself. He liked plenty of them. But Violet had a special talent for getting on his nerves, and she was in a unique position to give him a hard time right now.

All that would change in a couple weeks if Tyson could pull his final review off. He was up for promotion to become a full partner with Dr. Hartford.

He shook himself and gathered some clean clothes from the dresser, then headed to the bathroom to freshen up. He still felt groggy, but the adrenaline spike was working to clear his head.

By the time he got back to his room, he felt ready for anything. And it was a good thing, too. Any minute now, a portal would open up and take him halfway across the state in a blink.

Tyson zipped up his backpack, put his phone in a side pocket and stood with it over one shoulder, watching the darkness.

"*Tyson.*"

The whisper traveled down Tyson's back. He shivered at the breathy, ice-cold touch. A Cheshire smile glowed in the darkness.

"Cut it out, Violet." He swallowed against the fear, smoothing a hand down the back of his neck to rid it of the prickling sensation.

"*Tyson.*"

The voice again. Ice trailed down his arm. He jerked it away.

"Seriously?"

"Aw, can't we have a little fun?" A shadow emerged, silhouetted by the window behind it. The figure's chilly laugh echoed in the room. With the sound of two fingers snapping, a glowing, silvery-blue oval opened up in the air, and a woman stepped through.

"Taxi's here," she said, smirking at him. There wasn't anyone in the world he wished to see in his bedroom this time of night *less* than Violet Petrov, coven leader at Camp Silver Lake and his coworker.

"Har, har," Tyson replied, adjusting his backpack strap on his shoulder. "Let's just get this part over with. There's a new resident that needs me at camp."

"You better get used to the midnight calls, Miller. Tom's not going to be around forever. You could start by moving closer."

"I will, once I'm promoted." *And maybe then you'll give me some respect.*

"You know my signature of approval is needed to get there. You're not doing much to earn it right now." Violet dangled the leverage over his head without a trace of shame.

Tyson grimaced, flexing his fingers. He knew she wanted him to bow and scrape, and if he wanted that promotion, he had to do it. Never mind that he was the human here. "Thanks for the portal."

"My pleasure." Violet's grin widened, not so unlike the ghostly grin from before. "Step right up, my human friend."

She gestured at the portal like a model from one of those old TV game shows.

Tyson took a deep breath and let it out slowly. His stomach rolled at the thought of stepping through and having his insides all jumbled up in another dimension before getting deposited at their destination. Convenience or not, he hated traveling by magic.

Tyson's feet carried him forward until the tingling energy of the portal latched onto his foot, disintegrating it before his eyes.

He hated this part. He swallowed and took another step, letting the light swallow him whole.

The witches he'd talked to swore no one was supposed to feel anything. To Tyson, it felt like a thousand needles pricking every fiber of his being.

The ethereal winds of space and time blew him to bits and carried him across the universe and back again, throwing him together haphazardly at the end until he landed, barely catching himself on his hands and knees on the other side of a twin portal in another place.

For a moment, Tyson feared Violet had taken him into the middle of some ritual where he would be sacrificed and his entrails torn out and read like tea leaves.

Ridiculous. That kind of magic was banned years ago. A licensed witch wouldn't practice anything so dark.

He shook the paranoia off like a wet dog, scooting on all fours away from the portal so he wouldn't get drawn back in. His knees and hands stayed locked to the ground. Tyson didn't care how ridiculous it looked, he needed to remember that earth existed, that *he* existed.

A slight sucking sound behind him indicated Violet had come through, and the blue light of the portal disappeared.

"It's a shame I have to take it down. A permanent portal to your home would save you so much on gas, not to mention avoiding an interaction with the rogues."

Avoiding the wild group of paranormals that roamed the forest surrounding the lodge was a definite benefit, but Tyson wasn't about to admit that to Violet. He rubbed his chest, feeling like he was missing something, but his mind was still spinning from the transition and he couldn't figure out what it might be. All of his essential parts still seemed intact, at least.

Violet stepped around Tyson and grabbed a folder off the desk, dropping it so it landed between his hands. She crossed her arms and gestured with one hand at the folder. "We don't have much, as you can see."

Tyson sat back on his feet, still kneeling on the floor, and opened the folder eagerly. This part always excited him, meeting the new residents. He read as he stood upright.

Name: unknown.

Age: unknown.

Gender: female

Lineage: appears Native American.

Paranormal type: shifter, bird, Raven or Crow?

Abilities: flight, others unknown

Tyson lingered on the details they had about her pickup and what they found on the scene, then flipped the page over only to find more blank pages.

"Thank you, I guess."

Violet shrugged. "She's a hard one. You'll have your work cut out for you."

"I've had difficult cases before."

"I've unspelled the door for you. She's waiting inside. I'll be in my studio. However, if you want that promotion, you won't even *think* about needing me. I'm in the middle of a crucially important spell process." She walked past him down the hallway toward the stairs.

As always. Tyson scanned the file again, shaking his head at the lack of information. It was like Violet wanted him to fail. He could do this, though. His schooling and mentoring under Tom had prepared him for this. He had done it several times already, just not in the middle of the night and not without Tom to consult with.

Tyson turned the door handle in front of him and entered the room.

There she was. Sitting on a chair sideways with a hood up over her head, eyes staring out the room's only window into the darkness. *Could she see in the dark?*

Tyson took a deep breath, calming the slight tremor in his hands. Just nerves, he told himself. "It's locked and warded. You won't get far that way."

She twisted. Her brown eyes hardened their gaze, narrowing slightly. She crossed her arms and slumped back in her seat.

He took note of her posture. Completely closed off. Nearly everyone started out this way. Seeing that change was one of the most satisfying parts of his job.

"I'm Tyson Miller, your camp counselor. Welcome to Camp Silver Lake."

His introduction had minimal effects. She blinked once, then looked out the window again.

"What name do you prefer?" He was prepared to get a fake name. An alias. A lot of the residents had those.

She pursed her lips and rolled her eyes toward the ceiling. He felt like chuckling but suppressed the urge. If she only knew how predictable she was being. He took a chair opposite the shifter and set the folder and pen on the desk.

Intertwining his fingers, he took in her disheveled, dirty appearance; the ragged, short-cropped hair, her worn-out sneakers and jeans, her broken and chewed fingernails. She had a naturally pretty face, except for the scowl she wore whenever she glanced his way.

She had been on the road for a while by all appearances, but why had she come out of hiding? Tyson jotted a few things down on a lined sheet of paper, then tapped his pen while he thought about where to begin.

If only the official police report was in. The folder didn't have more than a statement from the S.T.F. team that picked her up. The full report would come in tomorrow, and possibly have her name.

Meanwhile, Tyson had to parse information from her like an interrogator. He could start somewhere less obvious, though, and work his way forward to what happened when they caught her.

"Where were you when the Paranormal Naturalization law was passed?"

She blinked rapidly at the question. "Why do you want to know that?"

Tyson put his hands in his pockets and leaned back in his chair. Best to play it casual with her. She was used to people demanding answers. "Curiosity."

She glanced to her left, then examined her fingernails. "Foster home."

Unsurprising, given her lack of trust. "Why did you leave?"

"Who says I left?" she shot back.

"You have all the marks of a runaway. Did they discover what you are?"

"No." She smirked. "They never caught me. I aged out. I've been on the run from *your* people." Her voice dripped with disdain.

"Then someone saw *something*," Tyson emphasized.

She bristled.

It wasn't usually wise to irritate a sleep-deprived, possibly starving and frightened paranormal being, but he was tired and didn't want to dance around getting answers.

It was nearly 2:00 a.m., but these check-ins couldn't wait. First, it was part of the law that allowed them to keep a program like this running.

Second, the residents needed some orientation before they got settled—someone to welcome them to camp, help them understand what would happen.

Except Tyson wasn't doing a very good job of that. Sleep deprivation or not, she needed to know someone was her friend.

He smiled, and the shifter squirmed, as if that simple gesture made her more uncomfortable than anything he had done or said so far.

"Yeah, okay, someone saw something," she said. "I wanted to stretch and chose the wrong moment, but you know what? I made it seventeen years without an incident. *Seventeen years.* You guys are so oblivious, you make it easy."

"To evade the law." He raised his eyebrows.

She showed no guilt, just pursed her lips again as if upset she had shared as much as she had. It wasn't lost on Tyson that she lumped him in with the people who caught her. She would see it that way at first—her against them. There were more sides to this than she presumed.

Tyson refocused on the numbers she gave him. Extrapolating from the date Naturalization laws were passed and her comment about how long she had been hiding her abilities gave away her age. Not much, but it was progress. He filled in *Age: 20* on the form. Only a couple years younger than him.

"What happened?"

She rolled her shoulders back. "That got your guys on my trail? Or that got me caught?"

Tyson lifted his hand, gesturing for her to speak, and waited. He wanted to hear whatever she wanted to share. Silence could sometimes be more effective than words.

"Isn't it in there?" Her jaw jutted out, gesturing toward the file.

"I'd like to hear it from you."

She bristled. "Why?" Her defensiveness seemed like a cover for embarrassment.

Because I want to help you. Tyson cleared his throat. "Nothing you say will make me think poorly of you. I've heard it all." Or near enough, especially with Tom's stories from ten years on the job. Tyson had nothing on him in comparison, but he'd still heard plenty.

She slouched in her chair. "The Stiffs grabbed a werewolf at the gas station, and my ride freaked. Stiffs saw me sack the driver. The only way out was to fly." She stared at her hands, fingers rubbing against each other.

Tyson sensed a tone of failure in her voice, and the disappointment in her expression was palpable.

"Were you supposed to meet someone?"

Her jaw clenched, and her chin tilted away from him. So there *was* someone else.

"I could get a message to them, if you let me know where to send it. What do you want it to say?" Tyson grabbed a pad of paper and set it on his knee, clicking his pen open again.

The shifter chuckled. "You really think I would fall for that? Allow you to deliver a note in confidence, only to have them—if there was a them—captured and brought here, same as me? You're insane."

Tyson smiled in spite of himself. She was sharp. He tossed the pad of paper and pen back on the desk. "You'd be surprised how often it works. Having friends and family with you can make the transition to Naturalization easier."

"Why do you care so much about making my *'transition'* easier?" she snapped. "I'm just a case number to you."

"No, you're much more than that." He softened his voice and looked directly at her. She adjusted her position, clearly uncomfortable. "You have a chance at a normal, productive life. Does that mean anything to you?"

"I can't live a 'normal' life. I wasn't ever meant to." She punctuated each word with conviction.

Her words sank their teeth into Tyson's brain. He'd never heard a paranormal phrase it that way before. Most of them voiced doubt and fear about the Naturalization process. He knew how to handle that. This was something different altogether.

"Why do you feel that way?" His pen hovered over the page, fingers twitching with eagerness.

She scoffed. "All you want is to fit me into your human box. Get me as close as possible to your ideal. Take away everything that makes me what I am. Have you considered that I can't be squeezed into your definition of a being that's worth existing? I don't need a camp to reform me. I need society to accept that some of us are different, and then maybe we could find a way to coexist."

Interesting. He breathed in and sighed, considering what she had said. He'd heard this position before, mostly by liberals protesting outside government buildings with angrily-worded posters. Coming from someone sitting in front of him, someone who didn't want the help he had to offer...He reached to his left and adjusted the picture frame there. It was the only thing in this borrowed office that was his. Everything else belonged to

Dr. Hartford. Tom. Tyson could wish his mentor was here right now all he wanted, but it wouldn't help him get that promotion. He had to do this on his own.

He forced himself to stop tapping his pen on the desk. The last thing he needed was for the new resident to pick up on his anxiety and use it against him. What would Tom say if he were there? *When a session steers in a direction I don't want it to, I reset it. Remember, you're in control.* Now seemed like a good time for that.

Tyson set down the pen and closed her file, then clasped his hands in his lap. "We have another bird shifter right now. You'll meet him tomorrow. You can't miss him." If anyone could break this shifter's rock-hard exterior, it was Fletcher.

He gave her an encouraging smile, initially wasted since she wasn't looking at him. The sensation that he was missing something passed through his mind again, but he dismissed it to focus on the situation in front of him.

Her head slowly turned, her eyes piercing his. "I don't need counseling. And I don't need friends."

Tyson's smile faded. "What do you need? We're here to help." He swallowed against the tension mounting in the air and started the breathing pattern from his training to keep his own emotions calm.

"What I need is to get out of here," she snarled, standing suddenly.

Her hands curled into fists as she advanced toward Tyson. There was a crackling sound, like a spinal adjustment, and feathers rustled as her wings extended from her shoulders, filling the room.

Tyson dropped his pen and slapped the panic button under the desk. Squiggly green characters spread through the room from the button under his hand. They crawled across his skin, tingling as they immobilized him, and he suddenly realized what was missing.

His lanyard.

He groaned internally. It was sitting on his bathroom counter. He'd been in such a rush to change, he'd forgotten to put it on.

The shifter's eyes widened at the sigils, making it clear she had never seen magic like this before. Just like Tyson, she stood frozen mid-step.

They could breathe but not move. They stared at each other.

The door behind Tyson opened and Violet, James, and Lilith stepped inside. The camp's resident witches. Well, and warlock. The lanyards around their necks, like the one Tyson had incidentally left home, were spelled to keep the sigils' activation at bay. James pulled out a piece of chalk and drew on the carpeted floor around Tyson. The moment he closed the circle, the spell lifted, allowing Tyson to move.

Tyson wiggled his fingers and toes, just to be sure nothing funny had happened, then nodded to the magic-users.

"Thanks." There were times, albeit reluctantly, that he had to admit magic was useful. Twice in one night should please Violet to no end, except her scowl indicated she was anything but pleased.

"Where's your lanyard?" Violet hissed, crossing her arms.

"I left it home."

James stepped in between them. "I would expect this from an intern in the early months, not someone up for promotion. It's sloppy, Tyson."

A massive lump lingered in Tyson's throat as he glanced between the three of them. He hadn't maintained a perfect record the past two years only to lose his chance at promotion over this stupid mistake. He straightened.

"It's never happened before and it won't happen again. You know that."

They exchanged looks.

Tyson cleared his throat. "Look, I think she was with someone, or looking for someone. If you can get her to fill out this questionnaire before I see her again on Monday, that would help. I can find out who she was looking for and maybe we can get a team to bring them in." He pulled open a drawer and slid a paper out, putting it on the desk. No one reached for it.

"Why did she attack you, Tyson? Two years and only one other incident, and that vampire was near-starved and raving mad." James still had his arms crossed and he looked pissed, probably about being woken up.

"She said she didn't want help, she wanted to get out of here. Then she attacked. Our conversation went as well as expected before that." There was nothing Tyson could do about Violet's dislike, but the turn this case had taken might have given James enough of a reason to withdraw his approval of Tyson's promotion. He needed four signatures to become Tom's partner. This shifter wouldn't ruin it. Whether she wanted his help or not, she would get it.

"I'll call Tom. He might have some insight into how to handle her. You can spend your night here thinking of a way to track down her friend," James said.

"Take it easy. I don't think Tyson did anything to cause this." Lilith smiled at Tyson, a smile he returned gratefully.

"There isn't any need to bother Tom over this," Tyson insisted. "I'll call him when I need his advice. For now, I'd like to go home and sleep."

Violet choked on her laughter. Was she drunk or something? "Is someone going to tell him?"

"What?"

"You can't leave camp without your lanyard." Violet's voice was suddenly hard as stone, almost like she had changed personalities.

Tyson's mouth dropped open. "You got me here without it. Open another portal."

She jabbed a finger in his face. "There's a twenty-four-hour restriction on raising portals after a license is issued, except when "a life or lives are endangered" or some other legal nonsense. You know they don't want us popping in and out all over the place."

It was a strict interpretation of the law, and based on the vengeful look on Violet's face, payback for Tyson's ordering her around earlier.

James stood up from the floor, dusting off his hands and sliding the chalk into his pocket. He adjusted his glasses. "Violet is correct. Additionally, the spells out and the spells in have different requirements."

"But they're your spells!" Tyson sputtered. "Can't you just...lift them for a moment?"

"Lift them?" Violet's tone became murderous. "I'm still patching holes from where that idiot flew through two months ago. Lifting it 'for a moment,' as you so loosely put it, would mean months of re-writing sigils and an alarmingly high potential for occupants to escape. Do you want to be responsible for that?"

Tyson shook his head.

Violet made a disgusted sound and stormed from the room. James watched her go, then looked back at Tyson, his eyebrows raised. "That won't win you any favors."

Lilith spoke. "It would be simpler to make you a new lanyard. James, would you start that? I'll get our newest resident unfrozen and settled in."

Tyson's gaze darted from James to Lilith. "How long will that take?"

"A few days. The spell has to cure," Lilith replied.

"I'll see to it." James straightened his vest, leaving chalk fingerprints on its pinstripe surface, and nodded to them both before leaving.

Tyson moaned, putting his head in his hands. So much for a quiet weekend.

"Don't be upset. The universe must have a use for you," Lilith said.

Universe be damned.

Lilith circled the immobilized bird shifter, eyeing her. "Magnificient, isn't she?"

Tyson's hand rubbed over his mouth. "It's a little invasive to ogle her like that while she's frozen, don't you think?"

Lilith tilted her head and smiled again, eyes glittering with something like wonder. Tyson might have considered her a friend if it weren't for her habits of manipulating the properties of space, time, and fate with crystals and chalk dust.

Blasted witches and their blasted magic. If Tyson worked at any normal camp, he could have called a Ryde and been home before morning.

"I'll get her settled. Why don't you go get some rest?" Lilith snagged a piece of chalk from inside her tight jeans pocket and knelt on the ground near the shifter.

Tyson grumbled, but filed the folder with the new shifter's information in the cabinet and gathered his stuff. From his two years working there, he knew one thing for certain: a weekend spent at Camp Silver Lake would be far from boring.

CHAPTER THREE
HARPER

"WE'RE GOING TO UNFREEZE you now. Please stay calm." The blonde woman had finished drawing some sort of chalk circle around Harper.

That idiot counselor had left the room. Good thing, too. Harper didn't think she could stand another one of his pitying smiles.

The woman held her hands out, a pink crystal shaped like a pointed rod in one hand. Harper couldn't do anything except glare until the witch tapped the crystal on Harper's chest over her heart.

The paralysis faded slowly, releasing her fingertips and toes, arms and head, and legs last. Harper gasped as a pins and needles sensation took over her extremities.

"There, now! I trust there won't be any more attacks?" The woman's voice was far too chipper for the late hour.

Harper rubbed her hand, shaking out her fingers, and nodded. For now.

"Good. You can call me Lilith. I'm a leader here at Camp Silver Lake." Lilith paused expectantly. When Harper didn't reply, the witch clicked her tongue. "Follow me, then."

She gestured and turned, marching out the office door and heading up a set of stairs in the dimly lit lodge. It looked like a cozy log cabin on the inside, not the prison Harper expected, but appearances weren't everything. She eyed the front door over her shoulder, just outside the office door opposite the stairs.

The woman cleared her throat, and Harper reluctantly followed her. The door was locked anyway.

"What should we call you while you are here?" Lilith stopped partway down the upstairs hall and unlocked a door.

Harper stepped inside. She crossed her arms over her chest and surveyed the sparse room. She wasn't about to give out her name. Names had power, especially in the mouth of a witch, and Lilith was definitely a witch.

"You might as well tell me now. We'll have it when the report comes in."

Harper tightened her lips. Let them find it out if they could. Quinn would tell her not to show all her cards until the best possible moment. *"Hold 'em close until they force your hand or until you're confident you'll win."*

Lilith put her hands up. "Very well, then. Can't say I blame you, after everything. You'll stay here tonight. We can find you something more comfortable in the morning."

A single cot and a chair shared the windowless room. It felt like a cell. Lilith hesitated for a long moment, but when Harper didn't speak, the witch shut the door and clicked the outer lock without another word.

Harper ran her hands on the walls, searching for a light switch, but when she found one, flipping it did nothing. The bulb had been removed, or maybe the lights were on a timer. She crawled along the floor next, pressing on baseboards and walls to determine if there was a window or secret door, anything she could use to escape. Nothing. She jiggled the handle a few times and tested her weight against the door. It seemed solid. The room was sealed tight. If this was a tactic to get her to talk, it wouldn't work. She'd stayed in much worse places.

Harper leaned her back against the wall, sitting on the floor with her arms wrapped around her knees. She was frustrated. Not at the room, but at herself. First, getting cornered and caught. Then, getting her hopes up when that idiotic counselor mentioned another bird shifter. Could he have meant Quinn? Harper knew better than to hope. At best she could expect another disappointment.

She stood and unfurled her wings, shuddering through the pain of transformation, then crossed the room to where she remembered the cot being. First thing tomorrow, she could ask around about Quinn. Not by name, of course, but no doubt if he had been here, or was here, someone would point her in his direction.

Harper curled up on the thin mattress, tucking her feathers around her like a protective cocoon, and fell into a fitful sleep.

A knock woke her. Judging by the slit of light under the door, morning had arrived. She groaned and withdrew her wings, taking human form again.

"Good morning, Harper King!" Lilith's chipper voice permeated the door. "Breakfast is nearly ready. The door is unlocked. I'll wait for you out here."

So they had gotten her name, after all. A face-match in public school records, maybe. *Damn them all.* Did they know about Quinn, then? There was no way they didn't see his name.

Harper threw open the door, squinting in the sunlight that streamed into the hall from the large windows on the first floor. People moved around downstairs, chattering in a mix of voices.

It was a completely different atmosphere from last night, but she wouldn't let its bright appearance distract her: it was a vehicle for government-enforced procedures. Chain-like laws at best, mutilation at worst. The government kept the details as hush-hush as possible, but when you spent time in the underground, you heard things. They might try to win Harper over, to convince her that they meant well, but she knew better.

"It's so nice to be on a first-name basis at last. Bathroom?" Lilith indicated down the hall, looking far too pleased with herself. While the witch waited outside, Harper utilized the facilities, using a little water to flatten her hair where it stood up awkwardly. She'd cut it weeks ago in an effort to stay hidden. A lot of good that did her. She missed her long hair.

"You don't have anything to drop off here," Lilith said as Harper unlocked the door and entered the hall, "so we'll get you some clothes. There's a community closet downstairs. I'll show you around and help you find something suitable, and then you can shower, all right?"

Harper nodded, the jagged edges of her cropped hair brushing her cheeks.

Lilith led Harper downstairs and gave her a tour of the laundry, handing her clothes in her size.

"Where is everyone?" Harper asked, holding the stack of clothes under one arm.

"Breakfast. Are you hungry?"

"Not much." Being in this place made Harper's stomach clench. She couldn't imagine eating anything. She had to get out of here.

"Ah. Well, maybe after you shower." Lilith banked right without warning, and Harper nearly went past the hall she turned down. Harper kept expecting to head back upstairs, but there weren't any stairs in sight. Lilith stopped in front of a door indistinguishable from any other door in the hall.

"There is a more community-based shower area with curtained stalls, but it's less private. This is normally reserved for group leaders like myself, but I'll make an exception for your first day." Lilith unlocked the door, and Harper moved past her, flipping on the light as she went.

"Everything you need is in there," Lilith said. "If you don't see something, just holler. I'll be right outside."

Again, that winning smile. She could be a model with those teeth. Harper tended to steer clear of magic-users on the streets; the witches here weren't what she expected.

"Oh, and Harper?" Lilith said.

Harper hesitated. "Yeah?"

"Don't be too long. The hot water doesn't last forever."

Harper shut the door, setting the clothes down, and sagging against the counter. She wiped her hands down her face. A tightness gripped her throat. She couldn't let go, not where someone could hear her.

Harper stripped her shirt off over her head and unbuttoned her pants, facing the mirror as she did. The grime on her face almost hid the deep circles under her eyes. The stress of being on the run. She looked gaunt and a bit haunted.

She emptied her pockets, pulling out a hair elastic, the crumpled receipt from that gas station a lifetime ago, and a candy bar wrapper. Her underwear went straight into the trash. It was more holes than not. She was small enough in her chest she didn't wear a bra. Too restrictive with wings, anyway. Harper stepped into the shower.

Bliss poured from the showerhead in the form of hot water. She eased into it, acclimating her body. It was the best ten minutes she'd had in a while.

Properly washed, Harper wrapped herself in a towel and stood in front of the mirror again. Damp and still-matted hair aside, she looked much better. She tried on a smile. It faltered. Those had never come naturally, even when she was younger. Made it hard to get adopted, not having a ready grin for every couple that came looking for a brown-eyed girl to take home. Her history and the package deal with her older brother didn't help, either. She had always been fine with that. Harper didn't need anyone else.

She pulled on the fresh undergarments and jeans. The pants were a bit long, so she rolled the ends into a cuff. The black tank-top went on next, then a zip-up hoodie. She relished in the softness of the nearly-new fabric. Maybe it was just the shower talking, but she couldn't remember a time when she'd worn something more comfortable.

Harper gathered her dirty clothes and opened the door.

Lilith stood outside, arms crossed, staring down a massive, snarling wolf. It glanced at Harper, then leapt, jaws snapping.

Without thinking, Harper dropped everything and bolted down the hall.

"Harper, don't run!" Lilith's cry followed Harper down the hall. *Don't run?* Was she insane?

The wolf panted, its fur brushing the walls. Harper slammed into a wall, not turning fast enough, and stumbled into the next hallway. The staircase leading up was just ahead. The itching in her shoulder blades grew to burning, and the tip of her wings pierced her skin on either side of her spine. A trickle of blood trailed down her back. *No. Not yet.* She pushed harder, sprinting for the stairs.

The wolf's forepaws slammed into Harper's back, and her chin hit the rug, burning. She threw her arms above her head, heart pounding, waiting for teeth to sink into her. Instead, she heard a garbled shout, followed by a yelp. The weight disappeared from her back.

Harper pushed up from the palms of her hands, turning her head behind to see what had happened. The wolf had an electric blue lead around its neck, like a collar and leash. It whimpered, cowering as Lilith stormed up.

"Keith, you just broke so many rules I don't know where to start. Let her up." Lilith crouched at Harper's side and helped her to her feet. The wolf disappeared, turning into a teenager wearing nothing but a pair of spandex shorts. As he shifted, the magic leash vanished. He was built like a body-builder, but the acne on his face made Harper think he was younger than her. Seventeen, maybe?

"What's with this one, Lil? Any of the others would have attacked me back. She chicken?"

"She's none of your concern! I thought you had stopped this nonsense."

"Safety of the pack first. She's an unknown. Had to see what she was made of." He gave Harper a feral grin, and she shuddered, having no doubt he meant that in a literal sense. The aftermath of the adrenaline rushed through Harper's veins, leaving her shaking. She rubbed her left arm and breathed through her nose.

Lilith's lovely face contorted in a furious grimace. "Your Naturalization Report is a few missteps from being withdrawn, and you know what happens then."

"Sorry, Lil," Keith muttered, averting his gaze from Harper and making wide, brown puppy-dog eyes at Lilith.

She sighed. "Keith, this is the last time. Truly."

Keith pumped his fist, then clasped his hands together like he was praying. "You're the best."

"I didn't say there wouldn't be consequences," she said. "Come see me after dinner."

He grinned at her and bounded off.

Lilith focused back on Harper. "Are you all right?" She waited for Harper's nod before continuing. "Sorry about him. He's had a difficult time acclimating to how we do things here. He's a particular breed of werewolf, one of the more violent types. Mauled his little sister with his first turning, and it has made him excessively protective of the new family he has in the pack here. He's an experiment, really. Most werewolves of his kind get put in higher security facilities. You'll receive protective wardings today so this won't happen again."

She seemed to be waiting for Harper to answer.

"Uh, thanks."

Protective wards meant no chance at escape. Harper had to find out if Quinn was here before then.

"Let's head upstairs. I can introduce you to a few of the others."

They ended up in a common room where a few small groups hung around. Harper shrank into herself, hugging the doorway. As much as she hated to admit it, her run-in with Keith had thrown off the "no-nonsense" vibe she wanted to emit. She needed a moment to recollect herself. Lilith prattled on beside her, talking about chore assignments and classes.

At one point, Lilith turned her sympathetic eyes on Harper.

Harper forced her hand to stop rubbing her arm and peeled her back off the wall.

"Don't worry about Keith," Lilith said. "Now the rogues, they're something to be wary of."

When Harper didn't respond, Lilith pointed through the doorway behind her. "Maybe you're hungry? The kitchen is through here."

They entered the kitchen where about a dozen others stood, or sat on chairs, or leaned against the counters. Harper couldn't tell what they all were just by looking, only that Quinn wasn't among them. Some were obvious, like the two vamps sucking red liquid from I.V. tubes like smoothies. A shudder rippled through Harper's body, and her wrist ached as if remembering that night in the tiny back-alley room where the pasty-skinned vamp drained her nigh unto fainting, just so she could get a lead to Quinn—an address that became useless the moment she got caught.

Harper itched to fly away from this place, but she couldn't risk escaping until she knew if they had the information she needed.

A group of six large males sat in a breakfast nook. Shirtless and lounging back like they owned the place, their eyes glittered in a predatory way. One of them, a large black guy with long dreads, sniffed the air and grinned at Harper, then winked. She bumped into Lilith as the witch stopped and gestured at the room's occupants, a glowing smile on her face.

"Everyone, I'd like you to meet Harper. Harper, everyone. No time for individual introductions, but you should know a few significant names. Some of our residents naturally form packs, and we do recognize those leaders. Zeke is the werewolf alpha."

The black guy with the dreads waved a hand. Harper crossed her arms and scowled, trying to let off a tough vibe.

"Heath and Lexi lead our vampire faction. Though there are some divisions there. Being resolved, I hope?" She raised her voice and a thin blonde-haired girl waved, her back to them, not pausing as she sucked her bloody breakfast. Harper swallowed hard. Witches. Wolves. Vampires. Why couldn't there be more were-rabbits in the world? She could handle a few rabbits.

"Of course, there are many species at Camp Silver Lake. We have sirens and several other shifter-types, a few witches, warlocks, and seers, nymphs and fae of various kinds." Lilith ticked them off on her fingers. "We're not the largest in the world, but we're getting there. We had to expand our borders last year. You'll find our grounds extensive, even for a flyer like yourself."

Escape wouldn't be as simple as walking to the border, then. Harper would find a way out. Surely others had.

"A flyer, huh?" Zeke leaned forward, arms resting on the table in front of him, golden-brown eyes shining. "Is she a drake, Lilith?"

"Fortunately, no. Harper is a bird shifter with raven or crow-like wings. Be nice while she adjusts."

"Chirp, chirp," one of his muscled buddies mocked. The table erupted in laughter.

Harper threw off her hoodie and flared her wings, knocking a plastic pitcher of juice off the counter to the ground. She dove forward, landing in a crouch on their table amidst the remains of their breakfast.

Her hand darted out and gripped the guy's jugular. A peculiar sensation built in her chest, like she had taken a deep breath and was about to burst into song. She felt instinctively that if she released that pent-up pressure as sound, no one in the room would survive.

CHAPTER FOUR
HARPER

THE WOLF WHINED LIKE a pup, and his hands scrabbled against Harper's vice-like fingers. Her feathers beat back against the other werewolves at the table, holding them at bay.

Fur grew on her victim's knuckles, and Harper tightened her grip. He froze, mouth open as he gasped, revealing pointed canines.

"I've met one of your kind already this morning, and it wasn't pleasant, so forgive me if I'm on edge," Harper snarled.

"Harper, that's quite enough," Lilith snapped, her voice rising to a higher pitch.

"I'll handle it, Lilith." A thick hand landed on Harper's shoulder. "Down."

The single word carried a weight that tugged on Harper's insides. She unclenched her hand and the werewolf collapsed, gasping against the bench, his golden eyes resentful. Zeke's hand pressed down, and Harper slid off the table, dusting off her hands and shaking her wings.

"How did you do that?" She demanded.

Zeke shrugged, sticking his hands in his pockets. "Alphas have a way, even outside their species."

"That's what wards are for," Lilith emphasized, her lips drawn in a thin line.

Harper turned her head, meeting every stare with a steely one of her own as she slowly drew her wings back in. She wasn't here to make friends; hopefully now that was clear. She let her gaze linger on Zeke. He seemed unperturbed by what had just happened, sliding back into the breakfast nook bench with his packmates. He also seemed like the kind of person who would know about Quinn, but who might understand too well why Harper asked. He caught her gaze and stared her down until she looked away.

She needed someone observant, friendly, and a bit naive to ask about her brother. A few others stood out, including one girl who gave Harper a hesitant smile as she walked past her out of the kitchen. Harper made a mental note to find her later.

Lilith cleared her throat, breaking through the tension in the air. "Would you like breakfast?"

Harper pressed her lips together. Between the scent of strange food and tension in the room, she couldn't imagine eating.

"We'll continue our tour then, shall we?" Lilith took Harper through another hallway. Halfway down, she paused and put a hand on Harper's shoulder.

"I thought after what happened with Keith you might understand why we have to work hard to control our instincts and not attack fellow residents. I know you're tightly wound after everything that has happened; you feel scared and insecure, but you should know that from now on, any incident will go on your Naturalization record. I'll let this one pass."

It sounded like the same deal she gave Keith, which was fair enough. Harper nodded, and Lilith's hand dropped.

The hallway opened up to the front entrance landing. Two closed offices stood on either side of the front door, and Harper recognized where she had been brought in the night before. To their left rose the staircase to the upper level.

A group of loungers leaned against the railing. One had bright magenta hair and a half-shaved head. Her eyes were a vivid, glowing pink. What the hell could she be? The girl moved her hands and fingers in strange, rapid gestures. The others laughed and signed back. A deaf paranormal? First Harper had heard of it. She turned to ask Lilith about the girl, but the witch was already several steps ahead.

Harper's shoulders ached. She rolled them and swung her arms back, grasping her hands behind her and stretching as she walked. To her right, the wall opened up in the middle of the hallway, guarded by a banister, and looked down into the first level at the center of the house. Harper's heart lifted a little at the height.

The feeling was brief, and any shot at flying out of here was just an illusion. She looked down into a common living area of sorts, where several others mingled and chatted, while some read or stared off into space. There was a television mounted to the wall, though the screen was blank. Three fireplaces and at least twenty different couches, chairs, and beanbags filled the massive common area. There was no sign of Quinn.

Lilith's voice drifted to Harper from farther ahead. "Stay with me." She rounded a bend, and Harper rushed to catch up. Her quick, short steps carried her past an open doorway, and she realized Lilith was inside and had to backtrack. Harper hovered in the doorway, staring into the brightly-lit room.

Violet stood across the room, draped in loose fabric with her permed brunette hair down. Harper recognized her from the night before. The witch ground away at some leaves in a tiny stone bowl and muttered to herself, not looking up as they entered the room.

Lilith cleared her throat. "Our newest resident to see you, Violet."

"Not during the retrograde, Lilith. I lost too much time processing her. You know I need to take advantage of this window. Could you do it?"

Harper sensed deference in Lilith. What was a group of witches called? A coven? Violet must have been the leader then, but Lilith was still in a position of leadership in the camp.

"You know I'm not as skilled at personal wards, Violet. If you're available later, I can bring her to you then. Besides, you usually like to give them the rules yourself."

"You give her the tour, and the rules. I'll ward her around dinner time." Violet's tone made it clear that it wasn't up for discussion. She put a stick of sorts in her mouth, one hand grinding away at leaves in the stone bowl in front of her while the other sketched marks on the table with chalk.

Lilith ushered Harper into the hall and shut the carved wooden door behind her.

"Sorry about that, Harper. This is a once-in-fifty-years opportunity for Violet to prepare some unique and potent remedies and spells. I'm afraid it makes her a tad edgy. She's normally quite warm and friendly. For now, I'm your guide. Perhaps you have some questions you'd like to ask me?" She smiled so hopefully that Harper struggled to maintain her typical uncaring attitude. Lilith waited a moment before launching into what sounded like a script. "Camp Silver Lake is one of three hundred branches of the American Paranormal Naturalization Program. Similar programs exist internationally, but ours has been deemed the best for its sixty-percent Naturalization success rate. It's the highest in the nation, and second highest worldwide."

Harper's stomach churned. They thought they had accomplished so much. "What happens to the other forty percent?"

Lilith waved her hand. "Don't worry about that now. You'll find out in your classes. You'll attend classes every day. No grades, just pass or fail. You will also meet with Mr. Miller—whom you've already seen—twice a week for the first few months here. Attendance is required. If you choose not to participate or show no sign of compatibility with Naturalization within the allotted time frame, you'll be shipped off to a higher security location and programs where you're treated with a lot less leniency."

It was the same old "new home" lecture Harper had received in every place she'd ended up. She could hear the same tone in Lilith's voice telling Harper to *"make this place work, they only get worse from here."*

Harper's stomach clenched. She didn't want to make any place work without Quinn.

Lilith stopped in front of a closed door, her blonde hair swinging down her back as she faced Harper.

"You'll have a roommate assigned once we know where you fit in here. Don't get used to having it to yourself." Lilith cocked her head. "I don't know what you've heard about these camps or the Naturalization programs, but you should know that the media doesn't always portray things accurately. We're all just like you here. With the exception of Mr. Miller and Dr. Hartford, but only because the state requires that a human be the one who determines whether you're compatible. The rest of the staff have been through Naturalization. If you ever have any questions don't hesitate to ask."

Lilith smiled warmly.

"So, wait, if you're Naturalized, how come you can do magic?" Harper asked.

"I struck a deal with the devil, so to speak." Lilith winked. "I work for the government, so they get to take advantage of my abilities. Most of which I utilize to keep everyone in the camp safe and secure."

"So, you're like a warden?"

Lilith laughed, and her laughter was musical. "I guess you could see it that way. I prefer the term guardian."

Harper had the feeling that if she stuck around long enough, she might grow to like Lilith. But Harper couldn't stop thinking about Quinn. If Violet got a hold of her with those wards, whatever that entailed, she wouldn't be able to leave. She needed to find out if her brother was here, and if not, break out. If Harper succeeded, she might have a chance of disappearing before they tracked her down again, and she could find him. Then they could find their parents together like they'd always planned.

Lilith opened the door and walked inside the room. Harper followed, noticing two narrow bunk beds pushed up against opposite walls. A lot of space for one person.

"This is one of our most warded rooms. It will act as your protection until you have a personal set of wards from Violet."

"Why all the wards? Why not just let us kill each other?"

Lilith blinked. "Contrary to popular belief, we're preserving the paranormal population, not culling it. There are people who want that, but just as many find us fascinating individuals who make life a lot richer."

Harper hadn't considered that. she wasn't sure how she felt about it, either. Why all the strict laws, then? Why the camps? Some humans might have liked paranormals, they might have even thought they were interesting, but humans were still afraid of what they could do. That wasn't likely to change any time soon.

"If you ever have questions about all this, or just need someone to talk to, you can come to me day or night. Violet seems aloof now, but she'll be more available once the retrograde is over. Mr. Miller is here as well, though usually not on weekends."

No way in hell Harper would trust them with anything. Well, except perhaps Lilith. Harper had to admit her respect for the witch was growing. She didn't force answers. Although, she could already know everything about Harper and just be waiting for her to reveal it in her own time. Harper cursed mentally. It was foster care all over again, except at a whole new level.

Harper realized Lilith was waiting for her response. "Where is your room?"

"The blue door we passed next to the apothecary, where you met Violet earlier."

The buzz of a cell phone vibrating startled both of them.

Lilith took her cell phone from her pocket and checked the screen. Her face paled. "I've got a grocery delivery happening any minute. They have to be escorted to the cabin from the border or those rogues I told you about will get to the truck before I do."

She glanced over at Harper. "I'll take you back downstairs. Kamri will look after you."

"I'm fine here. You said it was safe, right?"

"I'd rather you weren't alone on your first day. Come on," She gestured.

Harper thought about fighting it harder, but Lilith had been so nice that she didn't want to cause her more trouble.

They passed the lounging signers on the stairs, circumvented the kitchen and took another hall to the open common area.

Guitar music played, ethereal and distracting. Harper almost didn't hear what Lilith said next.

"Kamri has the bright red hair. There, see her?" Lilith pointed to a freckled girl with cardinal-red hair.

Harper grimaced. She needed a bodyguard like she needed a tooth pulled.

"Just be yourself. This is the one place you can do that." Lilith pressed a hand into Harper's shoulder, then leaned in.

Harper braced herself for more inspirational drivel.

"Your brother isn't here. He escaped." Lilith squeezed Harper's shoulder one more time and ducked through the doorway.

Harper stood, gaping, a tingle traveling through her spine and making her head spin in giddy circles. *He's not here. Quinn isn't here. And Lilith knows.*

What kind of torture was that, leaving her with the knowledge that her brother had been here, that she'd missed him? Why hadn't Lilith said anything earlier?

The music broke through Harper's dizzying thoughts and drew her further into the room against every instinct she had. She stood behind the couch, hoping no one would notice her, and lost track of all thought as she listened to the strummed song.

The guitarist was a man with shaggy black hair and super pale skin. His face was pretty, slightly pointed and utterly flawless.

Harper's jaw dropped when she realized he was the one singing. The voice was high and feminine, and she had assumed one of the girls in the room were accompanying his playing.

When he looked at her, she saw emotions swelling in his gaze like an ocean tide. He had more raw feeling in his voice than Harper had in her entire body.

The last notes of his song faded from the air completely before the group erupted in cheers and applause. The guy ducked his head, but she caught his smile beneath his curtain of hair. Harper heard his name passed around.

Ian.

Harper was so caught up in the after-effect of the musical spell he cast that she almost missed it when someone finally noticed her.

"Hey, new girl. Join the circle. Most of us don't bite." The words came from the girl sitting at Ian's side. She flicked her ponytail over her shoulder. It was deep red with a black underlayer. Kamri, Harper assumed. Her freckles gave her a cute appearance, but she bared her teeth in a way reminiscent of Keith. Another werewolf?

"Kamri does. Watch out for her." A joking voice piped up from behind Harper. It was the girl who smiled at her in the kitchen this morning.

"Do you have a name?" Kamri asked. She sat close to Ian, the pinky of her hand barely touching his. They seemed shy with each other, occasionally glancing and looking away. Beginning stages, then. What were the policies on relationships here? In the real world, paranormal "breeding" wasn't illegal, but they took your kids if you had them. Probably put them in one of these camps from birth.

Harper let the thoughts go and looked up. "I'm Harper." She left off the part about Lilith wanting Kamri to watch out for her. She could take care of herself.

"And what's your superpower, Harper?" Kamri asked. She was bold, unafraid, but controlled. All the others looked at Harper. They must have missed her display in the kitchen earlier. If they didn't know what she could do, they wouldn't be expecting it.

Harper pressed her lips together. Groans erupted around the room.

"Where do these ones come from?" The girl from the kitchen turned her green eyes on Harper, flashing with an emotion she couldn't read. She swept back her hair, black with blonde highlights. "None of us are going to judge you. We try to live together like a family, you know? We're all each other's got. This is a place you can show off. Be yourself."

That "be yourself" crap again. And family? Please. Harper hadn't bought into that since she was ten. The girl looked disappointed when Harper didn't answer, but stuck her hand out anyway. Harper couldn't stand seeing it hang in the air like that, so walked around the couch to her armchair and took it. She gave Harper's a gentle shake.

"Anita. Witch." She smiled. Harper attempted to smile back, not sure she succeeded, and released her hand.

Another voice came from behind Harper. "Kamri, werewolf."

She spun around and met those bared teeth. How could someone with freckles look so intimidating? Ian lifted his head beside her, brushing the hair from his eyes. He raised a hand from his guitar.

"Ian. Siren." His voice had a normal tenor tone, now. Siren. That explained his singing.

"I thought sirens were women? And, like, half-fish?" Harper wasn't known for her tact.

The room went stiff for a moment, then Ian smiled. "Most are female. Males are rare. Guess I'm lucky."

"Don't you need to live in the water?"

He gave Kamri a look. He probably answered these questions a lot.

Kamri smiled warmly at him, then answered Harper's question. "We have a pool. He spends some time in it but can walk around on land like anyone else. He doesn't have a tail either. Mixed parentage. A selkie and a siren. His shifting follows his selkie blood."

Harper nodded as if it made any sense, but her head spun. Selkie? She'd never heard of that. "Your singing was incredible."

Ian blushed and ducked his head again.

"Cheri's our other siren. You might have seen her. Magenta hair and glowing eyes?"

The girl from the stairs.

"She's crossed with a Seer of some kind, I think," Anita piped up from behind. "Her voice is out of this world, like Ian's, but she's a bit more...nefarious with it. Violet warded her against speaking."

"Like the little mermaid," someone else said. Everyone burst into laughter.

Even Harper cracked a grin.

"Not mermaid. Siren. And don't let her hear you say that. She'll predict your death and leave a note on your pillow," Anita said, but she was smiling.

A bell rang and everyone moved. There were at least four others Harper hadn't met yet, and a dozen more streamed in from outside.

"Class time. You don't have a schedule yet, do you? Want to see what it's like?" Anita again.

Harper thought about looking for Lilith and demanding to know what information she had about Quinn, but perhaps

Harper could see what Anita knew first. She was friendly enough, surely Harper could find out *something*.

"Sure."

Anita unfolded her legs and stretched as she stood. She was about Harper's height, which said something because Harper was shorter than most people. Anita grabbed her bag and headed through the common room entryway leading into the kitchen, and Harper followed. Nothing about Anita's appearance screamed witch, except the slightly herbed smell coming off her dark hair.

"Wait until you meet Fletcher. He's totally cute, you'll see him in this class. We had another bird shifter a few months ago, but he's not here anymore. Such a shame. Quinn didn't talk much, but he was *hot* in that brooding sort of way."

Harper's skin tingled. She didn't bother enlightening Anita about her relationship to that "hot" brooding bird shifter. The confirmation that Quinn had been here was enough to send Harper's mind spinning to discover a mode of escape.

Anita put her hand up to shield her mouth and leaned over. "They don't want us talking about it, but he actually escaped. It was insane. Blew a hole right through Violet's wards. She has the whole coven working on patching all the layers that got wrecked. She's still livid that she doesn't know how he did it. I think he had help."

"Really?" Harper murmured, hoping she didn't sound too interested.

"Yeah, this human chick vanished at the same time. They spent a lot of time together. I'm sure they were, you know..." Anita tapped her pointer fingers together, indicating they were together? Kissing? More than that?

Harper determined that she would find out who the human was. Tyson would probably know, as a resident human. She might as well get *something* out of the mandated sessions.

Anita and Harper entered the other side of the cabin, a part Lilith hadn't gotten around to showing her on the tour. It appeared to be a hallway of classrooms. Some were empty, others filled about halfway. Not knowing how many others were outside or in other parts of the house, and judging based on what she'd seen so far, Harper guessed that maybe forty paranormals lived in the camp altogether. Not including the rogues Lilith mentioned.

Anita kept talking. "They told us his application has been withdrawn. Usually, that means they've been determined unsuitable for Naturalization and shipped off to a higher security facility. I think the government tries to train them for military and spy work. Otherwise, pretty sure they're executed."

Executed. Harper stared at Anita. How could she say that casually? Was she so confident that it would never happen to her? As a witch, she was physically more human than most paranormals. Harper assumed that made it easier for her to complete the Naturalization program.

The two entered the classroom and Harper withdrew into observation mode.

"We're in Naturalization theory, in case you were wondering." Anita looked sideways at her. Harper made a choked sound that she covered with throat-clearing and tucked her hands in her pockets. The itching between her shoulder blades flared as a dozen pairs of eyes turned on her.

"They did tell you about Naturalization, right?" Anita continued.

"Everyone knows about it. I wasn't born under a rock."

Anita held up her hands. "Okay, okay, but you never know. Some people come here after being literally kept underground. Their parents put them in hiding and told them nothing, or what they told them is wrong. It's the most crucial thing you need to understand here. It's your way out. Otherwise, you get tranqed and carted off by Stiffs and taken the devil knows where."

"That's a tad dramatic, Anita. Haven't I taught you better?" A tall man stepped out of a classroom on the right—one of the people who'd responded to the alarm the night before. He wore a button-down shirt and suspenders, topped off with a bowtie, of all things. Who wore a bowtie anymore? Harper smelled the gel in his hair, and something else, something sharp that she couldn't name. His eyes landed on her. "Our newest resident."

"I thought she might like to get a feel for the classes, so I invited her. Is that all right?"

The man's green eyes flashed. A tingle passed through Harper's body, and then his face relaxed. "Indeed. I am Mr. Petrov." His smile faltered at Harper's stony expression. He swept an arm out behind him. "Please, come in."

Anita hurried forward, but Harper followed more hesitantly, taking a seat next to her.

"Vamp?" Harper asked, gesturing at Petrov with her head. She was sure someone had told her what he was already, but all the information being thrown at her was all melding together in her brain.

Anita had already unpacked a notebook and pen from her bag. The blue cover of the notebook was covered with scrawled sigils, and it took Harper a moment to remember that she was a witch.

"No way. Warlock. James Petrov." Anita said his name with a sigh, her expression becoming dreamy. "He's married to Violet. You met Violet, right?"

"I mean, I've seen her, but…" Harper trailed off.

Anita tilted her head. "It's retrograde. She probably didn't want to miss it to deal with any drama."

Drama? Now I'm drama?

Harper's eyes were drawn to the classroom doorway, where a boy with tousled, frost-blond hair stood. He was almost as tall as Petrov but burly. And he had *wings*.

"It's rude to stare." Anita quipped from behind her. Harper shut her mouth, but she couldn't look away. His wings were blue as a jay's, with gorgeous black and white markings across the bottom of the feathers.

Harper's shoulder blades ached fiercely, and she pinched her forearm red, but it wasn't really working. The blue jay looked at her and smiled, then walked up, taking the desk next to her. His wings stayed tucked against his back, but they were so large that the aisle was blocked on both sides. The person sitting on the other side of him cursed and changed seats. Harper wanted to reach out and touch those stunning blue feathers. Instead, she swallowed past the dryness in her throat and laced her fingers together.

"No shifting forms allowed in Naturalization Theory, Fletcher," Petrov said, shutting the classroom door and crossing to his desk.

He snapped his fingers in Harper's direction. She slumped down, letting her shoulder blades slide across the plastic backing of her chair, just to make sure all was normal. He wasn't talking to her, of course.

"I've only got a short time left, teach. Can't you let me, just this once?" The baritone voice rumbled from behind Harper.

Petrov glanced up from the paper he was holding. "I sympathize, but no allowances." He cleared his throat. "We'll be continuing our unit on life after Naturalization today."

There was a rustling beside Harper, and one of Fletcher's wing tips brushed her arm. When she looked next, Fletcher's wings were gone. There were wide slits in his t-shirt near the shoulder blades. That explained his easy shift.

"Here." Anita handed Harper paper and a pencil. "I have extra. They're charmed to correct punctuation and grammar."

Harper's ears perked up as Mr. Petrov started talking. She had only ever heard the media blab their approved scripts on Naturalization. What would it be like to actually go through with it?

"Naturalization is a different process for every type of paranormal. The goal is to maintain an air of normalcy so no regular human will suspect what you really are while maximizing any advantages or talents your abilities give you, if possible. Werewolves can choose to either maintain humanoid form or pick a lifestyle that enables daily transformation, depending on the breed they're descended from. Giant werewolves, for instance, cannot choose service animal positions, as they're much larger than any natural dogs, but they're welcome in specialized branches of the military for the extra stamina and strength they have in humanoid form."

Petrov waved a hand and a life-sized image of a singer appeared in the front of the classroom, the blue outline of her form transparent. She moved at a microphone, mouth moving as if singing. A second later, an enchanting song wove among the class members. It reminded Harper of Ian's song earlier.

"This is Selena. Some of you may know her music. She's a siren. Sirens can be entertainers once they're taught to reign in their voice and can be trusted not to enchant crowds. Witches and warlocks have hidden among human populations for centuries without detection, some to a further degree of success than others. We've already gone over what happened in Salem and areas like it, so it doesn't bear repeating. Whatever you choose as your life path must be in line with your ability to maintain an appearance deemed acceptable by humans."

The hologram disappeared, the music lingering for a few seconds after.

Petrov tapped his desk to refocus the class. He cleared his throat. "We hope that, in the future, the unique talents of more diverse paranormals will be accepted and integrated into society, changing the employment options available. For now, the government Naturalization licensure program has a strict non-exposure policy among naturalized paranormal citizens. Violations can result in imprisonment or death. You will get one warning."

Petrov cleared his throat. "There is a place for everyone in the Naturalization program if you choose to participate. We've gone over the details of the program these past few weeks and most of you have met with myself or Violet to determine your path. Some of you have already proven capability with Naturalization, others are just beginning the journey. Still others of you won't make it through and will face recruitment or termination at the government's discretion."

He seemed focused on an empty seat until he snapped his attention back on the class.

"As much as we may not like it, that is the state of things. Consider your part in this: if you go through with Naturalization and go into law, you could be part of the generation that changes things for the better for all paranormals."

Harper snorted.

Petrov pointed at her with the pen in his hand. "Miss Harper, you have an opinion to share? We welcome discussion here."

Words bubbled out of her. "Why aren't we doing more about this? I mean, we might be outnumbered by humans, but we're stronger, faster, often smarter, and definitely less fragile. How did we let it get to this point?"

Petrov's expression grew stern. "You will find answers to that question as you continue to take this class. For now, consider the wars that occurred when paranormals were first exposed: accusations led to torture, torture led to a lot of death. Unregulated transformation and use of powers led to mass destruction in certain areas, and hunts happened in full force. The resulting bloodshed far exceeded that which happened during the Salem Witch Trials. Was that the best way to achieve the peaceful co-habitation of our races and species? No. The Naturalization Act was a compromise to enable paranormals to be less persecuted and humans to not have to fear for their lives."

Harper withheld another discontented sound. At this point, she just wanted him to stop talking.

"You'll come to understand better with time," Petrov said. "Now, where were we?" He muttered, pausing for a moment before continuing. "Options for Naturalization are as varied as your forms and gifts. Don't see it as a limitation, but an opportunity to avoid the persecution your parents and grand-parents went through. You'll have the chance they never did: to be accepted."

Harper rested her chin in her hand. She tapped the pencil against the blank paper before her. It all sounded like a bunch of brainwashing propaganda. She raised her hand.

"Yes?"

"So, if our shifting forms don't comply with Naturalization standards, what happens then? How do you keep us from shifting once we're out there?"

Mr. Petrov smiled a strange, disconcerting smile. "Naturalization is an agreement you enter into with the government. If you haven't been fully checked in yet, then you've yet to receive your digital tracking device, which can monitor heart rate and blood pressure. In other words, your paranormal activity will be monitored, and if it violates your agreement, you will be hunted and terminated. For the safety of human and paranormal alike."

Harper crossed her arms over her chest and pursed her lips. "But how is that in any way better than what happened before? We're being forced to compromise ourselves, to limit and hide in order to make humans more comfortable. How is that fair? Why should we accept the bare minimum for survival? I thought we lived in a progressive society."

"We do. It's just run by humans. And they're terrified of us." Someone piped up from the back of the classroom.

Petrov held up his hand. "This is not open for debate. The purpose of this class is to inform. If you wish to change the perceived unfairness of it all, I suggest you make it through the program and get out there and do something about it. Until then, I have an assignment for all of you."

The class groaned. Petrov explained the requirements for an essay with the topic of "What Career I'm Choosing After Naturalization and Why." It was the sort of thing Harper never turned in before she skipped out of school just shy of graduation. Not that she would have graduated anyway.

Her eyes wandered to the blue jay shifter sitting across the row. Fletcher stared down at a blank page, possibly the start of his essay.

"Fletcher?"

He looked up.

"What did you mean when you said you only had a few weeks left?"

He squinted a little, then smiled a small, sad, beautiful kind of smile that Harper had never seen on anyone before. "Bird shifters can't maintain their shifter form and be Naturalized. We're too abnormal, and our instincts are too strong to avoid shifting in an emergency. They've tried training it out of us, but we don't hide it well. When I agreed to Naturalization, I agreed to let them take my wings. They've perfected this nearly painless cauterization procedure. I'll be normal. Practically human."

His voice sounded strained, despite the ease with which he spoke the words. Harper stared at him in horror, then looked to the warlock standing at the front of the room. Petrov met her eyes.

"You're a monster." Harper spat the words, her chair screeching as she stood and bolted from the room.

CHAPTER FIVE
TYSON

TYSON'S EYES FLASHED OPEN in the pitch black of the windowless room. Stillness. He was safe.

Safe in this closet of a room with a door that locked on the inside. He might have made a career of working with paranormals day in and out, but that didn't stop his human instincts from buzzing every time he was around them. He was used to the feeling, for the most part, but the darkness made it worse.

He unraveled the tangled blankets from around his legs and waist and heaved over, turning on his phone to check the time. 5:44 a.m.

Tyson rolled back over, putting his arm over his eyes, despite the darkened room. The weight felt comforting. He breathed deeply. It had been a long time since he had that dream. A few months at least.

A wail started up in the next room over. Perhaps Libby. She was the non-verbal banshee resident at Camp Silver Lake. Or at least, Violet thought she was a banshee. She wasn't Naturalization material, but Lilith held out for her and several less favorable residents. If they weren't ready by now, the chances were unlikely that they ever would be. Tyson shivered as he listened to her keening. That could have been what woke him, but he knew better.

Why would he dream about Reya now?

He rubbed at his arms. The goosebumps seemed permanent. He'd hardly slept. Today was supposed to be his day off from this insane place, a blip of normal in his unusual life. So much for that. He would consider a career change, but the work he did as a counselor was too necessary.

A knock on the door made Tyson jump.

"Morning, Tyson!" Lilith's voice sounded far too cheerful for this early in the morning.

"Morning," He called back, relieved he wouldn't be fighting off any irate paranormals in his boxers. "Can I help you?"

"Since you're here, how do you feel about having an open office?" Her muffled reply came through the door again.

An open office meant a stream of residents coming in and out all day without appointments. Given the situation, with a new resident and his being stuck here, he couldn't pass up the opportunity to help. That was what he came here to do.

"Sure thing."

"I'll let them know!"

Lilith was gone when he opened his door.

The quiet kitchen was a refuge. Tyson grabbed a bagel with cream cheese and a hot cup of coffee and headed to the office. It was on the first floor near the front entrance of the lodge. Tyson unlocked his door, noticing the slightest chalk streaks on the carpet from the warding bubble he had activated the night before. They'd come out when it got vacuumed next. He ate while his computer started up. He had a notification from Lilith—the police report on Harper King, the bird shifter they had just acquired. The computer had tagged her description from a list of girls reported missing in the past couple of years.

Her foster care story was accurate. She had parents, who were reported missing, and an older brother.

A brother Tyson had met. His hand trembled as he picked up his nearly empty cup.

Quincey King. Also a bird shifter. Tyson took a sip, getting the cold dregs of his coffee, the bitterness coating his tongue. He'd only met Quinn three times. His mentor Tom saw him more often. Tyson remembered the shifter as brooding and blunt, not so unlike Harper. Perhaps their bitterness came from being in foster care, or maybe it was a family thing.

There wasn't much information on the rest of Harper's family, which was unusual, but not unheard of. The parents were marked missing, not dead. Intriguing. Tyson searched their names in the database, but found nothing. Wherever they were, it wasn't in a registered Naturalization camp.

The thoughts slipped through Tyson's brain like water down a drain. He squinted at the screen and picked up his nearly empty coffee cup. Time for a refill.

Tyson clicked out of the report and scanned the rest of his emails. His eyes slid past one from his cousin Becca that he'd already read, then drifted back to it.

He clicked into the email, dated over two months ago. In it, Becca prattled on, as usual, about her work in her dad's Cryptozoology museum. It was doing better now than when they had been kids; ever since the Reveal, tourists swarmed the place to learn more about the myths become reality. Tyson's uncle, Jerome Belinski, was in Egypt presenting at a seminar and furthering his research. He had gotten Tyson the counseling job through Tom, whom he'd met at a conference.

Tyson skimmed the rest of the email, and his heart grew heavy. He hadn't seen or heard from Becca since she visited last month. She disappeared at the same time as Quinn. Several people cried foul, but Tyson knew her better than they did.

Becca never intended to stay at the camp long. She was data collecting for her dad, and then one of his colleagues contacted her with some information she needed and she left. Her disappearance had nothing to do with the rogue paranormal who had rejected the benefits Naturalization had to offer.

At least, that was the official story. The longer she was silent, the more likely it seemed she could be involved...somehow.

Tyson brought up Quinn's file again, scanning the session notes Dr. Hartford had taken. He could have switched it with Harper's and hardly known the difference, though Quinn seemed more calculating and less prone to outbursts. He'd never tried to attack anyone while here, and his first escape attempt had succeeded, against all the odds.

A knock at the door startled Tyson. He minimized the screen and spun around in his chair.

"Come in."

Fletcher ducked his blond head into the room. His blue-feathered wings were tucked against his back, but the edges still brushed the doorway as he passed. His normally cheerful face creased with worry. "Sorry to bother you, Tyson."

"It's not a bother. Please sit."

Fletcher closed the door and sat without leaning back to avoid crushing his wings. Fletcher stayed silent for a long moment, twisting the chair back and forth, clasping and un-clasping his hands. He rubbed his palms on his jeans, and his eyes flickered from Tyson to the floor.

Tyson hadn't seen him this agitated in a long time, but he could guess the reason.

"Is it about your Reformation appointment?" Tyson asked quietly.

Fletcher swallowed and cleared his throat. "Sort of."

Tyson's stomach clenched, but he kept his face passive. This close to a successful Naturalization, doubt was a normal part of the process, but it still made him nervous. Fletcher's success would be Tyson's success. And his key to promotion, but Tyson couldn't think about that now. Fletcher needed him. He had to stay focused.

"What is bothering you about it?"

"Has anyone ever regretted going through the Reformation? I mean, long term?" Fletcher's voice wavered.

Tyson hesitated. "You've been preparing for a long time for this. It's a big decision. But you have some great role models. Both of your parents and your older sister have been through the program. When was the last time you talked to them?"

"I got an email from them last week."

"What did they have to say?"

"My mom and dad were encouraging, as usual." Fletcher adjusted his seat, crossing and uncrossing his legs. "My sister, though. She's been getting more negative. Saying cryptic stuff, like how I have no idea what I'm doing, how it will affect the rest of my life. I always thought she would support me the most, you know, since her Reformation allowed her to get that position at the aviary, but now..." He trailed off.

Tyson made a note in Fletcher's chart to talk to his parents. These last days were critical, and his sister shouldn't be allowed to email him if she was unstable. Tyson could recommend psychological evaluation for her, as well.

"Have you met that Harper girl yet? She was in Petrov's class."

The question startled Tyson, and his pen drew an errant mark on the page. "Ah. Yes, I have. She checked in last night." He frowned at the pen mark. Harper seemed like the type of person who ruffled feathers wherever she went. He focused back on Fletcher. "What did she say to you?" He watched the shifter's body language.

Fletcher rubbed his middle finger, and his wings shivered.

"Well, not to me, exactly. She called Mr. Petrov a monster when she learned what...what bird shifters go through for Naturalization."

"The Reformation."

Fletcher leaned forward, resting his forearms on the tops of his legs. "Yeah."

Tyson paused, breathing in through his nose, then slowly out of his mouth. He had to phrase this in just the right way, or it would go off in a direction that wouldn't serve anyone. "Fletcher, do you remember the first time you learned about what going through with Naturalization would require of you?"

He tilted his head. "Yeah, but I didn't freak out like she did."

"You were prepared. Your family was an example to you. You could see they were okay, so you did better with the idea. Harper doesn't have that. She's been on the run her entire life. Her family is gone. She's afraid of all the unknowns."

"I'm not afraid of the process. I just don't know if I'm going to regret it."

"What are you looking forward to about completing Naturalization?" The air hovered between them, fragile and uncertain.

Fletcher leaned forward. "Seeing my family, I guess. And fitting in with everyone. Being normal. I wanted that my whole life." His face cleared, and his shoulders relaxed. "I don't have anything to worry about, do I?"

"It's going to be hard. You still have the surgery and recovery to go through. But you won't be alone." Tyson smiled, and to his relief, Fletcher smiled back. The pressure in the room eased.

"I feel bad for Harper, you know?" Fletcher said after a moment. "She doesn't have anyone. I don't want her to end up like Quinn."

"What Harper could use right now is a friend who can show her that she doesn't have to be afraid. How would you feel about being that person for her?" It just might work if the information came from a peer rather than someone she perceived as a threat, and Fletcher could affirm his conviction to go through with it. Two birds with one stone, as the saying went.

A wide grin spread across Fletcher's face. He slapped his hands on his knees. "Yeah, man! I can do that. I see what you mean. I could talk to her, right? Reassure her."

"Absolutely. And if she says anything that upsets you, remember that she doesn't know what you know. You can see me again if you need to talk it out."

"Thanks, Tyson." Fletcher had relaxed since he came in, but some tension remained in his expression.

"Is there anything else I can help you with?"

Fletcher's brow furrowed. He shifted his seat, feathers rustling. "Is it...is it a problem if I find her...attractive?"

Harper, attractive? Tyson remembered her crouched in the corner of this room the night before, wings spread, a grimace on her face. Some might find her attractive. The camp had rules, of course, about resident relationships. They were supposed to get cut off if they got too serious. In this case, however...Fletcher's elbows rested on his knees as he leaned forward, waiting for what Tyson would say.

Tyson sighed and looked him in the eye. "You've had all the lectures, Fletcher. I won't repeat them. Just remember that your Reformation appointment is this week. You need to focus on moving forward." He had every confidence in Fletcher. They'd worked together through Tyson's entire internship. *Meeting Harper today just shook him up a little.* Tyson forced a smile. "That doesn't mean you can't enjoy this time you have to get to know her. We encourage friendships. And your friendship could be what gets her to where you are."

A plant could have thrived on the light in Fletcher's smile. He stood, shaking out his feathers. "I can do that. Thanks for the advice."

Tyson spread his hands. "It's what I'm here for."

Fletcher walked out with a spring in his step, and Tyson's heart soared. That was why he had gotten into paranormal psychology in the first place. He could do a world of good here.

After Fletcher, Tyson got a steady stream of residents from the class Harper spoke out in. Apparently, she said a bit more than what Fletcher mentioned. Everyone wanted to know if she was going to ruin their chances at Naturalization, and Tyson had to explain over and over again how Naturalization applications were based on individual merit, not what their classmate thought.

The clock read close to 2:00 p.m. when he closed his door behind the last resident and slumped against it, finally catching his breath. His stomach rumbled, reminding him that he hadn't eaten lunch. He cleared the clutter from breakfast off the desk and his hand bumped the computer mouse, waking up the screen. An email notification popped up on the desktop. Tyson maximized the internet window and froze.

A new email from Becca. He licked his lips and tapped his mouse nervously with a finger. The door was shut, so no one could possibly see. Were they monitoring his personal email? Probably not, but one could never be too sure.

Tyson clicked the subject line, which was blank. There was only a single line.

Safe. Wanted you to know. See you soon.

His breath whooshed out of him.

"What have you gotten yourself into now, Becca?" he muttered, opening a blank email to reply and give her a hard time about being cryptic. He stared at the blinking cursor so long he started to see spots. And then, for the sixth time since noon, a knock came at his door. Two fists banging instead of one. He knew that double knock.

James and Violet Petrov.

Tyson's heart skipped a beat, and he pressed the power button without thinking, hard crashing the desktop. Becca wasn't guilty, but one of the people knocking thought she was. They had already interviewed Tyson since no one could get a hold of her, but he didn't know anything except that he was certain she was innocent.

"Come in." Tyson spun around as the door opened, a mysterious wind whirling through James' and Violet's hair like a special effect in a movie.

"You're working rather hard," James said.

"Just passing time. Is my new lanyard ready yet?" Too much to hope for, but he had to ask.

James straightened his glasses. "It's in the process."

"We came to speak with you about Harper King," Violet intoned, a mysterious, heavy weight to her voice. With James here, Violet must have Seen something, something that involved Tyson or one of his clients. He'd seen one of her trances only once. Scary stuff. He swallowed past his fear as Violet continued. "This Daughter of Raven brings mayhem to our sanctuary. She has disrupted many of our residents with her rage over Naturalization."

"We've had difficult residents before. There's a transition period for all of them."

"We have reason to believe she is a particular danger to herself and others." James stepped forward, urgency on his face. "She isn't just a bird shifter. The Raven sings from her blood."

"Raven born," Violet hissed, her gaze still caught in the clutches of her prophetic Sight.

Tyson crossed his arms, feeling his hackles rise. "Whatever she is, we can handle it. No different than your pet banshee."

That jibe would have normally gotten him a sizzling glare from Violet, but she was still entranced, her stare flat and emotionless.

James raised his eyebrows, and Tyson reconsidered Violet's word choice. *Raven born.* Raven was a significant figure in the beliefs of the Inuit. Nana brought Tyson up with stories of the mischievous creator of light. Some even said Raven created man.

"You both keep referring to this 'Raven.' Are we talking about a god? I didn't know the great Raven had daughters." Tyson shifted his weight from foot to foot. If they were dealing with a half-deity, a demi-god...

"I don't believe Raven is classified as a god, although it's a near enough definition. With your Inuit heritage, we assumed you would know more than we do about her kind." James knew more about the hundreds of types of paranormal and supernatural beings than Tom, who was the resident expert.

Tyson put his hands up. "Look, I may have Inuit grandparents, but all I know are fragmented stories told as bedtime tales. Nothing about Raven people, though I'm not surprised they exist. Is there any evidence she's related to a deity?" His mouth went dry. His training had covered deities and demi-gods. As counselors, they were instructed to avoid them whenever possible and to report any interaction with divine beings in the directory being created for reference. If Harper was one, she couldn't stay here. A team would be brought in, more specialized than S.T.F. It wouldn't be pretty.

"We...we aren't sure. We need you to find out. There is very little literature available, and Violet has had a premonition of sorts, though it's harder to read than most of the others she's had," James explained. "You are in a unique position to talk to Harper and draw out information. She may not know herself what her abilities are. It's imperative we find out, while at the same time keeping her calm. Help her feel safe here. We don't want any errant powers manifesting if we can help it, and we can't afford for her to escape."

"If you're that worried, why not transfer her to higher security? We don't have the resources to contain her if she's that powerful." Tyson straightened in his chair, uncrossing his arms, then crossing his legs. He couldn't seem to sit still.

James pressed his fingers against the edge of the desktop. "We're trying to impress key players in the Administration. Since the other Raven Born shifter escaped, we intend to keep a tight hold on this one and find out everything we can."

Tyson could play this angle to his benefit. He steepled his fingers, swiveling the chair slightly. He pointed his hands at James.

"You're willing to put a lot of people at risk for this information and to improve your reputation with the state. I'm not sure I agree with your methods, though."

James hesitated, glanced at his wife, whose expression remained stony, and drew his lips in a thin line. "Your full cooperation would be appreciated, of course. And we could guarantee that our appreciation takes the form of two essential signatures."

"Two?"

"Tom and Lilith are not our puppets, Tyson. We can put in our word for your recommendation. Your influence on them is up to you. We do ask that you don't tell them about Harper, at least not yet."

Dr. Hartford, Tyson understood. He would insist on shipping Harper off to another facility. Tyson wasn't sure about Lilith, but by James' insistence not to tell her, he assumed the warlock had a good reason. Perhaps it came down to who would take credit for unlocking the Raven born's secrets.

What James implied was risky, but if successful could turn into more funding, more land, and more benefits for everyone working at Camp Silver Lake. And Tyson wanted this promotion. As a full-time counselor at the camp, he would help more paranormals achieve a normal life. James' and Violet's signatures would otherwise be the hardest to get.

Tyson clapped his hands together, a satisfied smile coming to his face. "You can count on me."

Violet broke out of her trance and wrapped Tyson in her familiar, fiery gaze. "Do whatever it takes, Miller. Make her think you have something on her, her family, whatever it takes to earn her trust." She pursed her lips, never taking her eyes off his as she tilted her head.

Together, they turned to go.

"Oh, and you have an appointment with her in fifteen minutes," Violet said without looking back.

Fifteen minutes. Tyson groaned internally. Fifteen minutes to eat lunch, use the bathroom, and book it back here before he missed an appointment with a possible demi-god, or near enough.

"Thank you," he said sarcastically to the closing door.

CHAPTER SIX

HARPER

THERE WAS A GLASS door leading outside at the end of the hall. Harper pushed it open and stepped onto the grass, chest heaving.

How far could she get if she took off now? She searched the skies. They were a dark, stormy gray, and lightning crackled from the clouds with a frequency that made her nervous. *Never fly in a storm.* The ever-practical Quinn. Would he give the same advice if he were here?

Worse than the storm, someone would certainly spot her before she reached the clouds. She'd have to hike through the woods for a couple of miles to get out far enough to reduce the risk of being seen. Lilith's warning about rogues in the woods rang in her head. But how else could she leave this place?

Harper cocked her head at the sound of something scraping against metal. To her left was a large white box truck. Burly men went in and out with loads no normal human could lift. She recognized Zeke among them. The others must have been from his pack.

She jumped down the steps and headed toward the driveway where they stacked crates. Produce and various foods peeked out of the crates as Harper drew closer. Dozens of massive cooler chests sat next to them, she guessed for meat and dairy.

A guy with a clipboard stood on one leg near the garage. One pant leg was tied off beneath the knee of one leg as if the leg had been amputated. Harper recognized him from Zeke's table at breakfast. The guy spotted Harper and gave her a huge, teeth-bearing grin. Did all werewolves smile like that? She inched toward him.

"Harper, right? I'm Beckett." He held out a hand, which Harper ignored. He wiped his hand on his pants and retrieved his pen, then looked over at the others still unloading and checked a few things off on his clipboard. "Finishing up grocery delivery here. Almost didn't make it before the rogues today. We'll have to change the delivery time again. Hello, Lilith." He said it without turning around.

"You have the best nose, Beckett," Lilith said.

Lilith. Did she know more about Quinn than Anita? Harper's heart rate increased. Lilith could tell her about Quinn's escape, maybe the name of the human who helped him. But could she be trusted? Would she help Harper escape?

"And you have the best perfume," Beckett responded.

"I don't wear any."

"*Eau de naturale* is the best kind." He wiggled his eyebrows, and Lilith smiled, obliging his flirting, but she didn't return it.

Zeke set a large box down with a thump. "If you'd let the packs war, we could cut the rogues down. We're nearly three times their size."

"I'm not having a war, Zeke. Especially since they're more than just werewolves."

"The bloodsuckers aren't an issue," Zeke said, rolling his eyes.

"Drake nearly killed you last time. He's no vamp, Zeke, and you know it. No wars. The Hunter's Guild has the equipment."

"I hate being shut in when they come," Zeke mumbled. "My pack gets restless. They destroyed half the cabin in the two weeks the Guild was here last year. Couldn't we work together or something?"

They didn't seem to remember Harper was there. It was the perfect opportunity and she wouldn't let it pass her by, not with the knowledge that Quinn wasn't here any longer. She could find another lead on her own. She didn't need Lilith.

Harper inched away from the group. The truck engine rumbled as it turned over.

Zeke was nearly nose to nose with Lilith now, and Beckett stood between them looking conflicted about whose side he should be taking.

The others unloading the truck had disappeared. Harper darted around the side of the truck, shrugging off her jacket as she leapt up.

Itching and burning, her back erupted with fire and feathers. Black wings arced past her head and flapped, creating a massive downdraft and lifting her into the air.

She thrust her wings down again, grabbing the top edge of the truck to pull herself up. The tires ground on the gravel driveway as the truck pulled away. With one last flap, Harper clambered to the top then flattened down, wings covering her.

Harper grinned into the wind as it ruffled her chin-length hair and rippled through her feathers. Pure delight overcame her. She longed to spread her wings and launch into the air, but the threat of discovery kept her pinned. Her wings, flattened, held her to the roof of the truck with their comforting weight.

The truck wound down the forest road. Harper wanted to get through the boundary of the wards before leaving the truck, but it was getting harder to hold herself down as the vehicle picked up speed.

THUMP.

Something struck the truck and it veered wildly to the right, heading off the road. Harper leapt free, flapping her wings to stay aloft and avoid the tangle of branches scraping the truck top as it drove into the forest and crashed into the trees, smoking. She landed on a thicker pine branch, crouching low.

Did it hit a deer? Harper glanced down. *Oh hell.* A wolf, not nearly as large as Keith but still menacing, braced in the road. Its dark brown fur raised in a ridge along its back and stared straight at her, teeth bared.

She got the sense that it was Zeke; something about the human chastisement in its eyes. She pushed off from the branch, headed for the stormy sky and freedom. In her peripheral, the wolf jumped from the ground and ran up the tree trunk.

No way. Jaws clamped onto her foot. They plummeted downward and broke apart as they hit the ground. Harper rolled across the road, landing on her back. The wolf was there in a moment, and then it was gone, replaced with Zeke laughing in her face.

"One of the more clever attempts at escape, I'll give you that."

Harper glared at him. "I would think you'd be on my side."

"Naturalization gives us options, Harper. A chance to live a normal life. And keep others safe."

"Amputation isn't normal, Zeke!" Her voice grew shrill. She pushed against his chest, which was like shoving against a boulder. He moved off her, but not because of her pushing. He rolled to his feet and offered her a hand.

"I didn't say the options were great. I hope to change some of them."

Harper ignored his hand. She stood on her own, brushing off her pants, then curled one of her wings inward and looked over it for any damage. Nothing more than ruffled feathers. She was lucky.

"So...bird shifter? Have you met Fletcher?"

"Yeah, I have. Too bad he's due to have his wings cauterized," Harper snapped.

Zeke closed his eyes. "I thought I talked him out of that. He wants so badly to be normal. I told him that wasn't the way, but..."

"But what options does he have? You people put us in classes to brainwash us into believing Naturalization is the only way, and then put us in warded boxes thinking you've done us a favor?" She stopped. Her stomach heaved—from hunger or disgust, she wasn't sure.

"Save the speech for Violet. She's the one who has any influence here. I'm just the muscle."

"You could've let me go."

"I'm not convinced that's best for anyone." Zeke looked at the truck. A man dressed in nothing but biker shorts, like Zeke, dragged the driver from the front seat. Blood trickled across his forehead. Harper's mouth dried up.

"Is he dead?"

The other guy gave Zeke a thumbs up, then hauled the guy out and swung him over one shoulder.

"He's alive, for now. Violet can tell us the extent of his injuries and heal him. Come on, she'll want to see you too."

Harper gazed over her shoulder at the empty road. How many miles until freedom and Quinn?

Zeke eyed her. "It's not worth it to run."

"You have no idea what you're talking about. So shut up."

He gripped Harper's shirt at the neck and gave her a push forward. The rough treatment was unnecessary. She didn't plan on running again. Yet.

They walked the rest of the way in silence. By the time they reached the cabin, fatigue replaced Harper's anger. She tucked her wings in to fit through the front door, ignoring the stares from the gathering dinner crowd as Zeke led her up the stairs to the apothecary.

James and Violet Petrov waited for Harper, storms flashing in their grey eyes. They parted to let her into the room and exchanged a few quiet words with Zeke before shutting the door. Harper closed her eyes and prepared to be warded.

One thing they didn't mention was that wards were *heavy*. She had no fewer than fifteen sigils inked on her neck, arms, legs, and back. They were heaviest on her back.

"The marks are temporary. A couple hours and they'll start to fade." Violet handed Harper the jacket she'd left in the road before her botched escape attempt. Harper pulled it on, knowing she'd get more stares without it.

To be fair, most of the sigils on her back were for healing, and there was a thick poultice and bandage too. Bird-shifters' wings erupted straight out of their skin. She'd always bled during transformation, leaving thin lines of caked blood down her back until she was able to get her next shower. Violet said she could fix it, and Harper saw no harm in that. Violet did something to Harper's skin, made it more resilient. No shifting for twelve hours, she said. And now Harper knew why Fletcher's back didn't bleed when he shifted back to his human form. The only perk to being in this maddened place. But why heal her if her wings would be gone in the end? It was a puzzle Harper couldn't figure out the answer to.

Violet kissed James and he left the room. He had helped place the wards. Some of them were for keeping Harper within the bounds of the camp, from all directions. They'd had to ward her extra heavily because of her flying ability.

Violet turned. "You're late for your counseling appointment. Why don't you clean up a bit and then meet Mr. Miller in his office downstairs?"

The witch brushed her hair from her face, peering at the stained page of a book in her hands, having already moved on to the next thing.

Shocked at the lack of lecture, Harper stood in the stillness of flickering candles shuffling her feet.

"Do you require something else, Harper?"

Harper cleared her throat. "You, uh, knew my brother?"

She closed the book with a loud clap, and Harper jumped. "Yes. He was here, and he left."

"What...what would happen if he were found?"

She blinked. "You wonder if he would be brought here."

Harper bit her lip.

"No." The word hung in the air, and something severed in Harper. A whoosh of breath left her body. Was it relief? Her feelings were jumbled.

Violet continued. "Naturalization is an opportunity once lost, never regained. And the same would have been true for you, had your foolhardy attempt today been successful. I suggest you consider that the next time you think about escaping."

"I couldn't now if I wanted to." Harper gestured to the sigils under her jacket sleeves.

"And yet, Quincey King did." Violet moved to the shelf and placed the book in its slot.

Harper's eyes lingered on the titles. They were marked with dates, ranges of years handwritten on the spines. A few at the end seemed to be about biology and herbs, but her eyes drew back to the record volumes.

"If you'll excuse me, I have work to catch up on." Violet made a dismissive motion with her hand.

Harper walked backward a few steps, then pivoted and passed into the hall, shutting the door behind her. She jammed her hands into her pockets and went to the bathroom to take care of the dirt on her arms and face. She straightened her hair and scowled at the mirror. Why did she bother?

When Harper emerged, the lodge seemed empty. Where was everyone? Not that it mattered. She had an appointment, after all.

She hesitated in front of the office door. She usually ditched this sort of thing. Mandatory counseling sessions weren't new to her. She could ask about Quinn, maybe try to find out how he had escaped, but she sensed this Mr. Miller wouldn't take questions about her delinquent brother lightly.

Besides that, Harper felt a smidge guilty about injuring the truck driver during her botched escape attempt. Violet said he'd be okay, but last Harper heard he was sleeping it off in a guarded room.

Harper pulled her hand out of her jacket pocket and knocked loudly.

"Just a minute!" Tyson's voice sounded muffled through the door.

Moments later, The door opened wide. A piece of lettuce clung to one of Tyson's teeth and crumbs decorated his t-shirt.

"Let's get this over with," Harper muttered, brushing past him. She avoided the chair she was meant to sit in, walking around the room for a minute. "You have something right there, by the way." She pointed to her tooth. Tyson frowned and wiped his own teeth clean, then cleared his throat.

Harper spoke before he could. "You married?" She jutted her chin at a picture frame on his desk, a girl with brown hair holding a baby in one arm and the hand of a little girl with the other. Tyson smiled.

"That's my sister. Meagan. And my niece and nephew. Their dad was a police officer."

Was. The way he said it, Harper didn't have to ask if his brother-in-law is still alive. "Paranormal incident?"

He pressed his lips together, grabbing the back of the rolling chair behind the desk and leaning on it. "He responded to a werewolf attack. Those were the days before Supernatural Tactical Forces were engaged." He spun the chair and sat down, turning back to face her. "How has your first day been?"

Really? Harper gave him a long, hard look, not bothering to hide her disbelief. "They told you I tried to escape, right?"

His pen froze over the paper on the desk in front of him. "No, actually. They didn't. Zeke catch you?"

"Yeah. What's with that guy, anyway?"

Tyson looked up, tapping his pen against his opposite hand. "Thought he might help you?"

No. Harper was just surprised he helped *them.* Surprised anyone in this place did what they were told. They could rebel. Overthrow the whole system. But something told her that no one would take an idea like that seriously. They were too married to the utopian idea of getting licensed and living happily ever after with the humans.

Violet and Petrov were the worst, leading them like lambs to the slaughter. Did they get perks for being in charge? Points for each paranormal they Naturalized, bonuses for the crippled ones?

"If I could read your mind right now, what would I find?" Tyson asked in his shrink talk.

"Guess," Harper shot back.

Tyson fiddled with his pencil and let his chair drift side to side. "What do you want, Harper? Do you want us to let you go? Let the Hunters track you down and cart you off to an experimental facility? Or worse, kill you?"

"Just between us, death would be preferable." She plopped into the chair across the desk, slumping with her hands in her pockets.

"You're angry. I can see that."

She leaned forward. "Oh, can you? Because I—"

Tyson held up a hand. The pleading in his eyes made Harper bite her lip and sit back.

"Harper, yours is not a unique case. I get someone just like you in here every few months. They've lived in foster care, they've been in the streets, they've been in hiding. Taunted, persecuted, hunted. They killed their brother, their sister, their parents, their neighbor, mostly in horrible accidents. They don't know their own abilities. They come in here fighting. Some of them settle down, but others never do. They're the unlucky ones.

"I know you won't agree with me right now, but it's true. They're missing the point. With Naturalization, you have a chance at a normal life. To have friends, to have a family, to build a career, a home, a life for yourself. Why would you pass that up?"

Rage trembled in Harper's limbs. She drew her hands from her pockets and shook them out, loosening up the energy that compressed in her body. Breath flowed in and out of her lungs. She focused on it, blocking out his face and that glaring white paper on his desk. If he knew what she had been through to get this far, what would be taken away if she stayed...to never find her brother and parents...The words wouldn't form. Harper didn't speak.

"Think about it." His voice dropped, becoming gentle. It was a tactic. Perhaps an honest one, but a tactic all the same. Manipulation by any other name would hurt as much. Harper hated him for it, but she had to focus on keeping her anger beneath the surface. She feared what she might do if he kept pushing her toward that edge. Would he have time to get to that panic button under his desk this time?

"Are you willing to try, Harper? How about this—if you're going to give this your best shot, tell me something about you."

Harper stared at him, deadpan. What would happen if she didn't answer? Would they take her away from here? Withdraw her Naturalization application? The minutes ticked by. She couldn't see any clocks, but she felt the passing of time and wondered if Tyson's patience would run out, if he'd give up on her. He wouldn't be the first.

"I know my brother was here," Harper blurted. The words surprised her. She hadn't planned them, they just...happened.

Tyson snorted. "Okay. We'll go there." He interlocked his fingers on the desk. "Yes, Quinn was here." He separated his hands in a "ta-da!" motion.

Harper rolled her eyes.

"You already know he escaped. I assume that's why you tried to leave. Is that who you were looking for when you got picked up?"

She huffed. "I don't have to do this."

"No. You don't. We could sit here in silence for the next..." He glanced at the clock on the wall. "...twenty-five minutes. Or you could utilize the free therapy session, paid for by taxpayer dollars."

Harper considered him. He seemed sincere in wanting to help, but she wasn't about to sob on him about her family or anything else. Naturalization aside, she would sooner walk a thousand miles than talk about her feelings.

"Would it be okay if I asked you some questions? Just things I'm curious about. Answering optional."

Harper grunted, which actually drew a smile from him. He was starting to think he understood her. "Where is your family from?"

She could answer that one. "Oregon."

"You grew up here?"

"Yeah."

Tyson's lips quirked and he bobbed his head affirmative. "Okay, then. So did I. But my dad's the one who brought my mom here. From Alaska."

"Cool." If she cared, maybe.

He arched a brow. "What about your parents?"

"Look, I don't know what happened to them," Harper snapped, sitting bolt upright, gripping the chair seat and breathing deeply to keep from shifting.

"That isn't the question I asked," Tyson pointed out.

She reigned in her breathing, bringing it back under control. Her shoulder blades throbbed. She would kill to have them rubbed right now, but she wasn't about to ask anyone for any favors. "Aren't you a bit…I don't know. Young? To be counseling someone your own age?"

"Tom probably would have seen you, but he's not here. You can switch when he gets back. I'm here to put out fires."

"How long have you been doing this?"

"We're getting off-topic."

"Just want to be sure I'm speaking to a real professional. You know, someone who can fix all of my emotional issues." Harper put quotes around the last word. It hung in the air until Tyson cleared his throat.

"I know you don't want to be here, Harper. You've made that abundantly clear. But would it hurt to try?"

"Yes. I think it would." She leaned forward, hands clasped between her knees.

Tyson tilted his chair back, looking at the ceiling for a moment. Was he praying? Harper snorted at the thought.

"What if we just"—he spread his hands—"got to know each other? You know, likes and dislikes, that sort of thing?"

"Sounds like a date," she taunted.

"Uh, no. This is not a date. This is a *professional* counseling appointment."

"Sorry, *Mr. Miller*. I got confused." Harper said in a mocking voice as she bit back laughter. It was too fun getting under his skin.

Tyson shifted his shoulders. "You don't have to call me that."

She arched a brow.

"I just meant that a lot of the residents prefer to call me Tyson." He ran a hand through his brown hair, and some of it stood up for a bit before falling.

"Okay, then. Tyson it is."

"Do you go by Harper?"

She pressed her lips together in a line and let her head nod.

"Great. And, what's your favorite thing to do?"

Harper tilted her head and stared at him. He didn't get it. She put a hand to the side of her mouth. "It's sort of illegal," she stage-whispered.

Tyson laughed. It was the least annoying thing about him. Sort of rich and sincere, the kind of laugh that made you want to know the joke. Harper tightened her lips, holding back any sort of indication that she shared his mirth. He hadn't earned that yet.

"That's something. I mean, I asked for it. Where do you like to fly most?"

"Mountains," Harper said before she realized he'd asked two questions. Trickster. "My turn," she interjected before he asked another one. "What made you decide to be a paranormal shrink?"

"Counselor," Tyson corrected. "And I like to help people."

"Oh, ha." She shot him a fierce look, but he crossed his arms and gave her a self-satisfied grin like he'd done something clever.

"Seriously, though, the real reason is that I had this friend. She was like you, in a way. Shifter. She could change into a fox." He stared down at the pen rotating through his fingers and smiled. "We were best friends. When she told me, I was just amazed. Well, not at first. I was scared the first time. But after that, I thought it was the neatest thing in the world. I even wished I could do it. She told me not to tell anyone."

"But you did."

His face fell, and Harper suddenly wanted to make him laugh again.

"You know, I don't tell anyone this story. That's one reason why." He stared her down.

"Try me."

He shook his head and sat back in his chair. "When the people came and asked me questions, I answered them honestly. I was ten, and they assured me that Reya and her family would be safer, that they would learn to be normal and that others would be safer too, that I could be part of that change for them. I'd seen my friend's fear about being caught, I wanted her to not be afraid anymore. After that, her family disappeared. My parents assured me they were all being helped..."

He trailed off, then cleared his throat. His hand drifted to the pencil on his desk and rolled it back and forth. "I never saw them again."

Harper was shocked by his transparency and the depth of the lies he'd been sold. Bitter words rose to her lips, but Tyson wasn't done yet. He continued.

"A few years later, my sister's husband was killed, and I wondered if there was anything that could be done to get harmful paranormals rehabilitated, to make the world safer for everyone. I looked into Naturalization, everything they let the public know, and then I found Dr. Thomas Hartford. He came to speak on campus about a revolutionary program he'd pioneered—psychology for paranormals—and everything changed for me. I knew that this was the career for me. The past two years have been incredible, showing me again and again that this is what the world needs in order to integrate paranormals into society."

"That's what inspired you?" Harper curled her lips, withholding a desire to spit at his feet. "You destroy families."

He shook his head. "No, I help them get back to their families, back to a normal life where they aren't persecuted anymore. They're not hated and hunted the rest of their lives."

It made sense in a twisted sort of way. The way a psychopath justified murders.

"Tell me about your parents. Are they like you?" The counselor voice was back. It was like a persona that he put on and took off. For a moment, they'd shared something real. Now the insincere, syrupy gentleness was back, coating his voice and gaze.

Harper sat back in her chair. Tyson was utterly brainwashed if he thought after that inspiring little speech she would open up.

"I get it, you're protecting them," he said. "I respect that. Let's talk about something else." He put the pen down and leaned forward, pursing his lips and raising one eyebrow. A ridiculous expression. He scrutinized her. "I've asked enough questions for today. What else do you want to discuss today?"

Harper scoffed. "How about how messed up it is that you think you helped your friend. That you have ever helped anyone. Is that up for discussion?"

He bit his lip, then caught himself and stopped abruptly, changing his position in his chair. He maintained a carefully crafted expression of indifference.

She forged ahead, finally free to say exactly what she thought. "How brainwashed are you? You and everyone else in this place who tries to help, you do far more harm than good. How can it *help* to take people from their homes, their families, their lives, and put them in a facility that teaches them that what they are, their very essence is an abomination that must be suppressed, even terminated?"

Harper paused, chest heaving, waiting for him to respond, but he said nothing. Just looked at her with his chin in his hand. She released the next tirade as it built inside her.

"You would never tell a human who came into your office that they should stop being who they were, cut off their arms and send them back into the world expecting them to thrive! That's insanity, but it's exactly what you do here. There's a whole other side to this, and you can't see it. You can't see how your methods torture and hurt those who are subjected to them because they have no other choice!"

Breathless, she stopped. Her words were spent. She could have said more, but she wanted to hear him say he was wrong, that he understood her side.

It seemed an eternity before he moved. He sighed and adjusted his position in his seat. "There. Feel better?"

Harper gaped. Was he for real? "Feel better? How could I possibly...? You haven't said or done anything that could possibly make me feel better!"

Tyson nodded. At what, she didn't know. "Sometimes we just need to get words out to realize how ridiculous it sounds. Harper, I'm not here to hurt you. I'm not going to maim you. You're going to come to the realization that there are opportunities to be had here that you won't find anywhere else."

He smiled, then grabbed a piece of paper from the folder on his desk and slid it across to her. "This is a Naturalization application. How about you look it over and see what's required. We can talk about it in a few days at your next appointment."

Harper stood, laughing more out of nerves than humor. "You are certifiable. I don't know what they taught you at whatever crackpot shrink school you attended, but here's a fun fact: I don't care about your application. I'll keep my wings, thank you." Her stomach lurched at the fact that he felt fulfilled in giving her the 'opportunity' to be maimed for life. She had nothing more to say to him, at least not anything that would be productive.

"I thought you might respond better to someone telling you like it is. I thought you would appreciate the transparency."

"Oh, I do," Harper snapped back. "And I'm not afraid to tell you that it's horrifying what you do to my people in the name of progress and peace. What you did to your friend. They keep records on everything, don't they? Haven't you found out what happened to her yet? Or are you afraid of what you'll find?"

Tyson finally lost his cool. He stood, finger jabbing into the paper on the desk, sputtering as he struggled for words. "You don't know what you're talking about. If I could make you see—"

He ran his fingers through his hair, then pushed his chair out of the way and strode to the door, throwing it open. "I think we've both had quite enough conversation for today. I'll see you next week."

Satisfaction flooded Harper, seeing him so agitated. She grinned broadly, not bothering to hold back the laugh that bubbled up. "Look at you! Pretending to help people. Bless your heart."

He gritted his teeth. "I'm not pretending. I'm *trying* to help you."

She walked past him into the hall, glancing back over her shoulder and pulling her upper lip into a snarl. "I don't want your help."

Tyson grabbed his coat from behind his door and shoved his arms into the sleeves. He slammed the office door behind him. Harper lingered, still amused at his anger.

"I'm going for a walk," he growled, marching past her.

"I won't wait up," Harper called after him.

He straightened his jacket and threw open the front door, walking straight out into the windy afternoon. The door banged shut behind him.

She ignored the guilt that tried to ply her with reasons to feel bad about what she said to him. She honestly didn't care. Truly, she didn't. Next chance she got, she would leave this place and never see him again.

CHAPTER SEVEN

HARPER

AFTER TYSON LEFT, HARPER wandered aimlessly through the house, avoiding areas with people, familiarizing herself with the place. The heaviness of the wards Violet placed on her had lifted slightly, though her sense of agitation lingered. The wards might be meant as protection, but they were also effectively shackles.

Eventually, Harper's growling stomach forced her to the kitchen. A few stragglers remained, picking at their food. Another group argued in the common room. Something about a movie?

Kamri leapt up from the breakfast nook where Beckett and several other werewolves lounged. She sauntered toward Harper like she owned the place. Based on what Harper had seen, the werewolves were pretty high up on the social ladder. Or maybe it was a food chain thing.

"Glad you made it! You don't want to miss movie night," she said. "You're probably hungry. It's fend-for-yourself tonight."

"I could eat," Harper said, rubbing the inside of her wrist.

"So, do you like your meat dead or alive?" Kamri wagged her eyebrows. Harper couldn't tell if she was joking or not.

"I've always had my meat cooked before I eat it. Guess I don't know the difference."

"You're missing out! But if that's not your jam, we can cook." She said it without mocking. She headed to a large metal door behind the long kitchen counter and opened it up with a gust of cool air. A walk-in refrigerator, one of the industrial kind found in restaurants.

"I see hamburger patties, sausages, hot dogs...Man, I love delivery day. You pick, I'll cook." Kamri turned back to Harper, who must have had a strange expression on her face, because Kamri's changed in an instant becoming a mask of politeness. "Oh, I'm sorry. Here I am assuming you prefer meat. Are you vegan or something?"

Harper snorted. "Not likely. Hamburger sounds great. And...do you have any cereal?" After a day like today she wanted comfort food. All the stress of escaping, being warded, and her talk with Tyson had caught up with her, and her stomach complained in full force. She had skipped lunch, after all.

Kamri grinned, tossing a crimson strand of hair out of her face. "You betcha! Like milk with it?"

"Nope."

Kamri looked at Harper like she had two heads. "You bird-folk are strange." She carried a large package of hamburger to the counter. No way Harper would eat more than two patties. The werewolf probably knew that.

"Have you known many of us?" Harper asked.

Ian walked into the kitchen, hands in his pockets. Kamri grinned at him. "Just two. Three, if you count yourself. Haven't really gotten to know you, though, and the other one wasn't here long."

Quinn. Harper's lip trembled. She rubbed it, hoping her anxiety didn't show. She'd been so close to escaping, but Quinn felt farther away than ever now. Harper stuffed the feelings down, groping for a question to ask Kamri to find out more about how Quinn had escaped. Maybe Harper could mimic his success.

"Are you a LIFE or Fruit Loops chick?" Kamri grabbed both kinds of cereal and closed the pantry. As they walked away, Harper heard a faint beep. The coded lock on the door went from green to red. The fridge had the same red light next to it. As Kamri set the cereal boxes on the counter, she slapped a hand over her mouth. "Sorry about that. I wasn't thinking how derogatory that could have been."

Harper shrugged. "Calling me chick? I mean...yeah, okay, I'm a bird. But you didn't mean it that way."

Kamri raised her eyebrows. "That's a big thing, here. You should learn the terms that others find offensive. We avoid a lot of violence that way."

Harper rolled her eyes. She understood, but it still seemed ridiculous that anyone could get offended over a figure of speech like that. All the politically correct stuff made her uncomfortable, especially when groups of humans took it on themselves to protest similar 'offenses' but didn't lift a finger to protest what happened in the Naturalization camps.

Time to change the subject.

"So, I met Fletcher already." Harper tried to sound casual. "What happened with the other one? The other bird-shifter?"

"He tried to escape, like you. He didn't give up after the first time, either. He tried every single day he was here. Then this Cryptozoologist, Becca, showed up to collect our latest data and interview a few of the residents. It's, like, this month-long process? Anyway, she grew pretty close to Quinn and the next thing we know, they blow the joint together. That's not the official story, though. The human is off the hook, as usual." Kamri opened the box of cereal and grabbed a fistful, putting it in her mouth and chewing rapidly.

Harper's heart pounded as if she was the one escaping. Anita, that witch from the other day, had been so caught up in Quinn having a *girlfriend* she failed to mention they might have escaped together. Was that why Quinn hadn't come looking for Harper? She frowned.

Ian fired up a pan on the stove. He smiled at them through his curtain of hair.

Kamri beamed at him. "I never thought I'd see a vegan cooking burgers."

"I eat fish," he protested.

Kamri fetched Harper a bowl and spoon. She reached for the cereal and poured it herself. Kamri eyed her serving. "Do you eat like a bird too? I'm always famished after I shift out of wolf."

Harper hesitated, then poured some more. Kamri threw her that signature grin.

Harper cleared her throat. "How does that work, anyway? I thought werewolves were a full moon thing."

"Best we can figure is French blood. The *loup garou* is a breed that can transform at will. We also shift during the night of the full moon; that one is obligatory. Mostly just inconvenient. Apparently, the French werewolves were highly prolific breeders, too. Most of us can do it. Only a few do the half-crazed full moon transformation. They don't last long here. There isn't a cure."

Harper nearly spit out her cereal. "It's *genetic*?"

"At least the French version is. I couldn't turn someone if I bit them, but if I got pregnant the babies would be just like me." Kamri said, shrugging.

Ian blushed deep red at that, for some reason. "I might burn these. How do you like it?"

"Any way I can get it," Kamri said suggestively, snaking her hand over the one he held the spatula with. He stuttered. Kamri grabbed the spatula away from him and bumped him over with her hip. "Preferably bloody, though. Harper?" She indicated the burgers.

"Medium rare." The cereal was good, but Harper definitely needed more.

Kamri tsked, sliding a second bleeding circle of meat onto her plate. "Thanks for getting us started, Ian. Wanna make sure they don't pick a terrible movie?"

"It's already chosen. Some superhero thing. I'll go save our spot."

"If it's taken, tell 'em I'll bite 'em," Kamri said around a mouthful of meat.

Harper joined in a minute later, grease dripping down her chin. It was the best burger she'd ever eaten. Just meat, no bread or limp veggies to work around. Harper moaned and Kamri laughed.

"At least we agree on one thing. Thank God you're not vegan."

Harper laughed with her. Looking at the smiling faces, Harper realized she was in a place she could actually belong. She could never show her true self or talk about anything related to her shifter form while she was in hiding, but now...too bad it was temporary. The bite of meat in her mouth grew tasteless, and she swallowed. She needed a drink.

"Kamri, can I get—" The back door leading from the kitchen to outside burst open, and Fletcher strode in, windswept hair and feathers sticking every which way. His cobalt eyes landed on Harper, then darted around the room as if looking for someone.

"What's up, Fletcher?" Kamri asked, wiping her face.

"Where's Zeke? Or Lilith, maybe?" He had a wild look in his eyes, something like fear.

"I think Zeke is with Mandi. Not sure about Lilith," Ian said.

Kamri put down her burger. "Is something wrong?"

"Rogues are on the move. I saw them as I flew over the forest. They look like they're hunting. Is everyone inside?"

All activity in the room froze. People exchanged looks and murmured, most of them shaking their heads. Kamri counted heads, then ran into the common room and made an announcement. "Is anyone missing? Did anyone go out?"

Harper's mouth felt parched. She still hadn't gotten a drink, but that wasn't the main issue. She licked her lips.

"Tyson," she said. The chatter in the room was too loud for her small voice. She cleared her throat. "Hey, Tyson went for a walk earlier."

Fletcher heard her. "Kamri!"

Kamri ran back into the kitchen. "Everyone accounted for, I think. Did you find anyone missing?"

"Harper says Tyson left earlier for a walk."

"By himself?"

"Did anyone see him come back?" Fletcher's eyes darted frantically. Panic palpated around the room, washing across various faces like a wave.

"Why would Tyson go off into the forest alone if he knew they were out there?" Harper asked.

Ian answered from her left. "They're not active until after dark. He probably figured he was safe to go for a stroll. But there's a storm rolling in, so it's darker earlier than usual."

Kamri mentioned something about gathering the pack, and Fletcher said he'd find Violet or Lilith. No one else moved. Harper stood, scooting her chair back.

Ian glanced up. "What are you doing?"

"He can't have gone far. I'm going with the pack. I'll fly overhead and help them find him faster."

"No, you won't." Violet's voice came in behind them. Harper turned around. Violet's eyes had lit up, they were literally glowing. She must have been casting some sort of spell.

"It's my fault he's out there. If he's in danger, I want to help get him out of it," Harper said.

Violet held up a hand. "I healed your back too recently. If you shift now, you'll undo all of it. No, you'll stay here with the others.

Harper curled her hands into fists. It was a problem she had caused, and she wanted to fix it. She opened her mouth to retort, but Violet interrupted, moving on as if Harper weren't still standing there, glaring at her.

"Fletcher? Are you up for flying?"

"I was just out there and that wind's a beast." Fletcher was breathless. "I'm not sure I can last in it, but I'll try."

He walked from the room, blue wings tucked against his back until he stepped outside. Harper watched through the window as his wings unfurled and he launched into the evening sky. The wind immediately buffeted him, but he corrected his course with ease.

A moment later, a pack of werewolves ran through the same field in the back, splitting up in groups of two and three and heading in different directions. Harper counted ten, including the black one she recognized as Zeke.

Inside the cabin, everything returned to normal for movie night, although a palpable sort of tension lay thick in the air. Harper stood in the kitchen as everyone trickled toward the common room. Someone flipped off the lights in the kitchen except for a dim one above the bar-like counter that Harper leaned against.

Her eyes remained trained on the storm brewing outside as if she could see across distances through walls and trees to find the person everyone worried about. Was she worried about him? It wasn't her fault that Tyson had decided to wander off near dark. He knew better than she did the dangers that existed here, and she hadn't intentionally goaded him into leaving. Guilt gripped her chest in a tight fist.

A click on the countertop drew Harper's attention back inside. A woman stood beside her, skin and hair black, eyes milky white.

Harper squeezed the counter's edge with her hands. "Who are you?"

"Which stone?" The woman asked, dipping her head toward the counter.

Two polished rocks gleamed there—one a muddy red color, streaked with white. The other was white with soft gray lines through it.

"You want me to pick one?"

"Yes." She clipped the word so short that Harper assumed she might say something else, but she pursed her lips together, staring sightlessly to one side.

Harper wasn't one to linger on decisions like this. She pointed at the red stone, hardly knowing what she was choosing. The blind woman smirked and snatched the white stone from the counter.

"You've chosen your fate in the red amethyst. I knew you were a fighter when I first felt your aura, Harper King. Take your stone and go find him."

Harper palmed the stone, staring at it. "Why the rock?"

"For courage. For strength. For protection."

Harper snorted. "Are you some kind of Seer?"

"No. I See nothing." She passed Harper, entering the common room without looking back.

Harper shoved the red amethyst into her pocket and faced the back doors, taking in a breath and releasing the tension in her shoulders. Lightning flashed, lighting up the field briefly before thunder permeated the sky, rattling the windows of the lodge.

The door opened effortlessly and no one stopped Harper as she shut it behind her. The back deck of the cabin had an overhanging roof.

For a moment, she was sheltered, watching the rain clouds, barely feeling the wind. She breathed deep. Violet said she shouldn't shift for twelve hours after receiving the healing wards, but the witch could redo them, right? Wasn't it more important to find Tyson before the pack of rogues did?

Harper walked down the front steps, shrugging out of her jacket. Faint marks still decorated her arms, like whispered warnings against what she was about to do. The wind lifted the hair off her neck, and a few drops of rain struck her face. Her shoulders grew numb.

Would the spell suppress her ability to change? Harper breathed out, mentally probing her body. Feeling nothing different, she released her wings.

Pain split down the center of Harper's spine. She shrieked, falling to the ground, knees striking the gravel. Her fingers curled into the loose rocks. Slowly, and with agonizing pain, her wings pierced through her back and stretched toward the sky.

Damn that witch.

Harper's hands curled against the ground, and she panted, blinking tears from her eyes. Blood soaked through the tank top, now damp against her back, but it stopped soon enough.

Standing, Harper stretched her wings and flapped them a few times. She could move them. Her shoulders ached fiercely, but she could fly.

The wind caught her wings as she leapt into the air. All she had to do was find a single person among the trees. Hopefully, she would be looking for a moving target, not a body.

CHAPTER EIGHT

Tyson

Tyson stormed through the forest on a familiar path, keeping the cabin in sight and letting his thoughts whirl around his head. Anger took over his body, kicking loose rocks and sticks on the trail, berating Harper's foolish stubbornness in his head.

If she would just accept his help it would make *all* the difference. The counseling program worked; Tyson had seen it time and time again. It wasn't perfect, but wasn't it better than running and hiding from the government forever?

Tyson kicked a large rock that didn't budge from the path and his toe throbbed. He stopped and shook it out, cursing at the rock, the dirt, and the light rain that had started falling.

Mostly, he cursed himself. He hadn't gotten anything from her about her abilities or her family. Instead, he'd lost his temper. He had never gone off like that with the other residents. No matter how abrasive, how critical, how much they rejected what he offered them, he could always let it slide and do his job.

Harper got under his skin. Around her, Tyson felt like he had no idea what he was doing.

Tyson's mind turned to Reya. Mentioning her to Harper had been stupid. How could she understand? He believed that he had helped Reya and her family, but he couldn't know for sure. The records he'd searched had brought no results. It was as if her family had vanished, fate unrecorded. Could they have escaped?

Back then, methods of containment were harsher and less organized. Many records, if they were kept, were locked and Tyson wasn't sure how he would gain access. He'd given up a while ago, but Harper's criticism lit the fire in him again. He wanted to find Reya's record—not just to solve his own curiosity, but to prove to Harper that he *had* helped someone.

Tyson's stomach lurched. He paused, putting a hand to it and rubbing. He was hungry. Maybe that was all. But he wasn't ready to head back. He walked a little further.

The more Tyson thought about finding Reya's record, the more it felt wrong. He should focus on the here and now. Fletcher would be Tyson's first successful Naturalization. Tyson could prove that he was an effective counselor when Fletcher was Reformed and had completed the Naturalization process in a few days' time. Then Harper would see, it wasn't all empty promises with no return. The methods *worked*.

Tyson's feet slowed to a meander. The raindrops grew heavier, striking his head and shoulders. He looked up into a foreboding sky filled with electrified grey clouds. *Shoot.* He'd have to head back.

He looked around for the cabin, but he didn't see anything but trees. Blurry trees. His stomach lurched again, a completely different sensation than hunger. Had he wandered farther out than he expected? He hadn't been walking long enough to do that.

Nothing looked familiar. Tyson wheeled around and headed back down the path. The crisp smell of pine and rain mingled in his nose as he rushed along the path. Furtively glancing between the trees, Tyson expected to see the cabin at any moment, but minutes passed and thunder rumbled overhead and he saw nothing but trees for miles, and no end to the path ahead.

The trees blurred again.

Something was wrong. Tyson broke into a run. The density of the air increased. He had chalked it up to the storm and changing air pressure before, but now the hair on the back of his neck rose. A branch snapped. The sky grew darker, and rain clouds loomed thick and ominous. A loud crack penetrated the air like a gunshot. Tyson whirled around, sending leaves scattering along the ground. Just thunder. It was just thunder. He jogged, hands stuffed in his pockets, head jerking left and right. Shadows kept pace with him on both sides, their strides almost leisurely.

Tyson sprinted.

A crouching figure leapt between the trees ahead, springing off one tree trunk and landing against another before falling right in front of Tyson. Tyson scrambled to a halt and nearly fell backward. Laughter echoed around the forest, a dozen different tones. A group of people emerged from between the trees.

Rogues.

The nearest shadow pacing him turned out to be a short, pale-faced red-head. Heath. The blonde to his right was Lexi. Both vampires. Tyson recognized one or two of the others in their company. Their clothing hung in rags. Their hair lay knotted and tangled, and their faces were filthy, scratched, and bruised. They didn't carry any weapons, but then, they wouldn't need any.

Tyson wiped his hands on his jeans and breathed in through his nose, swallowing his fear. How could he approach this situation and still get out alive? His training didn't cover what to do in a forest ambush.

"Hey." Tyson managed to squeeze the inadequate word from his constricted throat.

A guy stepped forward, buzzed head gleaming. He smiled, though it was more a baring of teeth.

Tyson had to get a handle on the situation fast. "Heath, Lexi, what's this about?" The couple had once seemed like ideal Naturalization candidates, but they had deliberately avoided counseling appointments for quite some time. Trouble always brewed in the vampire faction. As a whole, they were moody and extremely unpredictable.

Heath's mouth twitched upward in a sneer. "Fresh blood." He had an arm loosely draped around Lexi's shoulders. As if they weren't standing in a forest at twilight with raindrops peppering them.

"Let's see if anyone at the big house misses him. Should send the right message," a raspy-voiced female snarled. A shadow darted around the clearing, faster than Tyson could follow, coming up behind him. Her nose nuzzled his neck from behind, and she inhaled. The others drew closer, murmuring. Tyson's pulse pounded in his ears.

"Mmm. He is fresh. O-positive." Her lips mouthed Tyson's neck. He pulled his head away from her, but she grabbed his hair in one hand and locked his arms behind his back with the other. She jerked his head back again, licking his neck.

Tyson shuddered, which made her laugh. His arms ached, twisted behind him in her impossibly strong grip.

"No, please. Just don't—"

"Don't what?" she teased. "You can relax, kid. It's not what you think."

One of the paranormals bent down as if picking something up, but he didn't straighten. Instead, his back hunched, and a dark mass spread over him. He lifted his head, showing snarling fangs on a narrow snout, straightening on four legs.

The woman holding Tyson whined at the back of her throat, like a cat warning another cat just before the squall. "Stand down, Rudy. Boss said I get first draw tonight."

The wolf snapped and growled, but bowed its head deferentially.

Her mouth touched Tyson's neck again, the unnaturally long points of her canines grazing his skin.

Tyson's heart raced. He never should have left the lodge, let alone entered the forest. The only one who had any idea he left was Harper, and she hated him. This was the end, and Tyson couldn't think of a single person who would care if he died. Megan might. Sisters were good for some things. But what about the residents? Would any of them mourn his death? He doubted it.

Maybe Harper was right about something.

Tyson couldn't draw breath. The vampiress chuckled. "They all cry, curse, or pray at the end." Her tongue flicked his ear as she hissed the words.

"I can't wait to hear what you do." Harper, suspended by a pair of dark wings that almost blended into the clouded sky, soared above them. She looked like an avenging angel, backlit by a flash of lightning, the wind pulling her hair back from her face.

Tyson sucked air into his lungs. She shouldn't be able to remain suspended that way, as if held by the wind.

The vampiress wrenched Tyson's arms back further, and he stumbled against her. More of the gathered mob shifted, some baring teeth, others crouching and making the stomach-churning transformation into beasts.

Harper folded her wings and dove. The vampire dropped her hold and leapt. She met Harper mid-air and they fell in a tangle of wings and limbs, rolling to the dirt.

Tyson sprinted for the trees away from the scene of madness. These weren't the tame paranormals he worked with every day; these were nightmares from hell come alive.

A shoulder rammed into Tyson's back, knocking the breath from his lungs and sending him crashing to the ground. A man sat on top of him, his weight pressing Tyson into the muddy ground.

Tyson tried to roll, but the man's bulk was too much to throw off. His eyes lit up silver, tinted with red. He bared his teeth and lunged for the throbbing, pulsing vein in Tyson's throat.

Enormous jaws clamped down on the vampire's midsection and tore him off Tyson. The vampire bolted, gone in a blink. The werewolf took his place over Tyson, the black blood from the vampire dripping from his teeth onto Tyson's coat. He didn't have time to do more than whimper as jaws darted toward his face.

A shrill whistle broke through the air. The werewolf froze, teeth inches from Tyson's throat. Tyson's head buzzed, and the sound rattled around grasping for purchase on his mind, but it kept slipping. He dragged his hands over his ears, muffling the whistle. The grasping sensation disappeared.

The werewolf turned to the source of the sound, apparently transfixed. No longer facing down immediate death, Tyson felt dampness on his jeans and realized he'd wet himself. Any sane person would have done the same.

He slid out from between the wolf's legs and clambered to his feet, slapping his hands back over his ears the moment he was freed. The whistle became a song, somehow winding around Tyson without touching him.

It came from Harper.

She hovered in the center of the clearing, mouth open. She was singing, although it was like nothing Tyson had heard before—ethereal and otherworldly, rising and falling with the gusting of the wind.

The other figures in the clearing stood enraptured, though their eyes seemed glassy and unseeing. Harper's song commanded the attention of a force of two dozen supernatural beings. No ordinary bird shifter had any abilities like this.

Harper drew a breath and held a final high note that reverberated in the air. Tyson's teeth rattled and his pulse quickened. An invisible force built up around him, and his eardrums compressed until they might burst. Tyson squeezed his hands over his ears harder and the pressure lessened.

The note ended abruptly, and the entire mob force dropped in crumpled heaps—vampire, man and beast alike. Tyson's knees wobbled, and he struggled to remain standing but somehow managed. Harper turned and Tyson's heart clenched in awe and fear. Her hair disheveled, her feathers outstretched, her gaze wild...He could see it. *Raven born.*

Harper surveyed the road filled with still bodies.

Tyson swallowed. "Are they...dead?"

Her eyes flickered up to meet his. The wild edge lingered there, but it was giving way to something more...normal. "I don't think so. We should go." What was she thinking? Had she done it on purpose?

Harper's wings flapped open, and Tyson jumped. She reached toward him.

He didn't move any closer. "For a moment, I thought you would join their side."

"Yeah, well, don't think about it too much. I still might."

A joke. Definitely a joke. She had an odd sense of humor.

Rain fell steadily around them as Tyson stared at her extended hand. What did she expect him to do?

"You managed to get yourself out here pretty far. What were you doing, running?" she asked.

Tyson furrowed his brow. "I think one of their group is some kind of illusionist. Or a transporter? A mentally enhanced being. I could see the cabin before..." He trailed off. The realization of how close he'd come to death clenched in his stomach.

"You're miles from there." Harper stretched her hand out further. "Come on, I'll take you back."

When Tyson didn't take her hand, she sighed and dropped her arm, then flapped her wings and launched into the air as she grabbed him under his arms. Tyson yelled as his weight forced her to dip toward the ground, and he braced for a crash. With several powerful thrusts of her wings, Harper pulled up into the sky.

If Tyson hadn't already peed his pants, he would have then. Harper tightened her grip under his arms, adjusting until she clasped them around his chest and locked her hands on her wrists. Her chest pressed against his back, almost like an embrace except his legs dangled toward the ground, and he was too terrified to enjoy it. The wind whipped past his face, numbing his ears.

For a few minutes, Tyson saw from Harper's perspective. The trees and ground rushing below, the horizon ahead, the air buffeting him. His heart lifted above the terror, and for a second he understood why Harper wouldn't want to risk losing this.

Then Harper tilted down and the fear clenched at Tyson again. She touched down in the driveway in front of the lodge and nearly dropped him. He stumbled a few feet, then straightened. He rolled his arms in their sockets, armpits sore.

His mind reeled between terror and gratitude. He stared at Harper and those black wings arching from her back. Wings that just saved his life.

She watched Tyson with her hands on her knees in a hunched position, and he realized she was catching her breath. Did demi-gods get winded? Looking at her now, demi-god seemed too strong a word. She might be descended from some divine being, but the gene pool had almost certainly been diluted. Gifted or blessed, then.

The moment stretched out between them. It was too quiet on the gravel driveway for having been assaulted and nearly killed.

The front door flung wide, and Lilith rushed out. "Tyson! Thank the goddess." She hurried down the steps and threw her arms around him. Maybe someone *would* have cared if he'd died. Even Harper came after him and he thought she would be the last one to care. Tyson looked over Lilith's shoulder at Harper, who stood off to the side with her arms folded, frowning at them. He smiled at her and the frown deepened.

Lilith released him and stepped back, glancing over his body. She tsked, her hand going to his right cheek. "Oh, dear. We'll need to do something about that."

Tyson reached up. His right cheek felt sticky, and when he took his fingers away, the tips were covered in drying blood.

Lilith addressed Harper. "Violet wants to see you. She's not happy." Her sympathetic tone had a hard edge to it, so unlike her that Tyson blinked in shock.

"Of course not. I only saved someone's life." Harper's voice was sharp with bitterness. Her feet crunched against the gravel as she walked. Tucked tightly against her back, the lowest feathers of her wing tips brushed the ground. Tyson walked beside Harper, following Lilith.

"Thank you for that, by the way." Tyson's face felt hot on the injured side. Now that he knew it was there, he couldn't stop thinking about it.

"Sure." Harper picked at an invisible thread on the hem of her tank top.

Why pretend indifference? Most people didn't fly off to save someone from certain death at the expense of their safety. Especially not someone they hated, and she'd made it pretty clear that she didn't like Tyson. It didn't make any sense. He wanted to ask her about it, but with Lilith there, he was sure Harper wouldn't admit to anything.

The group walked through the front door and up the stairs in silence. Because Lilith's room was beside the apothecary, they were headed to the same part of the house. Every once in a while, the edge of Harper's wings brushed against Tyson's arm. They were softer than he expected.

Most everyone seemed to be gathered in the common room for movie night. Mandi, the witch apprenticed to Violet, stood at the top of the stairs and grabbed Lilith's arm as she passed, whispering in her ear.

Lilith gave a tight nod and continued. Mandi stared sightlessly with her milk-white eyes as Tyson and Harper passed.

They arrived at the apothecary and Harper paused with her hand on the door. What was she waiting for? Her gaze was somehow softer than usual.

"I'm not sorry for the things I said. Most of them. But the way I said them..." She looked toward the ceiling. "My tone was harsh. I'm sorry."

"Thanks." It sounded abrupt and lame, but Tyson couldn't think of anything else to say.

Harper grimaced and pushed on the wooden door, letting herself into the apothecary.

"Tyson?" Lilith called, already standing in her room next door. She smiled. "Let's get you fixed up."

Her room was dimly lit with lava lamps. Dozens lined the walls on shelves, all of different colors.

"I've never seen so many of these in one place." Tyson gazed at the floating, colored blobs of light.

Lilith laughed. The light cast grey and purple shadows across her skin. "I love them, don't you? So soothing. Now, I know you're usually the one to talk others through their traumatic experiences, but I think you might benefit from the same treatment. What made you run off into the forest alone before a storm?"

Her eyes gleamed, reflecting the dozens of multi-colored lava lamps.

Tyson squirmed where he stood, avoiding Lilith's gaze. Put that way, it sounded pretty idiotic. "Harper had an appointment with me. She...she got under my skin. I needed some air. Didn't mean to go far, but the forest, it moved I think."

"We've been trying to catch Meredith for some time now. She's a troublemaker." Lilith said with a chuckle.

As if warping someone's surroundings and transporting them to a distant location was a mild inconvenience, like throwing rocks at a neighbor's cat or tying people's shoelaces together. Her hands reached and brought a white box down from a shelf.

Wait, Meredith? He'd heard that name before. "Isn't she, like, nine?"

Lilith lined up her supplies: a small jar, some gauze, little white bandages. Every movement was deliberate, done with an air of grace most people would envy. "Thirteen when she arrived, actually. Very small for her age, though."

"And now she's...?" Tyson didn't remember her being brought in, which meant she got to the camp and joined the rogues before he started his internship.

"Seventeen, I believe." Lilith lifted a cotton ball to Tyson's face and dabbed. The alcohol-soaked cotton stung. Tyson flexed his hands at his sides and bit his lip to keep from crying out.

"She's been hiding for *four years*?"

"Nearly. She was part of the first group of rogues we had, and has evaded every effort to capture her. Hard to contain someone who can warp anywhere they want to. Within the wards, of course."

How did they get her to the camp in the first place?

"She was brought to us." Lilith explained, as if she could hear Tyson's mental chatter. She set down the cotton ball and scooped some salve in her fingers. "Now hold still, this will soothe that sting right away, but I don't want to go smearing it all over your face."

Tyson stared forward and resisted asking more questions. Camp Silver Lake officially opened six years ago. He had just started college.

His face tingled from the goop she put on it.

Lilith wiped her fingers on a small towel and picked up some gauze and tape. "You can always check her file if you want to learn more about her."

Her mention of records reminded Tyson of Reya and her family. Lilith had been at the camp longer than he had, and she seemed like a safe person to ask. He waited impatiently to respond while she covered his face with the bandage.

"There. Not pretty, but it should heal pretty quickly." Lilith smiled.

"Thank you." Tyson hesitated for a moment. "Lilith, I've noticed something, looking through the files of past residents."

"Hm?" Her attention seemed focused on packing up the first aid kit.

"When I search for the names of some I know should be in there, I don't find anything. The database seems to have been tampered with, or something." Tyson squirmed. He hated even mentioning it knowing that if it was true, someone here that should be trusted had something to do with it.

"Could be. Not what you're thinking, though. Magic and technology don't get along well. We've had files wiped, sent randomly to different camps, buried deep in the hard drive...though fortunately never published to the public."

That would be a disaster. The identities of Naturalized individuals were kept secret for their protection. If their neighbors knew they were reformed witches, vampires, and shifters, the bloodshed would never end.

Knowing that paranormals were managed was enough for most people, and the civilian Hunts had mostly died out. A few rebel groups out there caused trouble once in a while, but the Naturalization laws in place prevent them from getting away with murder. Too many innocents mistaken for paranormal beings over the years due to paranoia. No one wanted a repeat of the Salem trials. Or the New York trials. Or...

"So, the files are just...gone, then?"

Lilith cocked her head to the side, considering, and clasped the first aid kit shut before setting it aside. "Violet keeps a written record of every paranormal who has gone through here. Has kept it longer than the camp has officially run. She's picky about who she lets see them, though. Is there a specific reason you're asking?"

Tyson stared at the wall, aware that Lilith watched him. No need to launch into a sob story about a long-lost childhood friend. He tapped his hand against his leg and shook his head.

"Thank you, Lilith."

"Of course."

A loud thud came from next door. The apothecary. Tyson swallowed. "Should we go see what that was?"

Lilith's face held a passive expression. "Oh, no. I'm certain something was just dropped. Violet is quite a capable witch. She can freeze even the fastest of paranormals before they cause her any trouble."

Tyson shifted uncomfortably. It wasn't Violet he worried for, but Harper. She'd tried to escape and that had failed. Was she having a mental breakdown? How would Violet react to that?

"We'll take care of Harper." Lilith's voice soothed over Tyson's fears. It had to be some kind of magical influence, but at the moment he welcomed the pleasant numbness tingling in his hands and feet.

He tried to form words into a response, but his mouth wouldn't obey. A gentle rapping came at the door.

Lilith sauntered over, hips sashaying, and opened it. "James! What a surprise."

"Tyson, what happened?" James pushed into the room, then glanced at Lilith. "Do you mind if I speak to him privately in here for a moment? Violet is using the apothecary."

"Of course." Lilith said, a little too brightly. She stepped from the room and into the dark hall. The light from the lava lamps glinted off her eyes, making them flash orange and purple before the door closed.

James straightened his glasses. The orange and purple lights reflected off of them, too. It made everything look ethereal and a bit spooky, now. Less amazing and more unsettling.

Tyson crossed his arms. "This is about Harper, isn't it?"

"She didn't simply find you, did she? Violet saw the rogues. She couldn't see anything after they attacked you. It went...fuz zy. Her visions never lose connection like that."

Tyson rocked up on the balls of his feet, then back onto his heels. He stuck his hands in his pockets. A sudden agitation made him tilt his head side to side, considering. He had promised to tell them everything he found out about Harper's abilities and her lineage, but he was still trying to figure this one out for himself.

"She can sing. No." Tyson shook his head. "Sing isn't the right word. But it isn't a whistle, either. Every rogue within earshot froze. It's like they were spelled or entranced."

"But you weren't?"

"It didn't seem to affect me. It couldn't hold onto my mind."

James visibly startled. "So it was mind control? Tyson, you're human. Does that mean her ability only works on supernaturals?"

Tyson shrugged. "She didn't explain it to me. All I know is when the singing stopped, so did the rogues. They collapsed. I didn't dare check to see if any of them were still breathing. We just got out of there as quickly as possible."

"She flew with you?"

"Yes." Tyson drew his lips together. The agitation had spread to his left hand, which was shaking at his side. He pressed it against his jeans, hoping James wouldn't notice. Why did he feel like he shouldn't have said anything?

James stared at Tyson thoughtfully. "She didn't give you any explanation? None at all?"

"No. And asking about her family...well, it's a sore spot. Her parents are from Alaska, that's all I got."

James clapped his hands together and held them up to his mouth. He glanced at Tyson. "Do you know what this means?"

Tyson shook his head.

James clapped a hand on Tyson's shoulder. "First of all, it means you've as good as gotten that promotion. You'll have my signature and Violet's, guaranteed." His hand dropped and his grin widened. "Second, it means I could be the first warlock to unlock the secrets of the Raven born."

A warning prickled in Tyson's chest. "She doesn't know anything, James. How do you plan to discover anything about her and her people?"

James' glasses gleamed orange as he turned. "There are ways."

The words had an ominous tone. Tyson meant to ask him about his methods, and whether they were ethical, or even legal, when another, slightly more alarming thought occurred to him. "Do you think she's dangerous to the other residents? The rogues were warded by Violet at one point. Harper's singing...it circumvented their protection, somehow."

James frowned, eyebrows drawing inward and creating deep creases in his forehead. "You're right. I hadn't considered...They might have done something to their wards, making them ineffective. I will speak to Violet."

There was still a gleam in James' eyes that Tyson didn't like, but when he opened his mouth to ask his next question, the room visibly darkened.

The lava lamps dimmed, and the air closed around Tyson and James, the temperature dropping. The electricity flickered.

James reeled around and bolted for the door. "Stay here!" he shouted at Tyson over his shoulder.

Tyson ignored him, following the warlock into the hall and freezing outside the apothecary. He glimpsed Violet standing too close to Harper, her hand raised in a tight claw, and Harper's bone-white, panicked face, before James flung the door shut behind him. All sound cut off. Tyson reached for the door handle and jerked it, but it didn't budge. A spell had been activated.

No one would be going in, or coming out, until it was lifted.

CHAPTER NINE
HARPER

TYSON'S PHONE BURNED IN the front pocket of Harper's jeans. He'd dropped it when they landed. She'd meant to return it to him, but everything had moved too fast. Or so she told herself. There had been time, but she wanted to double-check the name she'd seen on the screen.

Violet didn't look up as Harper entered, as usual. The witch's hair sat on the back of her head in a tight bun and she wore a suit coat and pants.

It created a discordance in Harper's brain seeing a business professional grinding herbs and rubbing crystals together. If she could ignore Harper for just a minute longer...

Harper slipped Tyson's phone out and swiped the screen. It lit up, revealing a white box with a blurb for the latest email received, including the sender.

Becca. There was a chance it wasn't Tyson's cousin, Becca, that he knew someone else by that name who would email him. Harper's excitement drowned out practicality. Becca could lead her to Quinn. She might even convince Tyson to help.

Harper jammed the phone back in her pocket, and her fingers brushed the red crystal the blind woman had given her earlier. She felt a jolt, followed with a surge of confidence and energy.

She cleared her throat.

Violet's hand froze, hovering over a bowl with a handful of flower petals. She crushed them slowly, sprinkling them into the bowl, then mixed the contents of the wood bowl with her fingers.

"You shifted."

It wasn't a question, so Harper didn't answer. Violet's hands pressed down flat on the countertop.

"Didn't I make it clear that you must wait twelve hours before using your wings? Can you not follow even the simplest of directions?" Her voice held steady, but beneath the calm, Harper sensed a tremor, like the precursor to an earthquake. Harper shifted her feet, wishing she could be anywhere but there.

"I found Tyson." Harper knew as she spoke that it wouldn't matter. She'd known people like Violet before. You followed their rules or paid the price.

Violet spun around and stalked toward Harper, a storm in her grey eyes. "We had a team searching for him. You weren't needed. You jeopardized yourself in a tremendous way, and you undid all of my previous work." Her clawed hands dug into Harper's shoulders and turned her to see her back. Harper spread her wings to make it easier, wincing as the witch prodded her spine and shoulder blades.

"They wouldn't have gotten there in time. I almost didn't."

Violet's hand ran along the base of Harper's right wing, then her left, making her shudder. Violet was feeling for injuries, but it felt like a violation. Harper forced herself to stand still and avoid yanking her wings from the witch's tight grip.

"While you are here, if you are to have any hope of your application being accepted, you do as you are asked by myself, my husband, and Lilith." But not Tyson. Violet seemed to ignore anything Harper said about Tyson. Did she not care for him?

"Tyson would have died if I hadn't 'disobeyed' you," Harper emphasized.

"I can't encourage your behavior, Harper. No matter your motives. There must be consequences." Her hands moved on from Harper's wings, and Harper breathed a sigh of relief until Violet's head slid close to hers.

"You are Quinn's sister." Her whispered words dripped like poison into Harper's ear.

She swallowed past the dryness in her mouth and licked her lips. What would she care about Quinn?

"He was here," Violet's voice lilted in a tantalizing sort of way. Her eyes dragged across Harper's face, searching for her response.

What did she want? "I don't know where he is. I haven't seen him for years." Harper's jaw tightened.

"Oh, I don't care where he is. His capture isn't my responsibility."

It wasn't? Harper gulped down the urge to say the words out loud and waited. Violet ran her fingers across the surface of a large wooden table then picked her fingers up and examined them.

"As soon as he left, he became a rogue. Rogues are hunted. Rogues are terminated." She snarled the last word, and Harper jerked. "Do you have any idea what his escape cost us? The administrators trusted us. They responded to our needs readily, they were willing to help. Now?"

Violet let out a harsh laugh. "Now it's phone calls day and night, answering machines and secretaries keeping me from talking to those who once supported us fully. Emails go unanswered for days, and the responses are canned and vague." She brought her fingers to her lips. "I can't remember the last time I slept. Did you know that?"

Harper slowly shook her head side to side, her pulse increasing. Violet was acting crazy; what could a mad witch be capable of?

"Damn him!" Violet shrieked and struck the table with a closed fist, rattling the jars on its surface. She brought her head up sharply. "And you're just like him. I should sign off on your release right now. You could be someone else's problem. Someone else's boon."

She paced around the table at the center of the large room. It was as if Harper didn't exist anymore, and she was talking to someone else, or herself.

"Someone else's reward. And they will think I'm weak. Word will get out. Another resident Violet couldn't handle. Someone else will take over. Someone harder, someone bad. What will they do to my precious ones?" Her lips trembled, and her eyes widened in horror, then she crumpled.

Harper backed away, and a board creaked under her feet. Violet's head snapped up.

"You!" She hissed. Her arms crawled along the edge of the table as she walked. Her green eyes dug into Harper's. "You could have cost me everything. You won't do it again." The storm in Violet's eyes raged. The air thickened, swirling around and lifting her hair slightly. A crackle of energy flickered in Violet's upturned hand. The beginning of a spell.

"What are you going to do about it?" Harper growled and flexed her fingers, wings stretching behind her.

Violet's face darkened and thick black lines appeared on her forehead, hooding her eyes. The air collapsed around them, like a black hole had opened up in a corner of the room. "You wanted me to heal you, and I will, pretty bird. But this time you won't ever fly again."

Violet advanced, raising her hand as if to strike Harper down, either physically or with a spell.

"Violet." A male voice barked.

The room immediately brightened. Violet's face returned to normal, creased only with an expression of grief so profound that Harper had to wonder if she was looking at the same person. Her hand drifted, trembling, to her mouth, and she covered up a gasping sob.

"I'm sorry," she whispered, then ran towards the door. It flung open with a bang in response to some magical influence from Violet, no doubt.

"You'll have to forgive my wife," Petrov said with an eerie calm. "She is under a terrible amount of stress."

More like insanity. Harper sagged against the table behind her, shaking at the thought of what that witch had nearly done.

Petrov cleared his throat. "Allow me to do the healing spell for you?"

Harper jerked her head up. "Go to hell," she snarled.

Petrov raised his hands. "Okay, I get it. After that I wouldn't trust me either. I just...I do not want to see you suffering. Could another witch do it? Perhaps Lilith?"

Harper's jaw tensed, and she opened her clenched fingers. Lilith, she would allow. She was the only one in this damned place who didn't make Harper feel like a commodity. Shegave a curt nod.

Petrov reached in his pocket and pulled out a cell phone, showing it to Harper before he held it to his ear. *He's afraid I'm going to attack him.*

His green eyes stared into Harper's, but he didn't move or speak until Lilith picked up. "Yes, Lilith, could you report to the apothecary please? Yes, immediately." He hung up, dropping the phone back in his pocket, then turned toward the bench and began putting items away and pulling others out, straightening jars and various rocks as he went.

"Please shift into human form," he said. Harper narrowed her eyes. "I am merely helping this move more quickly by getting things ready, Harper. I will not touch you."

Despite his assurances, Harper crossed her arms and waited, the shield of her wings at her back giving her more comfort than she cared to admit.

Petrov spoke again. "Violet is really quite a warm person, I want you to know. Most everyone likes her. You caught her at a bad time."

Harper didn't feel obligated to speak. The heavy feeling in the room lifted slightly, but there was still something there, a sense of ill-will. What would she have done if Petrov hadn't walked in?

"She's dangerous," Harper muttered.

"We all are, in our own way."

"Not that way." Harper swallowed. "She needs to see someone. Maybe those paranormal shrinks you people are so fond of here."

Petrov whirled on her with a furious expression on his face. His arms trembled, and for a moment Harper wondered if she'd just uttered her last words.

Lilith walked into the room, glancing between Harper and Petrov with concern on her face. "What's going on here? James?"

He broke out of the stare and shoved some bandages at Lilith. "She needs the healing wards. And tell her to stay the hell out of the sky for twelve hours this time."

"Oh, my." Lilith muttered, watching him leave. The wood door slammed behind him, making them both jump. "Let's clear the air, shall we?" She took down a wide jar filled with tied bundles of leaves and put one in a bronze bowl. A small purple flame sparked from her finger and lit the bundle. Smoke wafted into the air, and gradually, the desperate feeling lifted.

"There." Lilith smiled. "Sage always makes things better, don't you think?"

Harper made a small sound, something she hoped sounded like agreement. She brought her wings in before Lilith asked, knowing it was coming. She winced as they shrank, sliding past her wounds.

"Why does it hurt so bad?"

"You interrupted the healing process. It's quite delicate. Though I'm sure Mr. Miller appreciates what you did."

Harper sat in silence, unsure of what to say—especially since his phone bulged in her pocket. Her shoulders twitched.

"Hold still a minute longer," Lilith said.

"Sorry," Harper muttered. The sigils stung as Lilith placed them, working swiftly. Harper wondered why she hadn't done the wards in the first place. She seemed skilled enough.

"I thought you weren't good at personal wards?" Harper said.

"Oh, I'm not. These are healing sigils. We all have our gifts. Violet and James are protectors. I'm a healer. I think you'll find you can shift by lunch tomorrow." She cleaned off Harper's back with a damp cloth and stretched the bandages. "We'll wrap your shoulders. It will serve as a reminder for you to avoid shifting."

Harper jiggled her hand at her side, impatient to talk to Tyson about Violet. As a therapist, he might know what the hell made her act that way. Then Harper would ask about Becca.

Lilith kept talking, bringing the bandaging up and over each shoulder in an x-shape. Harper raised her arms at the witch's prodding. "You don't have to like Violet, but you should appreciate her. She works hard to keep the government from tightening their restrictions on camps like ours. They want more monitoring, more limitations for naturalized paranormal citizens. Some want to do away with the programs entirely and give the Hunter Guilds and mercenaries free reign. The world is a horrible place for a paranormal to live in. She doesn't want to worry our residents, the new ones especially."

Her words hit a place inside Harper that she didn't want to acknowledge. Everything was easier if she only had herself to worry about. She couldn't afford to become some kind of paranormal activist.

Harper's shoulder blades itched, and she resisted the urge to scratch at the bandaging. It criss-crossed on her back, binding her shoulders and chest over the tank top she wore. She could hardly forget it was there.

Lilith's hand landed softly on Harper's shoulder. "All of our residents have a hard time at first. I imagine it was difficult to hear that your brother was here, and now he's gone."

Harper closed her eyes in a long, slow blink. Yes, it was hard. Damn. She'd be lying if she said otherwise. But she would find Quinn again, and Tyson would help, one way or another.

Thinking about that gave Harper an idea.

"Maybe…maybe I could talk to Ty—Mr. Miller about it?" Harper said, trying to sound hesitant and uncertain.

Lilith brightened. "That's why we have him! Yes, if you're comfortable sharing with him, please do. Don't keep it bottled up inside. If you make an effort to get to know the other residents and attend your classes, everything will fall into place."

"And give Violet some space."

Lilith tossed her blonde hair over her shoulders, laughter bubbling out of her. "Yes, and that."

"Do you know anything else about my brother?"

"I wondered when we would get to that." She tucked her hair behind her ears, and Harper wondered how old the witch was. Her face seemed youthful and timeless, as if she would never age a day. "I've put a meeting with me in your schedule tomorrow. Come see me here, in the apothecary."

"All right."

"Less chance of being interrupted if it's scheduled," Lilith said cryptically. "Have a good night, Harper."

Harper took that as her cue to go, heading for the door. She would be thrilled to never see the inside of that room again, but she needed answers. Tomorrow, she would have them.

A hand waved in front of Harper's face, and she blinked, eyes clearing. Tyson. Just who she wanted to see.

"Harper? You all right?"

His concern caught her off guard. "Yeah, fine. Uh…How's your face?"

"Stiff. Moving my mouth is sort of difficult." He touched his jawline, which Harper noticed had a layer of fine growth coming in. Was it soft? Or prickly?

A memory. Rubbing her hand on her dad's face, sitting on his lap. It scratched when he kissed her.

Harper shook the memory out of her head. *Focus, Harper.* "I, uh, wanted to talk to you."

Tyson visibly startled, blinking as he looked at her. "You do?"

"Yep." Harper grabbed his arm and dragged him down the hallway. Two girls headed toward them from the top of the stairs. They giggled to each other, and Harper realized how it looked, dragging the camp counselor around. She dropped his arm like it had burned her.

Tyson rubbed it. "So, to my office, then?" he said.

Harper marched down the stairs ahead of him and waited impatiently until he caught up with her at the locked office door.

He put a key in the handle and jiggled it a bit. "So, what did you want to—"

"Violet is unstable. She attacked me in the..." Harper waved her hand toward the ceiling, forgetting the word.

"Apothecary?" Tyson supplied.

She snapped her fingers. "Yes, that. She acted legitimately crazy, Tyson. She threatened to ground me."

His shoulders relaxed, and he snorted. "Ground you? Like, the way a mom would, or...?"

"You're supposed to take this seriously."

Tyson straightened. "Yes. You're right."

Harper crossed her arms. "She threatened my wings."

"That doesn't make sense." He frowned. "I mean, Violet gets frustrated like anyone else. Isn't she doing some solstice, er, retrograde work right now? That has to be it. Everyone gets crazy during the retrograde." He leaned against his desk and jumped up, sitting so casually he couldn't be taking Harper seriously.

Then his arms folded and his expression smoothed. "What did you say to her?"

"Why do you assume I did something?"

"Because you attacked me once, if you recall," he ticked the items off on his fingers, "you have a volatile personality prone to arguing, and you're very good at pushing buttons."

"Sorry for that," Harper said. She meant it. "The attack in the beginning, I mean. I was scared. And pissed off. But I wouldn't do anything like that now. Violet was completely unprovoked, talking about how it was Quinn's fault that she was stressed and not sleeping. She was furious that I tried to do the same thing. She said it would mean the end of the camp."

Tyson blew air through his lips. "She's probably telling the truth, there. The administrators have hounded her from day one to keep this place in top notch running order. If they had a reason to doubt it, well, Violet would take the brunt of that. She started this place as a sanctuary for paranormals during the Reveal. When the government tried to break through and take those she protected, she got the place licensed. Then the Naturalization laws passed, and it all started going downhill."

"I thought she supported Naturalization."

"She does because she has to in order to keep the Hunters out. It's part of her agreement with the government. They even fund it now. She's fought for everything we have here, including my job."

Harper couldn't wrap her head around it, imagining Violet fighting for paranormal rights when she had just lost her marbles in the apothecary. "But why?"

Tyson clasped his hands together. "Because some people actually mean it when they say they care. Look, I've been here for two years. Long enough that I understand what Violet has gone through to keep this camp running. She does her best, and so do the rest of us. I know you don't like our methods, but if there were another way—a better way—we would change in a heartbeat."

He rubbed a hand down his face and seemed to be considering what to say next. "Violet, James, and Lilith all feel the same way. No one forced them into the positions they're in. Violet often expresses how she wishes her job didn't exist, but that doesn't mean she wants to help you any less."

Harper heard what he was saying, but she wasn't ready to believe him. "Why threaten me, then?"

Tyson frowned, shaking his head. "Something must have happened. It could have started with your brother's escape. How competent does that make Violet look, since it's her wards he had to break through to get out?"

"Yeah. I wonder how he did that?" A smirk twitched across Harper's face. "I mean, my brother isn't magic-savvy. He doesn't have secret ward-breaking abilities. How did he get through a powerful witch's wards?" She watched Tyson for his reaction.

"I told you, I'm not giving out the details."

"Because you don't know. But you do know who helped him." Harper pulled his phone out of her pocket.

"You stole my phone?" He slid off the desk and reached for it.

Harper danced out of reach. "You dropped it outside. I'm happy to return it. For a price."

He frowned. "That's blackmail. I should turn you in right now."

"Violet would love to hear it. Go ahead." Harper shook the phone in the air. She had him right where she wanted him. "You have an email from her. From Becca. She's your cousin, right?"

Tyson sat back into his office chair, letting it drift around in a half-circle. He ran his hand through his brown hair, making some of it stand up. Finally, his eyes refocused on Harper and he held out his hand.

"May I have my phone back?"

"Will you help me find Quinn?" It was a long shot, but she was going off a hunch.

"Harper, I can't do that. My job, everything would be at stake."

"I didn't say to help me escape. I just want to know that my brother is safe." Harper interlocked her fingers. "It's one small favor for someone who recently saved your life." She resisted batting her eyelashes. She wasn't begging.

"You know that you're the reason I was out there in the first place?" He sounded irritated, but a smile twitched at the corner of his lips. Harper let out a whoop.

"Hey, shhh!" Tyson gestured. His face creased with worry. "I'll talk to Becca and find out if she knows what happened to him. But that's it. I won't go looking for him, and I won't give you a free ticket out of here. I'm stepping way out of line as it is."

Harper sat down in a chair across the desk from him and flexed her fingers around his phone, then slid it across the desk toward him. "So. Becca."

"You do understand what you're asking me to do, right?" He tapped the back of his phone.

"Yes. Help me find my brother. Reunite a family. It's why you're here, isn't it?"

Tyson gave her a disapproving look. "You're twisting my words."

"What about Becca? Don't you want to help her? Or do you plan to report this to Violet?" Harper gestured to the phone. Tyson leaned forward and picked it up. His eyes flickered back to her.

"Becca is my cousin. Of course I want to help her."

"If she's anything like you, it's a wonder she ended up with my brother."

"Who said she was 'with' your brother? You know what, never mind. We'll sort truth from rumor soon enough." He adjusted his seat in the office chair and slid the screen lock off. "For your information, she's nothing like me. She's obsessed with paranormals, for one. Absolutely loves them in a geeking-out, spends free time researching different types sort of way."

"And you don't?" Harper raised her eyebrows. "I mean, why choose a career working with us, if that's the case?"

He stared at her, opening and closing his mouth like a fish.

Harper jutted her chin toward his phone. "So, what's the message about?"

"I don't know." He stared at the screen like a snake hid inside waiting to bite.

"Well, take a look, duh." Harper crossed her arms and leaned against the back of the chair, tipping the front legs into the air. The bandages pulled tight across her chest and back, and the healing wards beneath them made her shoulders itch furiously. The kind of itch that only resolved when she shifted, but that wasn't possible right now. She needed something to take her mind off it.

"You want me to read it right now?"

Harper didn't respond, just jabbed a finger at his phone. Tyson sighed and unlocked the device.

"She never said they were together, and I'm certain she had nothing to do with his escape. Don't get your hopes up."

"It's one of my last leads. There's nothing to lose." Even if her skin crawled at the thought of someone mixing up in their plans. It had always been just the two of them, Quinn and her, planning to get out of the foster system and find their parents. How would that change if a girl—especially a human one—was brought into the mix?

Harper could cross that road when she got there. For now, she needed to find him. She leaned forward, her chair slamming the ground with a thump, but Tyson didn't react, the creases in his forehead deepening. She blew air out of her lips like a horse, leaning forward with her elbow on the table, fingers of her other hand tapping the hard surface. If he would just tell her, already...

"Hold your horses," Tyson mumbled. The brooding look suited him. His thick eyebrows furrowed closer together, and his jaw clenched. A nice, strong jaw. Harper could imagine running her fingers along it...

What the hell? She shook herself out of the bizarre vision. Her foot jogged up and down, tapping on the floor. "What's taking so long? Did she send a novel?"

"Nearly. Look, she's chatty, okay? And I think it's in a code of sorts. She's talking about some memory from our childhood, but why?"

"Read it to me," Harper demanded.

"Okay. Here goes." He cleared his throat, and Harper held her breath.

This was it. This had to be it.

CHAPTER TEN

TYSON

...DO YOU REMEMBER THAT time when we hid under Nana's bed and no one could find us? We fell asleep and our parents called the cops...

There was a lot more to the email, but Tyson's eyes kept coming back to that line. What was Becca saying? Had someone called the cops on them?

"They're obviously in hiding. Who's Nana?" Harper's voice brought him back to the present.

"Our grandmother. My father and her mother were siblings."

"Where is your grandmother now?" Harper looked at him curiously.

"She's at a rest home. Not too far from where I live."

"Hm. That busts that theory. I thought they might be at her house or something, but assisted living doesn't allow for stuff like that, does it?"

Tyson's lips moved soundlessly as he read the line again. Then something about it struck him. "She was sleeping with me. With *me*."

Harper arched one brow, a strange smile creeping across her face. "You probably shouldn't broadcast that. I mean, she's your cousin..."

"Gross. Okay, you know I didn't mean it that way. In the memory she mentioned, we hid *together*." He set his phone down. "She's at my place."

"She is? What about Quinn?"

"She doesn't say anything about him." Tyson itched to get back to his apartment.

"Can I read it again?"

Tyson unlocked the phone and passed it to Harper, watching her face as she read. Her expression was so open, so earnest. Her brother was the key to opening her up, after all. They must have been close.

She dropped the phone back on the desk. "You're right. We're back at square one."

"Not necessarily. She might know where he is. Or they could be together, but she's protecting him by not mentioning him."

"When do you go back home?"

Tyson held up the new lanyard Lilith gave him. "Today, if I want."

Harper stared at her hands, and silence lingered between them. Tyson expected her to be excited, but she looked like he had shared the worst news with her.

"You ready to sleep in your own bed tonight?" she said at last.

"Yeah." He reached over to his computer and logged out, then grabbed the lanyard and phone, shoving both in his pocket. "Harper," Tyson said, locking eyes with her. "Are you okay? After Violet?"

She rubbed her wrist with the opposite hand. "I'm all right. I don't think she should remain in charge, though. Maybe Lilith. Someone who has it together."

Tyson shook his head. "You won't find anyone better than Violet. Give her a chance. I think you'll find your impression is wrong." Despite how annoying the witch was, that much he agreed with. No one else could run this camp like Violet.

Harper glanced away, then her eyes flicked back to Tyson. "What about you? Are you okay?"

She meant the rogue attack. Tyson swallowed, and his heart rate picked up at the memory. "I'll be better once I can relax at home for a bit."

She laughed. "Good luck with that."

A breathy, nervous laugh escaped him. "Yeah, thanks."

She walked toward the door. Tyson watched her go, noticing how graceful her stride was. Not the kind of thing a therapist should think about a client. He swallowed to bring moisture back into his mouth.

Harper paused in the doorway, hand on the frame as she turned back toward him. "When will you be back?"

"Tuesday morning." Vulnerability lingered in her expression, and he found himself wanting to reassure her. "Will you be all right until then?"

She slipped into the hall without answering. Tyson stared at the open doorway for a while, gathering his thoughts. His eyes landed on the locked cabinets under the desk where they kept the residents' printed records. He should have taken notes on this session, written down what he'd learned about Harper. Her brother, her repeated expression of her desire to escape and her distrust of Violet and James...

He'd do it when he got back. That would give him a chance to figure out which parts he could put in and which he wanted to leave out to keep Becca safe. His hand rested on the light switch just inside the doorway, and he looked back into the room. It seemed charged with some kind of foreign energy, both exciting and discomforting. He envisioned his mentor, Tom, sitting in the room in the chair across the desk, hands clasped in his lap, staring Tyson down with those grey-blue eyes.

Stay in this profession long enough and you start to feel like them.

Tyson hadn't known what he meant when he first said it.

Soon you won't be able to separate their feelings from your own. When that happens, it's time to leave.

Tyson remembered asking Tom if he felt that way. He chuckled.

Why do you think you're here? Someone has to take my place.

Tyson's throat constricted. He flipped the light off and locked the door, then headed up the stairs to ask one of the witches to open a portal and send him home.

The witches were not in. The apothecary sat quiet with the lights on, but nobody was home. Tyson was relieved to not find Violet inside, at least.

"Hello?" Tyson said the word hesitantly, as if it could summon a demon from among the books. No one answered.

Tyson stepped closer to a nearby bookshelf to read the titles, curious what type of books witches kept. One row of thick volumes caught his attention. The titles were dates. Each book contained a range of years. He ran his finger along them from the current year down to dates from before the Reveal, when Violet ran this place by herself for any paranormal needing refuge. Back before it was illegal to be anything other than human.

Nearly twenty years of books sat on the shelf. Tyson came back towards the middle, looking for a particular volume. It was a long shot, but it would have been about ten years ago, and this was the only camp in Oregon.

He dragged the volume off its shelf and nearly dropped it. It was heavier than expected. He opened it to find the names and records, including some photos, of everyone who passed through that year. They were somehow in alphabetical order.

Was the book spelled in some way? It seemed unlikely Violet did all this after the fact. Not that Tyson knew anything about it. He avoided the apothecary when he could, and these books had sat under his nose for two years.

Did they say anything about Reya?

Tyson flipped to 'R' before realizing his mistake. It would be by last name. He turned the pages closer to the end of the book to "T". Her last name was Todde. And there she was, nestled in the midst of the pages about her parents and siblings. Each person had pages of records, some more than others. Reya had four.

His hands sweated as his nerves set in. He wiped them on his jeans, staring at the door as if it would burst open of its own accord. Voices passed in the hall, then silence. He breathed deeply, trying not to sneeze with the herbal smell in the room, and brought his attention back to the book.

Her name stood out in bold. **Reya Todde.** The daughter of Stephen and Linda, and she had five siblings, all classified as fox shifters.

Voices sounded in the hall again. Blood rushed into Tyson's ears, and anxiety grew to a palpable point. What would Violet do if she caught him going through her private books? Were they meant to be private, stored unspelled on an exposed shelf as they were?

Tyson took out his phone. The battery had been saved by his turning it off at every opportunity, though the bar was in the red

He flipped through each of the four double-sided pages without reading, his eyes locked on the door, only glancing back to see if his camera was in focus. He caught a few pictures out of the corner of his eye, but his frantic glances kept him from processing what he saw. A flash of red hair, a blur of blue.

He slammed the book shut and thrust it toward its spot on the shelf. It rammed into a book on the right, making that book fall into the wrong space. He reached up to push it out of the way before the record book could slide into place.

The door creaked, and James strode into the room.

"Mr. Miller."

"You can call me Tyson."

"Mm." James jutted out his chin, looking Tyson over through his glasses. He lifted one side of his glasses, adjusting them on his nose. "I assume you would like to be sent home."

"I'll be back in time for Fletcher."

James gathered a few items and sketched on the ground, whistling slightly. In moments, the portal was up. "I had a standing order for a portal prepared in case you didn't want to catch a Ryde."

Tyson hesitated. James had assumed Tyson would use magic. That he would *prefer* it. Tyson rarely used magic, and yet somehow it was becoming a habit.

James sighed. "There are no shortage of them, and it's no trouble."

"I know, just, I...Thank you," Tyson managed. The spellwork might be nothing, but the paperwork associated with licensing a portal wasn't simple.

"You're welcome." James gestured. "And goodnight."

Tyson stepped through, holding his breath at the uncomfortable pricking sensation that traveled across his skin.

The problem with portal magic was that you had no time to prepare for arriving at your destination. If Tyson had driven, he could have thought about what he was going to say, how he would react. He had none of that advantage.

The portal's light died behind him, and he stared at the enormous, long-haired man sitting on the couch. Quinn. He looked as uncomfortable as Tyson felt, hands on his knees, sitting stiff and upright. Did he recognize Tyson?

Tyson opened his mouth to say…He didn't know what. Probably something stupid.

Becca bounded into the room. "Tyson!" She shrieked and flung herself into his arms.

Quinn jerked into action, rising off the couch halfway. A bit jumpy, apparently.

Tyson returned Becca's embrace and the tension that had been running in the back of his mind since she disappeared melted away, only to be replaced with a new kind of fear. She was here, but so was Quinn, confirming that she'd helped him.

"Your face!" she exclaimed.

"I'll explain later. For now, do you want to tell me why there's a felon in my living room?" Tyson asked, tugging on her arms to get her to loosen her grip. His hand brushed a bandage on one of her arms.

"Two, actually," Becca said, far too cheerfully.

"Wait, what happened to your arm?" Tyson asked, aghast. Her arm was covered wrist to elbow with a white bandage.

"You know, I'm not sure. It had something to do with the cursed half-snake mummy my dad sent to the shop before I left. I'm trying a few things on it. I think it's just irritated."

"Not infected, though?" Tyson searched her eyes, looking for any evidence of deception. She would lie to keep me from worrying.

"It's fine. Barely painful anymore. I think it's getting better."

Tyson closed his eyes, breathing out. "I hoped that you helping him was a rumor."

"You knew I liked him, didn't you?" Her eyes searched his, and then she laughed. "Tyson Miller, you're the most unobservant person I know! I couldn't leave Quinn in that place. Not with what they wanted to do to him." She crossed to the couch and reached a hand out to Quinn. He took it, and Becca swung their hands between them in her giddy way.

"I can't imagine your dad is proud." Tyson swallowed as he said the words, knowing at the same time that he shouldn't have said them.

Becca's face morphed into a scowl. Anger formed behind her eyes like a storm.

"You know I don't agree with my dad's methods and beliefs."

"Yeah. I know." *Sometimes I wish you had more sense, though.* That thought stayed inside Tyson's mind, fortunately. He rubbed the back of his head. "Circumstances aside, it's good to see you, Becca."

Becca grinned, tucking her blonde hair behind her ear. "I know you sort of already met, but last time it was under duress. So, Tyson, this is Quinn. Quinn, Tyson." She bounced on her heels looking fit to burst.

Quinn stood, towering over Tyson. Well, okay, that was an exaggeration. He was only about three inches taller, but it felt like a lot since he was built like a quarterback. He reached out a hand, and Tyson extended his to meet it, grasping as firmly as he could without coming off combative.

Harper and her brother seemed to have very little in common. Quinn was enormous, and all of it lean muscle. His hair flowed down his back much longer than Harper's, and he had the sort of face most girls died for.

Harper was pretty normal on that front. Not stunning, but not plain either. She just...blended in. Quinn definitely stood out.

They had the same intense brown-eyed gaze, though. Tyson squirmed under his scrutiny, wondering what he thought.

"I've heard a lot about you," Quinn said with a deep, baritone voice.

"Can't say the same for you. But then again, Becca loves to spring things on me." Tyson smiled, hoping it looked friendly. Quinn's Naturalization file was as thin as Harper's. Thinner, actually. According to Tom, Quinn sat in complete silence every appointment he had.

Becca grabbed Quinn's hand, smiling up at him. Eyes on him, she spoke to Tyson. "You don't look very surprised to see us. I knew you would figure it out. I was betting Quinn that you would *freak*." She sounded disappointed.

Tyson slid his hands into his pockets. "Brilliant, hiding it in the email like that."

"I know, right? Did you delete it, by the way?"

"Er, no." Tyson opened his phone. The battery was dead. "Let me get my charger." He moved toward his room, aware of Quinn's eyes following him.

In his room, Tyson could breathe. The whole apartment felt different with them there. Unstable. Not like the sanctuary it usually was when he returned from the camp each week. He reached over the side of his bed, grasping for his phone cord. It came up and he plugged in his phone, waiting while it powered up.

It was the perfect time to change out of his filthy clothes. He stripped everything off, grabbing a fresh outfit. He wished he could shower and wash away everything from the past couple of days, but there wasn't time. He had no idea how long his guests would stay.

As Tyson tugged his shirt over his head, he heard Becca and Quinn talking in the other room. He strained, but couldn't hear their low voices. He walked softly toward his door, listening at the crack.

"I don't know, Becca. He works for them."

"We've talked about this before. We can trust Tyson. He's more loyal toward family than the system." Becca didn't sound angry, just passionate. Her trust in Tyson settled like a weight on his shoulders, and his mouth went dry. Faced with the reality of harboring fugitives from the law, he struggled to make sense of what he should do. It didn't feel the way he expected. It was Becca, after all. Tyson would do anything for her. Except bury a body. A person had to draw the line somewhere.

Tyson's phone buzzed, indicating it had turned fully on, and he brought his attention back to it, flopping onto the bed. His finger hovered over the photo icon, tempted to scan through the pictures he'd taken of Reya's record, but it could wait. It had to wait. Instead, he tapped his email. He selected Becca's most recent messages and deleted them before he could talk himself out of it.

"Tyson?" Becca called out.

"Coming!" Tyson rolled off the bed, leaving his phone to charge. Becca and Quinn sat next to each other on the couch, glancing meaningfully at one another. Since she lived out of state, Tyson had never seen her with any of her past boyfriends. It was bizarre how nervous it made him feel.

Tyson stood awkwardly at the edge of the room. The only open seat was the couch, next to Quinn. He'd pass on that. Tyson sat cross-legged on the floor, determining once all this was over he'd get an armchair or something so he could have guests. He'd never had anyone else over. Of *course* his first guests would have to be convicted felons...

"There's some things you should know. More than you already do," Becca began. "We're together, first off."

"That being the most important thing?" He raised his eyebrows. Becca rolled her eyes. "I knew you had a thing for him when you were both at the camp. I'm a bit surprised it led to escaping and evading the law, but..."

She glared. "They wanted his wings, Tyson. If someone wanted to chop off your legs, would you let them?"

She sounded much touchier than usual. It wasn't like her.

"It isn't really the same thing," Tyson said, attempting to defend himself without offending her further.

"You know what, shut up," she snapped. "You're great at the whole counselor thing, except for this."

"Becca," Quinn said, his hand on her arm. She backed down, still fuming.

Tyson stared at her. Having heard similar from Harper, he was starting to realize Naturalization had a negative impact that he had never considered before. One he sort of just...ignored. No, not ignored. Justified.

Quinn stared steadily at Tyson. "I could function without my wings, but you don't realize how much they are a part of me. I could never see myself living life without them. I would rather die."

He glanced at Becca, who still seemed pissed even though she'd calmed down somewhat. The silence thickened the air in the room.

"Quinn is looking for someone," Becca blurted. Quinn tensed. "You might not know her, but—"

"His sister, right?" It was satisfying to see the shock on their faces. "She's at the camp." Tyson watched Quinn's expression morph from a smooth mask into something else. Fury? Grief?

"No."

He'd never heard so much anguish in a single word.

"Quinn," Becca said softly. "Quinn, it's all right. Nothing has happened to her. Tyson can tell us what he knows."

"She's all right," Tyson said in a rush. "Tried to escape once already, that's all."

Quinn snorted. "Of course she has. How many times did I try?" He glanced at Becca.

"A dozen, I think." Becca noticed Tyson's shocked expression. "They didn't know about all of the ones that failed. We aborted a few before they'd really begun. They knew about enough to decide they were pulling Quinn's application, though. It's what convinced us it was now or never."

Tyson looked to Quinn, then back to Becca. "How did you get out? Everyone is still pissed about that, by the way. No one can figure out how you did it."

"I made this." Becca pulled a device from her pocket and handed it to Tyson. He turned it over in his hands. A disc constructed of plastic and metal, unremarkable and with very little detail on it. "It works via an app I created. Basically, the pulse it sends out neutralizes magic in a targeted area."

"What's the range?"

"Only about twenty feet. I'm working on increasing it, but I'd have to increase the size of the device, and I like that it fits in my pocket." She laughed. "Quinn came up with the idea, but I knew how to execute it. It glitches now and then. It took us three tries to get it to stay functioning long enough to get out, and one of us almost got left behind."

"I'm surprised you escaped together. Why not just get Quinn out and then leave later?"

Becca shook her head. "We were already known to be too close for me to get out without scrutiny."

Quinn chuckled. "Is that what we're telling him?"

Becca stuck her tongue out at him, but Tyson saw the teasing in her expression. "What? It's true."

"Sure." He grinned, staring into her eyes. Becca gave a little laugh, putting her hand on his chest. It was like they'd forgotten Tyson was there.

Tyson cleared his throat. "Uh, guys? Anything else you want to tell me?"

Quinn broke their gaze. "Um, you're out of groceries."

"We're *starving*."

Tyson shook his head. Becca and her exaggerations. He crossed his arms and waited.

"Quinn's just really worried about Harper," Becca said. Quinn gave her a wounded look. "What? You are. And I wanted Tyson to know. It's critical that we get her out of that camp, for her sake and yours."

"Yes." Quinn rubbed at Becca's hand, agitated. "I haven't contacted Harper in months, and now she's stuck in that *place* without someone to support her." He looked at Becca, a smile quirking the corner of his mouth.

"I've been supporting her." Tyson straightened. Quinn raised his eyebrows.

Becca smiled sadly. "No offense, Tyson, but it's your job. I guarantee she knows that, and that she's either ignoring you or playing you to help her escape."

The truth stung. Tyson's shoulders slumped. "I know. I know that. I do."

"Also, we're going to Alaska. You could come." Becca's voice lilted up with a hopeful note.

"What?" Tyson's voice cracked. He cleared his throat.

"Would that be so bad?" Becca cocked her head. He stared pointedly at her. "Okay, I get it, you don't want to be a criminal. Too bad, it's kinda fun."

Only Becca would think that. Tyson tried again, nodding to Quinn. "Looking for your parents, right?"

"She told you?" Quinn asked.

"That's where my grandmother and grandpa were from. Alaska." Tyson replied. Strange to think their families were from the same place.

"I still don't trust you." Quinn stood, yanking his hand out of Becca's and approaching Tyson, who backed up until he hit the wall. Quinn loomed over him. "How well do you really know your cousin, Becca? He could still be on their side."

"Quinn, this is silly."

Quinn leaned in closer, his breath hot on Tyson's face.

Tyson turned away slightly to avoid the pungent, warm air. "You know what, you don't have to tell me anything about your plan. Just get out of my apartment. I'll take a message to Harper, but that's all I told her I would do. I won't tell anyone you were here, or where you're going."

There was a knock a few doors down, and Tyson jumped a little. He breathed a few times to get his heart rate down.

Quinn's golden-brown eyes watched Tyson with a hawk-like intensity.

"Okay." Quinn backed off, flopping next to Becca on the couch.

Okay. A single word that kept Tyson from being pummeled into his own wall.

Another knock came next door, sounding closer this time. The Stiffs? Tyson's mind buzzed, but he dismissed the anxious thoughts. Stiffs didn't knock politely. They bashed down doors. Probably just a friend of his neighbor. He tried to focus on Quinn's face, to read what he thought or felt. How did he keep his expression so stone-like?

"I thought you'd help." Becca's voice sounded small.

Tyson closed his eyes, then forced them open and looked at her. "Harper is better off in the camp. Maybe she'll do better knowing you're all right. I can tell her that."

Quinn clenched his free hand, the other gripped in Becca's. "That's not your choice to make."

"But it's the choice you're asking me to make. My whole career could go up in smoke. I could be imprisoned. Her blood would be on my hands if we fail." The full implication of the situation hit Tyson. He didn't see it before, faced with Harper's hopeful reasoning in his office. "I can't do it."

Becca's face contorted with disgust, and she pushed herself off the couch. "What is wrong with you?"

"Becca, please," Tyson widened his eyes, hoping she saw the pleading in them. He needed her to understand. "I know you're upset, but I can't see any good coming of this."

"Your priorities are messed up if you'll put your comfort and safety above someone else's *life*." She seethed with anger.

"She won't die if she's Naturalized," Tyson insisted.

"That's what you think." Becca paced the floor with clenched fists. "You're the psychologist. Has your mentor shared the statistics with you yet?"

"What statistics?"

Becca's eyes narrowed. "Suicide rates in paranormals after Naturalization."

"Well, of course I've heard some numbers, but ours are better than anywhere else in the country. We're improving them significantly with our new follow-up program." Tyson rubbed his hands on his jeans. "Look, you guys don't need me. You can use your device like before."

"Someone has to tell Harper where and when to meet us. For that, we need you." Becca stabbed her finger toward him.

Tyson considered what she was saying. A messenger. They just needed a messenger. He could do that, right? What Harper did with the information was none of his business. And he wouldn't be letting Becca down.

"Fine. I can send her a message when you need me to. But I'm not getting any closer to this." And in reality, he was only willing to do as much because Harper had saved his life. He owed her something for that.

"Fine." Becca's anger was far from fading. Tyson hated it, but he couldn't see another way without putting himself in their position. He couldn't help anyone else at the camp if he got put in jail.

Tyson stood, straightening his shirt. "Good. That's settled, then." Neither of them would look at him. He flexed his fingers, shaking off his nerves. That strange buzzing sensation plagued his head, growing stronger. It felt like a warning.

A knock came at the door, and they all swung their heads toward it. Tyson was right beside the door and his hand was on the knob before he could think.

"Tyson, don't— " Becca cut off with a shriek.

The room's only window shattered behind Tyson. He spun around.

Quinn stood on a skinny ledge outside the window, his black wings spread behind, balancing him.

Becca stood between them, green eyes shining with disappointment. She took a breath.

"Becca, I—"

"I'll call you." She stepped through the window and wrapped her arms around Quinn's neck. Tyson couldn't see her face anymore.

Quinn gripped her waist, and with a final stony glare in Tyson's direction, he pushed off the ledge and fell. The doorway behind Tyson exploded as four men in black tactical armor burst into the room.

"Where did they go?" one of them demanded.

"I-I don't know. I just got home and found them here."

The officer's chin jutted out, and he pointed to the couch. "Sit there."

The others fanned out, sweeping every inch of the apartment. One of them brought in the cell phone, and Tyson closed his eyes. He had deleted the emails, but it wouldn't take long for them to discover that she was his cousin.

"Just this, sir." The man held it out to the one who spoke to Tyson. He must have been a captain of sorts.

The captain gestured to Tyson. "Open it."

Trembling, Tyson took his phone and swiped it open. The man handed it to his captain, and Tyson watched with trepidation as he scrolled through it.

He glanced from the screen to Tyson's face. "You work for the camp?"

Tyson licked his lips. "I do."

"Why would they come here?"

"They wanted me to give them information about the camp." The lie came easier than Tyson expected. The least he could do was give them some time to escape.

"What kind of information?"

"They were just getting to that part when you got here." Tyson's leg tapped the floor, agitated by his nerves. He forced it still and tried to look earnest.

The captain considered Tyson. The other two men come up behind him. "Nothing here, sir," one of them said.

"You're free to go." Tyon's phone hit his lap. "But I'll be speaking with your superiors. One of my men will stay here for a while in the event they try to return." The captain nodded to a man on his left.

"Thank you," Tyson played the part of a grateful innocent and tried not to think about what Violet would say when she heard that Becca had contacted him, Quinn in tow.

The men filed out of the apartment. Tyson breathed in as the door shut behind them.

He stared at the broken glass on the floor. A breeze came through the permanently open window, exposing the sound of cars driving by outside.

No matter how he tried to convince himself he was doing the right thing by not getting more deeply involved in Harper's freedom, he couldn't get rid of the gut-wrenching feeling that it wasn't enough.

CHAPTER ELEVEN
HARPER

HARPER DIDN'T EXPECT HELL to have waffles for breakfast. She loaded up a plate, murmuring thanks to the guys serving, and made her way toward the tables. Where to sit?

A glance told her Tyson wasn't there. Facing the day felt harder knowing that he wouldn't be there to talk to if things bombed, which they were bound to.

Who was she kidding? She didn't need a shrink to make it through one day of Naturalization camp. Harper looked around the room.

Fletcher perched on top of a windowsill across from where she stood, making silly expressions with his eyebrows and grinning, his blue wings blocking all of the sunlight streaming in from outside like he was showing them off. They *were* gorgeous, but his cocky charm was annoying. He also ate what Harper thought was liver, which sounded divine...just not for breakfast.

Kamri messed around with the other werewolves in the breakfast nook. They played around pretty roughly, but Kamri seemed to have them well in hand, and Harper remembered that Kamri was considered one of the leaders of the pack with Zeke.

Zeke had left a few minutes prior, after a hushed discussion with Lilith in the hallway. There were six massive guys sitting with Kamri. They talked loudly, slapping each other around and tossing food across the table, mostly varying degrees of cooked meat. Did they eat anything else?

Harper chose a seat at the opposite end of the long table near Fletcher. At the other end, tucked away in the shadows provided by Fletcher's wings, three vampires sucked away at I.V. lines attached to bags filled with blood. One of them stared at Harper—a blonde, emaciated girl with hollow, haunted eyes. She drew long and hard from the tube, like smoking a cigarette, then locked the end of the line and crossed her arms.

Harper dropped her gaze too late.

"I heard you had a run-in with the rogues last night. Was Heath there?"

"I didn't ask their names."

"Did you kill any?" Her skinny fingers tapped on the table in front of her. Harper's shoulder blades itched, but the bandages reminded her there wouldn't be any escaping that way. Would she have any warning before the vamp leapt across the table and tried to suck her dry?

"I don't think so, but I didn't stick around." Harper rolled her shoulders.

"Too busy saving your poor human friend." The vamp's voice dripped with scorn.

"Yes, too busy acting on the shred of humanity left inside me. Do you have any?"

She stood up from the table baring her fangs, eye color bleeding to red.

"Jade!" Lilith's voice barked. "Stand down."

Jade's eyes faded back to a muddy brown. She leaned across the table, voice dropping low. "You won't have her protection for long, bird brain. And there are worse things than death here."

"Like being one of you," Fletcher said. He flicked his right wing back, flashing sunlight at Jade. She shrieked and spun toward him. An acrid, charcoal-like smell reached Harper's nostrils, and smoke rose from the back of Jade's neck, the only part of her exposed above the collar of her leather jacket. Fletcher grinned and pushed off from the windowsill, landing on the kitchen island behind Harper, then hopping down to the floor. Jade crouched on the floor next to her friends, and all three hid their faces from the sun, hissing and cursing in Fletcher's direction. He just laughed.

Lilith's face twisted in a furious expression that transformed her into something horrifying rather than lovely. "I expect better from the lot of you. Especially you, Fletcher. Your Naturalization Reformation is in a few days!"

Fletcher's head bowed and his wings drooped before they shrunk into his back, the blue feathers disappearing. The vampire girls vanished, leaving the room quieter than Harper thought possible. Fletcher lingered, glancing at Harper.

Lilith cleared her throat and Fletcher hesitated, then gave Harper a little wave and hustled out of the room as if he had somewhere to be.

Harper pushed a few bites of waffle into her mouth, then grasped a lock of hair from just behind her ear and fidgeted with it, keeping her head down as conversation slowly returned to the kitchen, more muted than before.

A bell rang a few moments later, and everyone scattered. Plate empty, Harper headed for the kitchen sink. The lights on the fridge and pantry shone red. Breakfast was over.

Lilith sauntered over to Harper. "I have your class schedule. You start out with Naturalization Theory, then meet Zeke outside after lunch. Then a special session with me." She winked, handing over a paper, a notebook, and a small pencil case.

Harper took the items from her. "Did Tyson make it home?"

Lilith raised her eyebrows. "Yes. Mr. Miller left last night. It's kind of you to be so concerned about his well-being."

Harper forced her mouth to widen in a smile. It felt false, but she did have something to be happy about. If Tyson's cousin was at his place, and maybe Quinn with her, then Harper's days there were numbered.

"Off to class, then," Lilith said, matching Harper's smile with a perfect one of her own. Harper walked past her toward the hallway on the other side of the house, where several classes were in session behind the closed doors. Harper stopped in front of the same classroom as the day before and gazed through the rectangular window. There were only five students with Mr. James Petrov standing in front of them.

Harper leaned forward and pressed her head against the door's surface. She could skip. But everyone would know she had, and there might be consequences she wasn't prepared to deal with. It would be better to pretend she was acclimating than to keep stirring the pot and causing trouble. Easier to escape if she got everyone to think she was going along with it all.

The knob turned in Harper's hand and the door swung open. She fell forward, stumbling to catch herself before she sprawled on the linoleum floor.

"Harper, it is good to see you in class. For real this time, I expect?" Mr. Petrov closed the door behind her and walked to his place at the whiteboard in front of the class. He gestured at the chairs, where the five students sat, staring. Ian was among them, to Harper's surprise. He gave her a small smile as he peered up through his hair.

Harper unclenched her hands and chose a seat on an aisle next to Ian, but one seat back so she wasn't right beside him. Hopefully, her anxiety wasn't too obvious. If there were any werewolves in the room, no doubt they could smell it on her.

"Welcome to Naturalization Theory. This first class of the day is for those who are new, and others who might be struggling to progress toward Naturalization ideals. We welcome debate and the voicing of all opinions, but not name calling or displays of paranormalcy." Mr. Petrov peered over his spectacles. Harper slunk down in her seat. "Now, who wants to give Harper a brief review of our recent week's discussion?"

"We were going over the ways in which those with paranormal abilities endangered human civilians, and the pros and cons of Naturalization to both populations," a girl with straight, pale brown hair answered from the front of the classroom. Harper hadn't met her, but remembered glimpsing the girl at movie night. Her body was model-thin, and her every movement was accompanied with a willowy grace.

"Thank you, Leah," Petrov said.

Harper straightened in her chair. "Pros? What pros could there possibly be?"

Mr. Petrov perked up. "Harper takes counterpoint. Who wants to go toe-to-toe with her? Leah?"

Leah, twisted around to face Harper. "There are many benefits to Naturalization. When civilians aren't in terror for their lives, or hunting their neighbors to root out witches and monsters, everything runs more smoothly. They become kinder, treat each other with less suspicion and more good will. It's for the good of the community."

She smiled with such self-assurance Harper wanted to fly across the room and deck her. Instead, she clenched her hands and forced herself back into the chair, feeling the top dig into her upper back.

Petrov folded his arms and tilted his head, looking at Harper over the top of his glasses.

She breathed in and let the words flow out. "But what about the community that's being eradicated? Who knows how each of our kind emerged? However they emerged, they're cultures now. Entire tribes, packs, flocks, and more are in danger of disappearing, forced into hiding or to alter their entire identity just to make others comfortable."

"Paranormal individuals cause damage on a massive scale, including deaths."

Harper let her breath out slowly to ease the anger she felt rising. She could have a rational debate about this, couldn't she? "How often are they alone when they change for the first time? How often are they met with terror, hate, and violence from those they love most, those who should support them? How often do those people become the first victims because paranormals don't know what's happening or why and they're afraid of dying, but afraid of themselves most of all?"

Murmurs of agreement rose from several others in the room.

"That's what Naturalization is for," Leah said. "If we give ourselves up to the greater good of safety for everyone, we must train our destructive instincts, reject our alternate forms, allow our reproductive ability to be eradicated and reduced, and strive to become as humans are. Then there are no half-breed children transforming without understanding. No new monsters created. Less chaos, less murder, more peace."

Harper stared at her hands. "What if we embraced it instead? Taught our children, and humans, how to live together with all of our abilities mixed together. If we accept Naturalization as the only way, we admit our lives mean less than the humans'. But why should they be the superior race?"

"Because they can control themselves!" Leah's voice rose.

Harper stood, slapping her palms on the desk in front of her. "Humans still murder! They still lie and abuse and cheat! You call that control? Some of us could stop those things, and some of us do, but how can we make any difference at all if our unique abilities are stripped away? It shouldn't be about making us appear like them. It should be about helping us act like the best of them. We don't have to give up the essence of ourselves to do that."

Harper's gaze burned ahead, not at her debate opponent, but at Mr. Petrov. She shook with anger, but for once she felt completely in control. The energy to shift built up beneath the surface, ready to harness, but it didn't overwhelm her.

Leah opened her mouth for rebuttal, but Mr. Petrov unfolded his arms and his hands came together in a slow clap. The rest of the class joined him, even Harper's opponent.

"Eloquently expressed. Perhaps you could consider a career in paranormal law, Miss Harper. We could always use forward thinkers like you to improve the lives of those who follow."

His praise reached his brown eyes and threw Harper off guard. She sat frozen in her seat, unable to think of what to say.

"Now, who wants to comment on the debate we just heard?"

Harper stayed silent, spent after giving the most impassioned speech of her life. A speech that, in the end, meant nothing. It didn't change Petrov's opinion, or Leah's. It had zero impact on the laws holding her here. Next time, she'd keep her mouth shut.

"That was brilliant." Ian leaned over, hair falling into his face. "I've never heard it put that way before." He brushed the hair back to reveal hopeful blue eyes.

"Yeah, but, do you think it can ever change?" Harper replied. "No one here seems to care."

"They care, they just hide it. They're afraid to feel it, even when they know what's coming. I think it can change, but like so many people throughout history, we might have to fight for it."

Harper snorted, crossing her arms. "The front line suffers the most."

"The front line values the changes most," Ian said. The bell rang, signaling the end of class. "If you ever start an insurrection, I'm in." He left.

Harper wasn't sure what to think of that. Start a rebellion? Yeah, right. She wasn't a natural-born leader, prepared to raise a flag and lead her people to freedom. She didn't need anyone besides herself and Quinn to be concerned about.

She glanced at the paper Lilith gave her. Zeke's class was next, something called Practical Paranormal, which sounded ridiculous. At least it was outside. Following that, the next class was Remedies with Lilith herself. Harper swallowed, thinking of what the witch said the previous night.

Hopefully, Harper would get some answers. She picked up the unused notebook and pencil and walked past Mr. Petrov, feeling his gaze as it followed her out of the classroom.

Harper stopped at her room to take off the bandages around her shoulders— it was nearly lunchtime—and dropped off the pencil and notebook, then bolted outside. The sun shone bright and clear, no sign of yesterday's storm.

The class had over thirty people in it. All of them seemed to be near Harper's age, but it was hard to tell with paranormals. The guy standing next to her could be a hundred, even though that was unlikely. A lot of the really old ones were too good at hiding, or they were killed in the chaos of the first years after the Reveal when they wouldn't turn themselves in.

Did they have Naturalization camps for adults? It seemed likely.

Harper squinted at the bulky figure at the front of the group. Zeke greeted the group with a bright white smile she hadn't seen on him before. His dreadlocks swung past his shoulders until he grabbed an elastic from his wrist and pulled them up out of the way. His loose gray t-shirt and jeans made him look like he was more ready to hang out with friends than teach a class.

The blind woman who had spoken to Harper before she rescued Tyson stood beside him. The red amethyst was still in Harper's pocket. Harper wanted to thank her, or at least find out her name, but Zeke spoke before Harper could move toward her.

"Hey, guys," Zeke called out. Everyone stopped talking. Harper eyed the crowd. Zeke's alpha ability was incredible. The compliance of the crowd was absolute. Even Keith quieted immediately, stanidng at the back of the group with several other teenagers.

Keith caught Harper's stare and a feral grin spread across his face. He nudged the guy next to him, the same guy Harper had choked at breakfast her first day. That one glared furiously, baring elongated teeth as if he was losing control of his human form just at the sight of her. Harper shuddered and looked back at Zeke as he spoke.

"Pair up, everybody. You know the drill. And don't hog the newbie." Zeke grinned at Harper, a fully-bared smile. Werewolves. Would she ever get used to them?

"Get going, then!" Zeke barked.

Everyone spurred into action. A dozen people surrounded Harper, asking her to spar with them, jostling each other to get close to her. Harper whirled around, not sure what to do or say, until Zeke strode up and started shoving people off in pairs.

"Exactly what I told you not to do, you cretins," he growled, throwing two more people away. He grabbed one by the shoulder and pushed her toward Harper. "Sharon, you'll be Harper's first match. Don't go easy on her just because she's new. I have a feeling this one will be harder to crack than you expect."

"Match?" Harper swallowed. What was going on?

"It's a duel." The tall blonde, Sharon, smiled down at Harper. She was built like a truck—broad shoulders and thick thighs. Harper almost expected a German accent to come out of her mouth, but she talked like any American.

"Circles up!" The blind woman shouted, standing where Zeke had left her. She raised her arms and the field crackled with energy. Large white circles burned into the grass, about ten feet wide. Shimmering globes erupted from the lines, arching into twenty individual bubbles spread across the wide field.

"Stay inside the circle," Zeke gestured. "On my mark, the duel begins. You take turns attacking. When it's your turn to attack, your goal is to make your opponent shift or reveal their magic or otherworldly abilities. When it's your opponent's turn, you must avoid revealing your true form and abilities. Winner is decided when ten minutes is up or the defender loses."

Loses what? Their life? Harper wiped her clammy hands on her jeans. "I thought we were discouraged from attacking each other?" Wasn't that the point of the wards?

Zeke chuckled. "Well, yes. But we all have steam to blow off. This keeps it controlled, organized, and relatively safe. Believe it or not, we have far less conflict this way."

Harper swallowed, wiping her hands on her pants. "Are there any rules?"

"Just stay in the circle. And do no lasting harm. Bumps, bruises, and scrapes are expected. Anything more will result in your being removed from the class for the day and given a citation. That goes on your Naturalization record." Zeke fixed his eyes on Harper.

Harper nodded, and he left the circle she stood in.

Sharon held out her hand. Harper gulped past the dryness in her throat, wishing she'd thought to get some water before leaving the cabin. Harper hoped Sharon couldn't feel the clamminess of her hand as they shook.

"So, uh, do I get to ask what you are before we start?"

Sharon's smile widened. "You can ask, but I don't have to answer."

"Fair enough," Harper muttered. If she had to guess, she'd say werewolf. She was huge, for one, and she acted cocky enough.

People were scattered all over the field, each facing their opponent, serious expressions or friendly chatter varying from circle to circle.

"Anything else you care to tell me? Any rules that Zeke left out?"

"The circles are warded." Sharon kicked toward the white line that marked the outside of the circle. "If you fall or try to get out after Zeke's call to start, you'll get a shock. It's a bit nasty."

Harper stared at the innocent white line in the dirt. "Right. Thanks. So, who's the witch?" she asked, looking back to where the blind woman and Zeke stood talking together.

"On your mark," Zeke called.

"Attacker," Sharon said, jabbing her finger at herself and avoiding the question. She pointed at Harper. "Defender."

Harper crouched, getting ready to run, or at least brace herself for whatever Sharon did. Harper's shoulders ached with soreness from her flight the day before. She rolled them a bit to shake off the sensation.

Based on what Lilith had said, she should be fine to shift. But the whole point of the exercise was to avoid doing just that. A queasy feeling spread through Harper's stomach.

"Anyone ever died?" she asked.

Shannon grinned.

A howl erupted from behind Harper, and she almost shifted. Judging by the activity that exploded in the other circles around the field, that howl was the signal to start.

And now Sharon had two heads.

One Sharon hissed, baring jagged teeth. She—they—lunged toward Harper, those two heads on a single body were tripping her out worse than the edibles she got a hold of when she was fifteen.

Harper dove out of the way, rolling through the dirt and barely avoiding the invisible warded barrier at the edge of the circle. She crouched, panting, and faced the two-headed girl.

"I thought we weren't supposed to shift." Harper's heart pounded, and her muscles seized with fear. Those two heads reminded her of a cobra, but without the hoods. Sharon looked like something else that Harper couldn't put her finger on.

"Defenders can't shift. Attackers can do anything shy of kill or maim." The talking head flicked out its tongue, now pointed. She darted forward, both heads aimed at Harper, green eyes flashing. Harper ducked and rolled between Sharon's legs.

"What the hell are you?" Her heads were freaky with their inhuman teeth and snake-like necks, but she didn't seem to have much else going for her. A little extra speed, possibly strength, but Harper wasn't going to let her get close enough to test those theories. Harper had a handle on it until one of Sharon's heads started spitting a translucent gel-like liquid. The substance hissed when it struck the grass, so Harper knew she didn't want it anywhere near her skin.

Ten minutes felt like an eternity. Sweat dripped down Harper's back as she dodged viper-spit and snapping teeth. If only she could fly out of reach...

Zeke's howl split the air as a sizzling glob of saliva struck the heel of Harper's shoe. She scrambled backwards through the grass, kicking it off before it could eat into the rubber and her foot.

Sharon smiled, and with a disconcerting slurping sound her second head drew back into her body and her neck shrank to normal. She still towered over Harper, but she held out her hand, looking as if she had a great time trying to not-kill her.

Harper eyed her hand, then took it.

"Way to go, newbie. Guess I won't be the one to crack your egg." Sharon cackled and Harper rolled her eyes at the pun. Sharon waved her hand and crossed out of the circle.

"Wait, don't we switch who attacks?"

"With new partners. Keeps it more exciting that way. We'll have another shot at each other another time. Can't wait."

Harper watched her go, wondering who would step into the circle next. There were several individuals making their way toward her. When they noticed each other, some of them broke into a run.

"Nice work against the hydra, feathers."

Harper whirled around. Keith stood casually in her circle. Her eyes narrowed. "What do you want?"

Keith grinned madly at those grumbling about him beating them to Harper. "What does it look like? I'm set to duel you."

"You and I already did this once. You lost." Harper folded her arms.

Keith's face tightened into a scowl. "That didn't count. You didn't know the rules yet. Besides, I'm changing my tactics."

Harper planted her feet in the dirt, facing him head-on. "I was defender last round, it's my turn to attack."

Keith wiped his nose on his sleeve, jamming his hands in his pockets. "I was defender too. We flip for it when that happens."

Harper gritted her teeth. "Fine. Get on with it."

Keith pulled out a quarter. Harper held out her hand and marched up to him.

"I flip."

He dropped the coin into her hand. "No problemo."

Harper threw the coin wildly into the air overhead. "Call."

Keith gazed up at it, watching it arch toward the ground. "Tailfeathers."

Harper's hands clenched tighter in their fists. Her nails bit into her palms. The coin landed with a soft thud and she ran to it. Keith sauntered, hands in his pockets, acting infuriatingly calm and good-natured. Harper leaned over the silver circle in the dirt.

Tails.

Keith laughed. "Look at that. Guess I get to choose my position. Attacker."

"Surprise," Harper muttered under her breath, taking a few steps away from him. She spotted Zeke across the field. He seemed to have just finished talking to two other students. One was limping. Then he raised his head and opened his mouth. His howl cut through the air.

Keith stripped down to nothing but a pair of tight biker shorts and transformed into a snarling, giant ball of fury.

Harper ran headlong toward him, yelling as loudly as she could, fighting the urge to shift and fly out over his head.

A flash of worry shot through Keith's eyes when he realized Harper wasn't going to stop before they crashed. He skidded to a halt, four paws sending dirt and rocks into the air.

Harper stopped too, chest heaving, staring at him, muscles tense and waiting for his next move.

He jumped.

Harper ducked, curling into a ball with her hands over her head, making herself a smaller target. He landed standing over her, belly fur brushing the top of her head. Harper uncurled and started to crawl out from beneath him. He thrust his snout under her side and flipped her onto her back.

Sickeningly fast, the wolf morphed back into human form and Keith was on top of Harper, a gloating smile on his face.

Wings blossomed from Harper's back, and she felt the song, waiting to burst from her chest. Had it really killed the rogues the other night? She couldn't afford to test it now. Instead, she emitted a screech, thrusting Keith off her with supernatural strength.

He flew at the white line, striking the invisible barrier and sending crackles of green rippling out over a sphere-like shape that encompassed the dueling ring. He crashed to the ground face-first, but picked himself up immediately, shaking his head.

Zeke's howl marked the end of the round, and the bubble around them disappeared.

"Got you that time, birdie."

Harper wanted to clean the smirk off his horrid face. He wouldn't be smiling if he knew how close she'd been to killing him.

Harper leapt into the air, wanting nothing more than to get away from his smug grin and that stupid circle and the stifling confinement of this prison disguised as a summer getaway.

She flapped her wings, enjoying the stretch and the air on her face. She climbed higher until the oxygen grew thin and the air chilled. It would be difficult for anyone else to breathe at the level she flew.

Sky stretched from horizon to horizon on the cloudless day. The field and lodge lay below, its residents milling about. Some of them gazed and pointed up. Beyond them lay miles of forest and a tiny road winding down the mountain.

Harper picked up a pocket of warm air and glided, wings spread, relishing the wind as it tickled through her feathers, and she realized that she didn't feel blood on her back. Nothing hurt, and she was as near to heaven as she could get.

How high could Violet's wards go? She squinted toward the sun. As she turned her head away, a faint glimmer of green overhead caught her eyes. It was similar to the warded barriers around the dueling circles. A bubble.

How did the witch maintain so many wards? The coven probably had something to do with it, but Harper wouldn't be surprised if the witch sucked magic from the residents of her Happy House.

Harper's ears picked up the sound of someone yelling. Zeke waved his arms, gesturing for her to come down. She lifted her face to the sky one last time, feeling the rushing air and the warmth of the sun on her face. Then she dove.

She pulled up at the last second, eliciting a few shrieks from people in the surrounding dueling rings, and landed on her feet in front of Zeke. She folded her wings in, but stayed shifted. She was done with this game.

Zeke's expression twisted with fury. "What was that?" He stepped up close, getting into her face. Her wings flared out, an instinctive response, and those watching gasped.

"He was straddling me. I think that's called sexual harassment. Is that a thing here?" Harper folded her arms against her chest, heart pounding with adrenaline.

Zeke took a long sniff, then huffed it out, moving his mouth like he'd tasted something gross. "The duels are meant to train you—"

"I don't give a damn about this training!" Harper yelled, her hands dropping to her sides and forming fists. "I have no future here, werewolf. If I choose Naturalization, my wings get chopped off. What do they do to you? Do they remove your heightened sense of smell? Do they lock you in your mutt form for life and sell you as a pet? No? Then I don't want to hear this Naturalization crap from you!"

She took off at a run, flapping her wings until she was airborne again.

Zeke hollered after her, but she ignored him, pushing until she felt the burn in her wings. She focused on putting as much distance between herself and that field of imbeciles as she could, ignoring the clench in her stomach that told her it was time to eat. She landed on the top of a tall pine, too far to even see the cabin any more. There was nothing but blue skies and pines. For a moment, Harper just breathed.

A glimmer of blue caught her eye. A blue jay in blue jeans. She wasn't the only one cutting class, apparently. Fletcher was supposed to be a role model for Naturalization, with his deadline coming up. So what was he doing out here?

CHAPTER TWELVE
HARPER

HARPER SPREAD HER WINGS, her movement making the tree dip beneath her. Thrusting into the air, she flapped hard to draw upward. Fletcher must have heard her panting as she caught up, because he turned his head.

A friendly grin spread wide across his face as he slowed down, letting Harper fly alongside him.

"Harper! I didn't expect to meet you up here. I mean, I hoped I might, but..." He ducked his head as if embarrassed. "Aren't you supposed to be in class?"

Harper suddenly felt uncomfortable. All she could think about were those gorgeous blue wings. She pushed the thoughts away. "Aren't you?"

He shook his head. "I don't have anything until this afternoon. It's my free period right now."

"Do you always spend it flying?" Harper squinted at him. The brightness of the sun glinting off his feathers made it hard to see.

"Usually." He glanced at her. "How are classes going?"

The anger Harper felt before surged up to the surface. She clenched her fists and her wings flapped hard, pushing her forward. Fletcher adjusted his pace to keep up.

"Hey, you're upset. Is it Zeke?"

"How did you know?" The hard, sarcastic edge of Harper's tone blocked the emotion in her chest.

"Yeah, Zeke can be tough. He's the kind of person who cares enough to be hard."

"It's not like it's all him. He's part of it, but..." Harper trailed off, at a loss for words.

"Not everything," Fletcher guessed. "Do you want to talk about it?"

The wind rushed into her face. The ground was covered with trees, but the cabin was in sight and they would be there in moments.

She shook her head in response to Fletcher, then ran a hand through her short hair. Time for another shower. It was amazing how just a few days in a place with free access to warm, running water made her want to be clean all the time. Before, she could go a week or more without showering.

"I can respect that you don't want to talk, but I think it will make you feel better. How about if I guess what you're so hung up about, we'll talk? If not, we'll keep flying." Fletcher watched her with those icy blue eyes.

Harper avoided looking at him. "Shoot," she said, as if she were entirely disinterested. "You only get one shot, though."

Fletcher paused, thinking. His eyes lingered on her. She kept her head down, determined not to let him see her smile. Why did this feel like a game? He was prying into her emotions, her deepest thoughts. With Tyson, it felt like an intrusion. Somehow, with Fletcher, it felt like the kind of attention she'd craved her whole life.

Silence stretched out. Zeke's distant howl marked the beginning of another dueling round. The arenas and their duelists were visible now, each one fighting for survival in more ways than one.

When he finally spoke, his words took Harper completely off-guard.

"You're afraid. The more you participate in these classes, the more you get to know the residents of the camp, the more you fear that you'll break down and succumb to the lure of living a normal, un-persecuted life as a Naturalized citizen."

Harper looked up slowly, her eyes connecting with Fletcher's clear blue gaze.

"It is tempting, isn't it? As unappealing and unacceptable as the price to pay is, some part of you longs for the day when you can stop running, stop hiding, and just be you."

"But I can't be me without..." Harper gestured to her soaring wings and the sky above.

Fletcher nodded, as if he understood. But he didn't. If he did, he wouldn't agree to have his wings chopped off.

"I used to think the same way. And then I realized that if I was in a freak accident and lost my legs, or an arm, or something like that, I would still be me. It just changes my appearance, but not the core of who I am."

"How do you know? You've never experienced it. What if you come back from that operation and you're not you?"

Fletcher cocked his head to one side. "I guess I've come to a place where I don't believe that would happen. I've accepted the outcome will be whatever it will be. I have family who have been through it too, which helps. You don't have that though, do you?"

"No." Harper thought about Quinn. He would never support Naturalization. Never. They were going to find their parents and a secret place to live out the rest of their lives. Maybe in another country.

When Harper didn't reply, Fletcher cleared his throat. "I could be that for you."

"What?"

"I mean, I could write to you. Support you in your journey, you know? Once I go through it, I'll leave camp soon after, but I could get permission to call. To visit, even. My family doesn't live far. It might help just to have someone who understands the decision that you're facing."

Harper licked her lips. He didn't know that she wasn't even considering Naturalization. Would he be so friendly if he did? "You don't know me."

"I've wrestled with similar thoughts and feelings. A year ago I was right where you are, thinking there was no way I could do it. I wouldn't have made it without my parents and my sister being there for me."

They flew in silence until the cabin and the dueling arenas came into view.

Fletcher dropped down and glided in a lazy circle. Harper watched him, her wings relaxing into a steady rhythm.

The dueling round ended as they landed on the ground outside one of the circles. Groans and cheers echoed across the field. The others left the arenas, some of them turning human and others staying in their shifter forms.

Beckett bounded across the field as a three-legged wolf, tongue lolling out. He looked ridiculously happy, more like a dog than a wolf.

Harper followed Fletcher out of the circle and off the field.

"I've got a class now, but I'd like to join you for dinner. Would that be okay?" Fletcher asked, grinning.

Had he asked Harper out on the paranormal camp-resident version of a date? In five minutes of conversation, this guy had drilled into the core of her feelings, even got her to talk about them. Harper found that she *did* want to spend more time with him.

"I'd like that."

"Cool. See you later." He waved and jogged off, wings disappearing into his back as he headed toward the forest. What class did he have there?

Harper went into the cabin, wings still out, where she got a lot of looks. Her wings were jet-black and gorgeous. Who wouldn't want to stare at them? The thought filled her with pride, and she gripped the edge of one wing, running her fingers through the feathers as she let the crowd carry her toward the smell of food.

She found an empty seat at the kitchen island and sat down on the high bar stool. Ian stirred some colorful vegetable dish that smelled amazing. Harper was tempted to eat it, but she knew her stomach would rebel later. It didn't do well with that much fiber, she had learned.

Another stir-fry sizzled in a giant wok beside it. Beef? It smelled different. Maybe venison. Beckett grinned at Harper's side, waiting in line for his food.

"Hungry?" He asked.

Harper opened her mouth to respond, but was cut off when someone bumped her wings, nearly throwing her off balance.

The guy grumbled an apology, but Harper caught the finger he gave her behind his back as he walked away.

Beckett growled at them under his breath, then turned his attention to Harper. "I see you're as talkative, as ever." He picked up a bowl.

Harper calmed her nerves and tried a smile.

Anita, on lunch duty today, handed Harper a steaming bowl of meat stir-fry with rice sprinkled on top. Harper's mouth watered. She had to wait for a fork, but as soon as the utensil was in her hand she dug in, chewing past the heat to get something in her stomach.

Beckett took the seat next to Harper, handing her a glass of water as she panted. She chugged the cool liquid with relief.

"Famished, apparently." He smiled again.

Harper took a few more bites, slowing down as her stomach felt less pinchy. "Why do they feed us so well?" she blurted out.

Beckett raised his eyebrows. "Not what you expected?"

"Nuh-uh." Harper said, chewing the savory meat.

"It's because they're afraid of us." Ian's quiet voice caught her attention amidst the chatter of the kitchen. He had finished serving up bowls of vegetables and rice to the hungry residents and had his own bowl now. He took a seat next to Becket on the end of the counter.

"What do you mean?" Harper asked, forgetting the next bite on her fork. A chunk of meat fell back into the bowl.

"What damage do you think a large group of half-starved paranormal teens and adults could do if they rebelled and broke out of camp? They've got to keep us fed, fat, and happy. Well, at least two of the three, I guess. I'm not sure the majority of us are thrilled with the regulations and limitations we have to put up with. You know, being tracked everywhere we go, warded against leaving, and then dealing with high-security surveillance and death as a punishment for any misstep once we pass Naturalization."

Becket shook his head. "If they didn't feed us on top of all of that, well, I'd be the first to rip the throat out of whatever hunter they put in my way of getting out."

His sudden blood-thirstiness shocked Harper. Her fork dropped back into her bowl.

"Yeah, I can see that," she said. "Wait, did you say we're being tracked?"

If there was anything worse than being here, it was the possibility that even if she managed to escape it would be for nothing when they caught her because of some tech she didn't know about.

"It happens during the warding. You might not have noticed. Warding is already super uncomfortable. They implant a tracker under the skin in your back, usually. Some say it's on your neck, close to your brain stem so you can't remove it, but I've felt some of my friend's trackers in their shoulders."

Harper reached her arm back as far as she could reach, rubbing the smooth skin of her back. "I don't feel anything."

"They could have put it somewhere different. Your wing placement might have made a normal implantation impossible," Ian suggested.

Harper dropped her hand to her side, fingering the primary feathers on the lower edge of her wing, then she looked between the two of them. "How long have you guys been here?"

"Three years," Beckett said.

"Nine months," Ian followed.

Harper wanted to ask about Naturalization and how close they were to getting out, but it seemed rude. She bit her lip instead and bent her head back over her bowl.

After lunch, her schedule said to meet Lilith in the apothecary. She stood in front of the double doors, mouth dry, food sitting heavy in her stomach as she recalled what had happened the last time she was in this room.

Harper pushed on the door. It swung inward before she put much effort into it, and Lilith stood there, smiling her perfect white smile. She gestured for Harper to come in. Harper stepped through the doorway, keeping her wings tucked tight. The door closed.

"Your wings are beautiful."

Harper shuffled her wings against her back. It was odd to receive a compliment after hiding them for so long. Something like pride flooded her chest. "Thank you."

"How has your first day of classes been? Made any friends?" Lilith asked.

"Hard to make friends when you're debating paranormal rights and dueling with your fellow students."

Lilith noted something on a chart that sat on the table in front of her. "Yes, James—Mr. Petrov—tells me you have a way with words. And that your ideas are...progressive. Zeke wasn't as thrilled with your performance." Her eyes scanned across the page in front of her.

"What did he say?" Harper tried to peer over Lilith's shoulder.

Lilith slid another paper over the chart with a swift motion. "It's not important just now. We're here to talk about something quite different."

"Okay...we're not going to talk about plants, are we?" Harper asked, thinking back to the word *Remedies* written on Harper's schedule.

"No. We're going to talk about this." Lilith reached up to the shelf with the large record books Harper had noticed before. She didn't catch the year before Lilith set it down on the table and flipped through to a certain page. She turned the book toward Harper, pointing at an entry.

"They were here." Lilith stared at Harper, but Harper didn't look up from the names in the book. The names of her parents.

Mick King. Sarah King.

Scrawled in the margins of the book with spidery writing were the words *Raven born* with a question mark afterward.

"Who wrote that?" Harper asked, pointing.

"Violet did. Fourteen years ago."

Harper gripped the table with her hands, eyes locked onto the page. They were here.

"Fourteen years ago...that was before the Reveal. Before this was a camp."

Lilith tucked her hair back on one side. "No, the camp was here. Violet ran a refuge for paranormals. It was illegal back then. She legalized it later when the Hunters came for those living here. What I'm wondering is why your parents were here."

"You don't know?"

"They were here for a single day, Harper, and weren't exactly forthcoming. They kept to themselves, rested, ate, and flew on. They were headed north, that's all I know. And this." She tapped the page again, pointing at those scrawled words. "Do you know anything about your heritage?"

Harper frowned. Her parents had disappeared when she was little. Quinn said they'd left on a trip, not meaning to be gone more than a week. They lived with a family friend during that time. When their parents didn't return, they became wards of the state.

Harper coughed at the emotion that came up. "I couldn't tell you anything about where they came from. I grew up in Oregon. It's the only place I've ever known, and Quinn is my only family."

Lilith's eyebrows drew together in sympathy. "I'm sorry to hear that, Harper. It's as I expected, however, and why it's crucial that I speak with you. You are a rare species, and I mean that very respectfully."

"What do you mean?"

Lilith closed the book and replaced it on the shelf. Harper had to withhold the urge to jump up and grab it from her hands, to open back to that page and see their names. Her parents.

Harper had hated them, been angry with them, claimed she didn't care if she saw them again, but she had always come back to wanting to make sure. Make sure they hadn't left on purpose. Make sure they weren't still alive somewhere. What if they were?

"Have you ever heard the lore of the Raven?" Harper's blank look must have served as answer enough. "Raven was a sacred being to many Native American people. Mischievous, creative, trickster. Some believe he created men and women to spite the other gods. He grew fond of them and wanted to protect them. So he created other people. Your people." Lilith paused, letting the weight of her words sink in.

"So, you think, because of my wings, that I'm related to a god?" Harper scoffed. "I don't have any god-like powers, Lilith. I bleed like anyone, I could die like anyone."

"Now, I wouldn't say that. You are stronger and smarter than any average human. You are creative. That escape attempt you made says as much, and the fact that your brother got out. You cannot be caged. Besides, I heard about the performance you gave when you found Tyson."

She was talking about the song Harper sang that knocked the rogues out. But how did she know? Had Tyson told her? "I didn't tell you about that."

"No. A friend did. You could say, a friend who was there."

Harper's eyes widened as she realized what that implied. "You are friends with the rogues?"

Lilith found a chair and pulled it over to where they stood. She sat down in it, and gestured for Harper to do the same. Harper realized she'd been standing next to one and brought it a little closer to where Lilith sat. They looked at each other.

"Friend is too strong a word for what we have. They are loyal to me, and they bring me information when I need it."

"Why do you let them do what they do? They seemed pretty sinister," Harper asked, skin crawling when she thought of the look that the vampiress had given Tyson as she breathed in the scent of his blood.

"They are so similar to you and me, Harper. They just want freedom. The fact that it's denied makes them act like caged tigers. Mr. Miller just got caught up in things, is all. I don't agree with all of their methods, and I assure you they had a stern reprimand after that night's events." Her eyes glittered with something. Satisfaction? Or was it something more like malice?

Harper shifted in her seat, uncomfortable at the parallel Lilith made between Harper and the rogues. Harper wasn't like them. She didn't want to hurt anyone, she just wanted freedom.

"What would you be willing to do for it?" Lilith asked. Her eyes watched Harper, as if knowing the answer before she would give it. But then, why ask the question?

"Do for what?" Harper knew what Lilith meant, but she wanted to be sure.

"Escape. Freedom."

Harper's head moved side to side, and her lips screwed together as she thought. "I wouldn't harm. I wouldn't kill."

Lilith held up a finger. "Ah. That is what you *wouldn't* do. I asked, what *would* you do?"

Harper threw her hands up. "What's the difference? I would do anything else. Anything other than those things. I would lie, I would steal, I would cheat."

Instead of the reprimand Harper expected from a person in Lilith's position, the witch grinned and clapped her hands together. "That's exactly what I hoped you would say. You, my dear, are in a unique position to help me with a problem I have, and I think you'll support the cause."

"The only cause I support is my own. I want to get out of here and find my brother, Lilith. I won't be distracted by anyone else's good intentions." Especially since Harper had no reason to trust Lilith. No reason other than the witch's honey-sweet words and general likeability. Her good nature. But anyone could fake that.

Harper avoided Lilith's scrutinizing gaze, instead, rubbing her fingers on the surface of the table next to them and staring at the myriad of jars filled with dried herbs and concoctions.

"I can reunite you with him. All I need is your help. A few days, Harper, and I'll have you flying out of this camp in broad daylight."

Harper eyed Lilith. "You could do that? What about the others?"

"That's what you're going to help me with. I need you to disarm Violet and James for me."

It was as if Lilith had struck Harper in the stomach. She gasped. "Disarm them? How?"

Lilith brushed her pants briefly and tucked her hair behind her ear. She seemed so calm, despite whatever she was about to say.

Tremendous energy building up in the room, creating pressure so strong Harper's ears popped.

"Those two have been thorns in my side since I arrived here. I try to make things better for the residents and they push back. Violet used to do this for good, but I wonder how many of the first residents paid her to keep their presence here quiet. Now she has a cushy government job as leader here, she's head of a coven with decent clout, and she controls everything that happens in these walls. She has power, and she's not risking it to rock the boat of the administrators who approve things for us here. You've seen the kind of change that needs to happen, Harper. We need to stand up for ourselves, not cower in our corner and take orders. That will never happen with James and Violet at the head."

Was Lilith talking about full-scale rebellion? Against James and Violet, or against the government?

"How far does this go? All the way to the top?" Harper asked.

"Eventually," Lilith said. She examined her nails. She kept them long, almost like talons, if talons had glittering turquoise gel polish. "We hope to appeal to the president and his committees ourselves. But Violet won't stand for that. All I'm asking is for you to help diminish her power. I'll do the rest."

Harper spread her hands wide and shrugged. "I know you think I'm the great-great-whatever granddaughter of some ancient deity, but I'm just a bird."

"No, darling." Lilith swung her head emphatically. "You are so much more than that! You have Raven in your blood, and you are unique in your ability to help me with this. I tried to recruit your brother, but he was only interested in escaping. He thought small. You, I can tell, think big."

She held her arms out, then brought them in close, leaning her elbows on her knees and putting her chin in her hands as she looked at Harper with wide, unblinking eyes. "What do you say, Harper King?"

Harper hesitated. What Lilith proposed sounded good. It sounded like everything Harper wished she could do on her own—leave camp and help those left here.

Violet was unstable, unfit for leadership, no matter how her husband denied it. But how could Harper possibly help remove a witch's powers? Why didn't Lilith do it herself? She was also a witch, after all.

"What can I do that you can't?"

Lilith clapped her hands together again and squealed. "Oh, I hoped you would catch my vision! You and I will do a great thing together, you'll see. Our time together here is almost up, but I can show you tonight. I have some people I'd love for you to meet, and I can explain the plan in detail. There's just one more thing I have to do first."

Her tone shifted, becoming almost apologetic.

Harper narrowed her eyes and tensed her muscles, readying herself to shift or run. "What's that?"

Lilith waved her hand. "Oh, do relax. You ravens are so intelligent, but it does make you get suspicious easily. I have a spell that will contact you when I need you. It's a simple thing. I'll draw an 'X' on your palm, like this." She traced an 'X' on her own hand and it glowed purple, then faded into her skin. "Instead of coming to your room, which might draw unwanted attention, I'll activate the mark and you'll be able to find me."

"All right." Harper reached her hand toward Lilith, who cupped one hand beneath, then placed the tip of one fingernail in the center of Harper's palm.

Lilith crossed it over Harper's skin. Harper didn't feel anything, not even the pressure of Lilith's touch, and then her skin tingled and a bright purple 'X' formed across the creases of her palm. Sweat broke out on Harper's forehead. Her ears rang against the pressure in the room, and a slight buzzing sound reverberated through her skull. Lilith's skin, even the entire room, was cast in lavender light.

"I'll trust you to not tell anyone about this."

Harper bobbed her head in agreement, but Lilith's stare indicated she needed verbal assurance. Harper cleared her throat. "Of course. I won't tell anyone." She tried to pull away, but Lilith clasped her hand in a grip like iron.

"Very well." Lilith's voice intoned. The room immediately brightened back to regular midday lighting, and Lilith's skin became a warm, blushing peach color. She patted Harper's hand, pushing it back, and her smile revealed its usual straight, white teeth.

Harper's head spun a little. There was a reason she usually avoided witches. She didn't think she would regret it this time, though. A simple meet-up spell sounded like getting a text message. Just a small convenience.

"This should wear off, right?" Harper looked at her palm, turning it over and seeing nothing but smooth skin.

Lilith opened her mouth to reply, but was interrupted as the door swung open. She snapped to attention, eyes riveted on the person at the door. Harper twisted, her left wing pressing into the chair back. Violet stood there, chest heaving, black, curled hair flying wild about her face.

"I've received a call, Lilith. I need to leave immediately. Will you take charge until I'm back? It should only be until dinner." Violet's eyes flickered to Harper, obviously avoiding details due to her presence.

"Of course." Lilith rose gracefully from her chair.

Harper stood, too, passing through the door moments behind Lilith. Violet's eyes seemed to bore into Harper's back, even as she disappeared down the hallway.

Harper's hand throbbed. She leaned against the wall just around the corner, staring at her palm. She half-expected that purple 'X' to appear again, but the skin remained smooth and unmarked. She couldn't shake the feeling churning in her gut that something terrible was about to happen.

And Harper might have agreed to be part of it.

CHAPTER THIRTEEN
TYSON

THE SANDWICH DELIVERY GUY'S eyes popped wide open when he saw the hole in Tyson's wall.

"Renovations," Tyson said, taking the plastic sack from his hand and shutting the door. He bolted it for good measure and slumped into the couch, closing his eyes. He ate in silence, except for the traffic sounds, louder now with the window missing.

Tyson's phone sat innocently on the arm of the couch, a small black void on the gray microfiber. He ignored it until the last bite of his sandwich was gone and the garbage tossed, then sat back down on the couch, straighter this time, and opened up to the images he had taken. He selected the first one.

The pages mostly held observations, formatted like journal entries by whoever wrote them. With a cup of coffee at his side, Tyson took his time flipping through them.

The four double-sided pages contained only a few weeks' worth of information—almost a year after Tyson remembered her family being taken in.

He noted the progression of the "treatments" as they were outlined. Potions and truth serums, with carefully calculated percentages, made him inclined to think a witch had indeed written this. Could it have been Violet?

Subject deemed incompatible. Tyson's eyes blurred as he read the line on the second to last page. Incompatible for what? Naturalization? These would have been the early attempts to merge paranormal citizens with the human population. Had Reya failed to meet the requirements?

His heart stopped on the last page. Reya's red hair spread out on a steel table, her face the only part visible. The rest of her body lay beneath a stark white sheet. Her eyes were closed. She could have been sleeping, except he knew she wasn't.

Subject retired after sodium thiopental, pancuronium bromide, potassium chloride injection. Higher than average dosages were required to achieve cardiac arrest.

The statement was followed by a full autopsy report, containing the exact percentages of the compounds and the time of death. Tyson tossed the phone away, stomach churning as bile climbed his throat. He stared at the screen from a distance, hardly believing what he'd read. Reya was thirteen when she received that lethal injection.

Did her parents and siblings all pass the same way? What transpired before then? Why did they deem her worthy of death? Tyson's chest gripped with the emotion that flooded him. He didn't understand. Reya would never hurt a soul. He could access the full record, find out more. Though, knowing that it sat on a shelf in Violet's lab made the nausea worsen. Violet had known about this. She might have written those words herself, or she knew the person who had.

Tyson retrieved his phone and poured over the pages, muttering the words under his breath, trying to understand why. Why was Reya killed? There wasn't enough. He needed to see the rest of the record; no doubt Violet would have moved it if she suspected he had seen something.

He fell asleep at some point, his phone dropping out of his hand.

The sticky drip of drool down his neck woke him, and he smeared it away with his hand, smacking his lips and groaning as he stretched. His neck ached from the angle it had rested on the couch arm.

With a start, Tyson remembered what he'd read the night before and scrambled for his phone in the crack of the couch. A zoomed-in shot of Reya's autopsy photo glared back at him from the screen—the last thing he saw before he fell asleep. The tightness in his chest released and the tears came. He sobbed on his couch in the still-dark hours of dawn, cool air blowing in through the hole in his wall.

When his tears subsided, his face tingled with the aftermath of emotion. He stared blankly at the open wall, seeing out onto the street below. A few stray cars passed, their lights golden beams shooting through the blueish dawn light.

Did it change anything? What Tyson had learned? The camps didn't use those methods often anymore, only when a truly unstable paranormal case was presented. They were treated as the highest of criminals, despite the fact that sometimes, they had never killed a soul. It was the potential to kill, to lay ruin, to destroy, that made the Administration decide that they needed to call for execution.

Did that await Harper? Were Quinn and Becca right to be so furious with Tyson's decision to side with the system?

His head ached. He put it into his hands, breathing through the tension pounding in his temples. Between Reya and the broken window and everything that represented, his apartment didn't feel safe anymore.

Tyson had just gotten there, and now all he wanted to do was leave. Where to go? He could visit his sister and her kids. He wasn't in a mood for entertaining children, though.

His thoughts drifted toward Nana, and he picked up his phone again, turning on the lock screen to check the time. It was after 5:00 a.m. already, not as early as he thought. Visiting hours at the rest home didn't start until 9:00 a.m. He could grocery shop at the twenty-four-hour store nearby and grab breakfast...

Tyson was too hungry to wait to eat. His first stop was a gas station where he bought a warmed breakfast bagel and coffee, deliberately avoiding any thoughts of Reya or Harper or anything to do with his job.

The small talk made by the cashier brought his anxiety down a few notches, but once he was in his car again, it crashed over him like a wave. He chugged the too-hot coffee like his sanity depended on it, hoping the buzz from the caffeine would hit and help him make it through the day without any more breakdowns.

The events of the day before and that morning feeling like a life someone else had lived until Tyson glanced in the rearview mirror and saw the gauze taped to his face.

He couldn't brush this off so easily. He pulled down the visor mirror and peeled the gauze and tape off, expecting an ugly-looking scrape. Instead, his hands brushed a cheek covered in two-days' worth of stubble and nothing else. It was smooth and clear of any evidence of injury—not a scab or even a scar.

Over and over Tyson touched the skin, wondering what could possibly have been in that salve Lilith used. Only, no salve could do this alone. She had to have used magic on him, and that thought made his blood chill in his veins.

He could talk to paranormals, watch them shift without too much discomfort, but magic was one thing that didn't sit well with him. It was too unpredictable. Too...volatile. The unease settled into his stomach. He flipped the visor up and started the car.

Grocery shopping passed without incident. Tyson only needed a few things; he'd be back at camp tomorrow. Putting away the food and doing a quick cleaning of the apartment, including sweeping up the glass, gave him time to put his thoughts in order before he got back in the car. He was beyond ready to talk to someone, even if it wasn't about work. Especially if it wasn't about work.

The drive to the rest home where Nana lived took less than fifteen minutes. Tyson parked in the lot outside the red-brick building. His keys went in his left pocket, his phone in his right, and his wallet in his back pocket.

Sometimes visiting Nana felt like going to battle. Tyson never knew if he'd catch her on a good day or not.

The doors slid open automatically, and Tyson walked through. It was too cold and smelled of antiseptic pretending to be some kind of floral air freshener. Photos of past residents decked the walls. Tyson thought he recognized one or two as he walked up to the reception desk to check in.

Visitor sticker on his chest, he walked to room 206. The door stood open, and Nana sat up in a chair. She wore a shawl, despite summer temperatures outside.

Tyson had adapted to the AC on his walk down the hall and felt pretty comfortable, but maybe getting old made her feel it more. He took her in for a moment. Her black hair was streaked with gray, and someone had done it in a braid down her back. There was something youthful about the expression on her face.

Tyson rapped his knuckles on the doorframe. "Hello, Nana."

"Nukilik?" she murmured, squinting at him.

Nukilik. Nick. Tyson's grandfather. "No, Nana, it's Tyson."

Her shoulders slumped. "Oh. I thought you were my Nukilik. He was so handsome."

She was caught in memories today. Days like this usually made Tyson wish he hadn't come, but then again, maybe it would help. He came to forget. They could be forgetful together. He pulled up the room's spare chair and sat down.

Nana's hand grasped for his. Tyson liked to think part of her recognized him, but more likely it was simply a comfort thing. Nana always treated anyone she met like family. "I see him so clearly like he was standing here. You look like him."

"Thank you." Tyson sat in awkward silence, though he doubted she noticed. She was used to silence.

"I miss my land of snow." She rocked in her chair, sadness written on her face. "My people were chased from the land, you know. Chased away with laws as sharp as knives."

Her phrasing struck him. Harper might have known what that felt like. Tyson didn't feel like responding, so he sat and listened, knowing she'd continue.

"If Raven's children knew, they would not let us be driven so. But they are in hiding." She whispered the last part like a child who thought they held a secret.

Wait. Raven's children? Like, Raven born? Violet's vision had been about Harper being Raven born. So far, Tyson hadn't learned anything, except that Harper didn't know about her heritage.

And that death song she'd sung to knock out the rogues...remembering the sound of it made Tyson shudder. James had said the Raven born were from the north. North, like Alaska.

"What was that, Nana?"

She muttered to herself, ignoring Tyson. He leaned closer to hear what she said.

"Raven sent them, you know, to protect us." She moaned. "Oh, to protect us. But we cannot reach them."

Tyson hesitated. "I met one, I think."

Her brown gaze sharpened, and she finally looked straight at him. "Met? One does not meet them. One worships them. Praises them."

"She's a descendant, I think." He considered Harper, her blunt manner and her rounded face. He snorted at the thought of *Harper* being thought of as sacred. "She's not what you would expect."

"Are any of us?"

So profound today. Tyson shook his head, not sure what to say.

"Where is she?" He jumped at the harsh edge in Nana's voice.

"Uh, in the mountains. Oregon. Why?"

"She is trapped." Nana's voice quaked. Tyson had never seen her so enraged. "The government. Their laws. Their terrible laws. Who could trap such a glorious creature? Cage her like an animal?" Her tone grew more upset with each question. He touched her arm, shushing like he was calming a baby, or an animal.

"She's not in a cage, Nana. It's all right."

"You will rescue her." It was a statement, not a question.

Tyson stammered. "It's...complicated. I tried helping her the way I knew how. She doesn't want to be saved."

"Bah." Nana blew a raspberry and brushed his words away with an irritated gesture. "She prioritizes the care of others, not being taken care of. You must rescue her. She will respect you, then. A woman with the soul of Raven living inside of her will always look after you."

"She's being guarded with magic. I'll end up in prison or worse."

Why did he defend himself to her? Nana would never know if he didn't help Harper, as long as he didn't tell her. But the guilt would eat him alive. He needed Nana to understand how impossible her directive was; then she'd agree that it couldn't be done.

Instead, she straightened to the full height of her curved back and jabbed her finger toward Tyson. "You carry the spirits of our shaman ancestors with you, Nukilik. How can you have such doubt?"

She thought Tyson was his grandfather again. Maybe he should just leave, but he didn't want to leave her so agitated. He hesitated, fingers tapping on the wooden arm of the chair. He was Nukilik's grandson. Wouldn't that mean the same ancestors watched over him?

He rubbed the back of his neck. He'd never been sure what to think of those tribal beliefs in the ancestors. He grew up listening to Nana preach about them. His Nana's Alaskan heritage made her believe the ancestors were always around them, providing for them. Protection. Power. Guidance. Was there such power for humans to wield?

Nana bent over on her hands and knees, hand sliding between the mattress of her bed and the frame.

Tyson cried out and reached for her, moving halfway off the chair, but her hand came back holding a package wrapped in a dark, unfamiliar kind of cloth. She handed it toward him, panting from exertion.

"Take it, Nukilik."

Tyson ignored the package. "Let me help you up."

She waved him off, sticking the package out toward him again. Hesitating, he took it from her. She pushed off the floor and back into her seat, rubbing her brow with her hand. "Open it."

The material was softer than anything Tyson had felt. Velvety and smooth. He carefully peeled the folds apart to reveal a strange, curved knife with a bone handle.

"You look as if you have never seen an *ulu* before." Nana's husky laugh barked from her like a cough. "I have saved it all these years. I knew we would need it, even here in the land where they have everything. They do not have proper *ulu*."

Tyson stroked the bone handle, his fingers itching to curl around it. He'd never held such a weapon before.

"What would I use this for?"

"To save Raven's daughter. Use it, and the ancestors will be with you. Raven himself will guide you."

Save her. Tyson thought of Reya. Where was this knife when she needed someone to rescue her? An even more sobering thought hit him square in the chest. Could he sit back and watch the same fate fall on Harper? Or at least, a fate she considered worse than death?

"Why do you hesitate, Nukilik? This is not like you. You are better than this." Her eagle-eye glare seemed to pierce Tyson. If she could reach, she would have swatted his head.

Tyson cleared his throat. Her words weren't meant for him, and yet, they were exactly what he needed to hear.

Nana's face drew together, looking old again, as if the conversation had drained all the life out of her. She blinked, misty-eyed, and her hands started trembling. "Tyson?"

He smiled. There she was. She remembered. He set the *ulu* aside and went to her, wrapping his arms around her. Somehow, despite not knowing him, she had helped him.

"Thank you, Nana," he said, voice muffled in her shawl.

She patted his back. "You're a good boy to come visit me. But I am tired. Can you come back tomorrow?"

"I will soon," Tyson promised, withdrawing his arms and standing. He picked up the package. "I have something to do first."

An orderly knocked on the door, drawing his attention away from Nana. "Time for lunch, Amka."

Nana smiled widely at the woman. "Have you met my grandson, Natalie? This is Tyson."

He recognized the tone in Nana's voice and did a ring check on the girl: single. Probably about his age. Natalie smiled, and he noticed her gaze flickered down to his hand, then swept across his body. He stood up.

"I need to get going, Nana. Thanks for the talk." Tyson's palms felt sweaty, and the girl hadn't said a word to him yet. She was pretty with her strawberry blonde hair and bright face, but his life was complicated enough without adding a relationship in the mix.

He gave Nana a quick hug and shot Natalie a smile as he passed her in the doorway. No need to burn bridges.

Tyson carried the *ulu* knife around his apartment, feeling a little lost. He placed it on his bedside table, but it looked awkward there, so he picked it up. Its weight seemed familiar, though he'd definitely never held it before.

He unwrapped the material and gripped the handle, then set it bare of its wrapping on the bed. Its bone handle gleamed against the dark comforter. How could this knife help with Harper? He had no knowledge of how to use it, even if he could think of someone to use it against. Maybe Nana was more far gone than he gave her credit for. And yet, sitting there listening to her, it felt like her words were meant for him. In the comfort of his apartment, her words didn't match up with reality.

Tyson turned the *ulu* over and over in his hands, accidentally sliding a finger on the edge. A fine red line opened along his left pointer finger from the tip to the end of the second joint. He sucked in his breath at the sting, watching the blood bead up. His head lightened and his pulse climbed from his hand to his ears, overwhelming everything.

Greenish-blue light bloomed in Tyson's vision. He shielded his eyes and stopped his hand halfway up, turning the gloved appendage over in the air. He glanced down and saw mukluks and caribou skin pants, barely visible in the ethereal light cast from the sky. There, dancing among the stars, a shimmering sheet. The Northern Lights.

"Nukilik!" Someone yelled. "You are needed, Nukilik!"

Tyson's body turned towards the voice and a large black bird swooped up before him, wings and claws reaching for his face. He ducked, cowering to the ground, and heard a great rushing wind. The snow whipped up into the air, faster and faster until a blizzard surrounded him. The voice disappeared in the wind. Tyson stood up in the middle of a swirling white vortex.

He was alone.

Tyson came to, facedown on the bed, blood trailing down his palm, the knife clutched in his opposite hand. He dropped the blade and hurried to the bathroom down the hall. He had to do something about the bleeding.

He ran cool water over his finger and rummaged through the cupboard above the sink until he found the bent cardboard box with the bandages. His mind was too scattered with fear to consider everything he just saw, or why he saw it. All he could think about was the blood. He didn't think he needed stitches, as the bleeding was already slowing.

Patting the wound dry, Tyson used his teeth and free hand to open three smaller bandages, applying them over the cut on his finger. The appendage throbbed as if all his blood was going to gush out from a single two-inch cut.

Leaving the bathroom, Tyson passed his bedroom doorway and stared at the *ulu* knife, which sat on the bed as if nothing had happened.

Where had that dream come from? Was it a vision of the past or the future? He'd never been to Alaska, but now he felt a hollow place inside him, yearning to be filled with the sights of that land. Was the knife enchanted, or had it been triggered by something inside him, some dormant ability? Tyson swallowed, running his hands down his shirt front as if to make sure his body was solid. It had to be the knife. He had never shown any propensity towards magic, and he wasn't about to start.

Tyson shook himself and headed for the kitchen. Something to eat. Yes, that would fix it.

Three bowls of cold cereal and a scrambled egg didn't touch that spot in his chest. Heat rose in his head, making him feel feverish. He turned off the lights and crawled into bed without touching the knife again. He left it at the end of his bed on top of the covers as he curled up, wide awake and trembling. His injured hand pulsed in the dark as his eyes drifted closed.

Tyson was nearly asleep when a shock of arctic air blew across the nape of his neck, and a female voice whispered in his ear.

Nukilik!

CHAPTER FOURTEEN

HARPER

HARPER TOOK ADVANTAGE OF her free afternoon and had a nap. Getting extra sleep was glorious. She wasn't sure what time it was when Fletcher knocked, but she answered the door with a sleepy stretch, feathers rustling.

She closed the door behind her and let Fletcher chatter as they navigated downstairs, without saying much in reply.

The kitchen was packed. To Harper's surprise, none of the residents were cooking. Instead, Violet, James, and Lilith worked the stoves while the familiar woman whose name Harper still didn't know tossed salad beside them. Her milk-white eyes contrasted against her dark skin.

Harper nudged Fletcher. "Who is that?"

He followed her gaze. "Oh, that's Mandi. She's training under Violet to take over the camp when she retires."

"And she's...?"

"A witch? Yeah." Fletcher blinked several times before he realized what Harper meant to ask. "Oh! Yes, she's blind. But don't underestimate her. She can sense a lot of things other people are oblivious to."

Harper glanced back to the woman, Mandi, and wondered why she had given her that stone. Was Mandi fond of Tyson? She seemed to spend a lot of her time around the other witches, and Zeke too.

Witches were people Harper usually avoided, and yet, the red amethyst Mandi gave her seemed to help when she needed a boost of courage to save Tyson. Maybe they weren't all bad, but it would take a lot more to convince Harper of that.

Violet called for everyone to be quiet, raising her hands so her flowing sleeves fell down to her elbows. The room slowly settled down. It was filled to the brim with the ragged assortment of paranormals currently residing in the camp.

"As some of you are aware," Violet began, "we've been working hard for the past year to change the legislature around some of the restrictions placed on Naturalized individuals."

Murmurs of agreement waved through the crowd, and a lot of heads nodded.

"Most specifically, the restriction of a two hundred-mile radius from the city of settlement after Naturalization. Through the efforts of several individuals here and in other camps like ours across the United States, I'm thrilled to announce that new technology has been implemented to enable an extension on the original travel radius." Violet raised her voice to speak over the cheers breaking out. "Naturalized citizens now have a radius that extends anywhere in the continental United States!"

The room erupted into exclamations, feet stomping and clapping. Harper simply watched the commotion, stunned by the response. Fletcher hugged her, picking her feet off the floor and squeezing her until she could hardly breathe. He set her down, his face flushed and eyes sparkling with joy.

Violet's hands went up again and Mr. Petrov delivered a piercing whistle until the chaos dulled to loud whispering.

"New trackers should arrive by the end of the month and will replace the ones you currently have. The radius will not go into effect until you've completed your individualized Naturalization program." Some booing came through the crowd, but it was quickly hushed.

Harper itched thinking of the device implanted somewhere beneath her skin.

"To celebrate this momentous occasion," Petrov said. "Classes are cancelled the rest of today and tomorrow, to give you a little taste of the freedom you'll soon be able to enjoy."

Harper's eardrums nearly burst with the reception that statement received. She wanted to clamp her hands over her ears, but she tucked her wings closer around her instead.

"Can we eat now?" someone—Harper thought it was Keith—shouted from the breakfast nook. Petrov laughed and filled a plate in response. Steak strips, rice, veggies, a salad for the vegetarians, and some fruit mix. It smelled delicious, but Harper wasn't feeling particularly hungry after that announcement. So much cheering over such a small change.

Fletcher ushered her forward.

"Can you believe it, Harper? Out of state! We can go anywhere now!" He handed her a plate piled with a bit of everything except the vegetables, giving her a huge smile.

She forced a small grin onto her face, not wanting to ruin this moment for him.

"I can't believe it's happened right before my Naturalization comes up. What luck, eh?"

"Yeah." Harper robotically followed him to a table filled with people. He pulled out her chair, but she just stared at it for a moment.

"Uh, Harper? You okay?" Fletcher looked concerned.

"Oh, yeah. Yeah." She sat down, setting her plate on the table and staring at her food. Fletcher handed her a fork, still giving her an odd look. He was too discerning for his own good. Fortunately, he was distracted as the others started talking about the new development, the places and people they would visit. He was drawn into the excited discussion, freeing Harper from his scrutiny. She picked up the fork and pushed meat around her plate, snagging a piece and chewing it without tasting it.

Ian and Kamri sat across the table with their elbows touching, listening but not participating in the conversation. Thinking of what Ian said to her that morning in Petrov's class, Harper wondered if they felt the way she did—that it was too little, too late.

Fletcher and the others might have been satisfied with this consolation prize of extra travel mileage, but why did they have to sacrifice who they were to get it?

A hand landed on Harper's shoulder, and she dropped the fork to her plate with a clatter. The chatter at the table paused, then picked up again. Harper looked up into Violet's smiling face.

"Harper, you've come to us at such an exciting time. I'm sure it's overwhelming, but the changes you get to witness are monumental. Perhaps you'll even be part of them. Some of our students have been fundamental in bringing this about. How do you feel about it?"

Harper blinked. Violet was asking *her*? As if their last encounter hadn't ended in disaster? And in front of all these other people? Luckily, no one paid them much attention, except for

Fletcher who grinned up at Violet with such a look of adoration in his eyes, Harper wanted to punch him.

Harper's hands clenched into fists beneath the table, restraining the urge to swat Violet's hand from her shoulder and storm from the room. "Honestly, I don't give a damn. At the end of the day, I still have to lose my wings to get these little perks you're fighting so hard for. So, you'll excuse me if I'm not thrilled."

Fletcher's eyes widened as he dropped his gaze to Harper.

Violet's hand squeezed her shoulder. "That's exactly what we need more of, Harper. Passion, motivation, vision." Was this her way of making up with Harper? Because it wasn't working. Violet gave Harper one last squeeze and drifted to the next table without waiting for a response.

Harper stared at the witch's back. Her hands ached, so she released them, flexing her fingers. She stared at the crescent marks left in her palms by her nails and thought about what Lilith had said.

We need to stand up for ourselves, not cower in our corner and take orders. Why didn't more of the others believe that kind of future was possible? *They're begging for scraps...and they like it.* The excited buzz of conversation filled the room—people talking about who they hadn't seen for years, family that could finally welcome them home once they'd been Naturalized. It was all part of a move to get more of them to comply, Harper realized.

They should be accepted for who they are. That's what we all deserve, isn't it?

She ate in a fog, responding enough to be ignored, except for that persistent look in Fletcher's deep blue eyes. He didn't seem to be asking anything of her, simply letting her know someone saw that she wasn't as excited as everyone else.

The group moved to the common room, where Fletcher grabbed a blanket and wrapped it around Harper's shoulders. He sat beside her with his arm encircling the blanket like it was the most natural thing in the world.

Fletcher was right; it was addicting, feeling like she belonged. But the price she would pay for this comfort lingered in the back of her mind. Sitting there with him, talking and laughing with Kamri and Ian and some of the others, Harper could almost forget about escape, about Quinn, about all of it.

And it terrified her.

The tingling in Harper's hand began at 1:34 a.m., according to the room's alarm clock. She shook out her arm and changed positions.

The tingling persisted and grew stronger, becoming pins and needles buzzing to the point of pain. She sat up in bed, rubbing the hand with her opposite one, which provided minimal relief. At 1:58 a.m. it glowed with a soft purple 'X' and Harper stared at it in fear and wonder. *Magic.*

She stood up, shaking her hand in a futile effort to get the painful prickling to stop. She moved closer to the door to find her jeans and the intensity lessened. She combed through her hair with her fingers, grateful that it was short enough not to be a total mess.

Harper padded quietly down the stairs. It was cooler in the entryway, and she rubbed both of her arms, the buzz in her hand still at an uncomfortable level. She wound down the staircase again until she reached the basement.

She hadn't been down here except to choose new clothes and deposit dirty ones. It was quiet, the only sound like distant water lapping in a pool. Kamri had mentioned a pool on Harper's first day here. She was tempted to go see it, but the sensation in her arm was too uncomfortable to delay.

Now which way? Harper glanced down both hallways, each one equally dark, and decided to take the one toward the laundry room. The buzzing intensified and she winced, rubbing up her arm and turning around to go the opposite way.

She didn't know what was down this hallway. The last time she came close to it, she was running from Keith and didn't pay much attention.

Doors lined the hall. Extra bedrooms, or maybe unused class-rooms. One of them had a light under it, though she couldn't hear any sounds coming from inside. She touched the doorknob and the prickling sensation stopped. Relieved, she turned the handle and stepped inside.

The moment the door closed behind her, the room erupted into roaring cheers. It was dimly lit and filled with a group of people, all residents, not many she recognized. Keith stood toward the middle, looking bored, while the rest had their eyes on Harper and wide grins on their faces.

"Your champion!" Lilith's voice called from the front of the room. Harper blinked in the light, dumbfounded, still getting her bearings. Lilith's arm stretched outward, and she gestured for Harper to come forward.

Harper walked through a narrow aisle between rows of metal folding chairs. Only about half of them were filled. She arrived at the front of the room, standing beside Lilith and blinking, dazed, at the crowd. This was what Lilith meant by having some people for Harper to meet?

Some of the crowd wore their shifter form, panting wolves and Shannon the hydra with her two heads. Harper also recognized Cheri, the pink-haired siren girl. She wasn't cheering vocally, the mute spell Violet placed on her in force, but her face showed the same enthusiasm as those around her. Her eyes, a very normal green-color, gazed from beneath a curtain of vivid pink hair. Had Harper imagined them glowing pink that first day?

Lilith motioned for the clapping and cheering to stop. It was a wonder they hadn't woken anyone else up. There must have been a spell on the room to keep sound in.

The residents in the room, about twenty or so, took their seats or curled up on the floor, depending on their physical ability to use a chair.

Harper rubbed at her arm, pinching the tender place near her elbow to make sure she was awake. *Ow.*

"The moon is nearly full, Mercury is in retrograde, and all is aligned for the dramatic and essential change that is about to take place." Lilith's arm snaked around Harper's shoulders, squeezing her close as the room erupted again.

Harper managed a half-smile, but she had no idea what Lilith meant.

Harper swallowed, eyes passing over the faces in the room. None of the people she'd really come to know were here. Fletcher, Ian, Kamri...It appeared they were all satisfied with scraps. She licked her dry lips.

Lilith continued her speech. "The rest of your number, waiting patiently near the borders of our prison, will be ready to do their part. Are you ready to do yours?" Hoots, howls, and roars shook the walls. The room *had* to be spelled. The sound rose to an ear-splitting level. Harper clamped her hands to her side, a plastic smile glued to her face.

"You'll have to forgive Harper," Lilith said once the tumult died down again. "She hasn't been clued into every aspect of our plan. But once she is, she will play a most essential part." Lilith's eyes flashed violet and the residents went crazy, howling and baring their teeth, even the human-looking ones.

It was madness and chaos, and despite Harper's conviction to bring better leadership to the camp, she wanted to go back to her room, pull the covers over her head and pretend to be ignorant of all of this. Her mouth stayed dry, no matter how many times she swallowed or ran her tongue through it.

"What do you think, Harper?" Lilith said quietly, her words meant just for Harper. She squeezed Harper's arm. "See how much we need you?"

"I...I didn't realize so many opposed Violet and James."

"There are more than could meet here tonight. And in camps across the globe. I am gathering my coven sisters to join me in rebellion. We'll take control of the camps first, then draw others in from outside to support our cause."

"What is that cause?" Harper asked.

"Freedom, Harper." Lilith breathed in and smiled, showing her perfect white teeth. "Freedom for us all. And it starts here. Are you with us? Or were all those words in Petrov's class hot air?"

It was so much more than Harper had bargained for. All she wanted was to find her brother and her parents, not spring the whole world out of the chains the law put paranormals in. And yet, if she wanted to see change...real change that enabled her to live with her family, to be who she was without consequence, it had to start somewhere. Didn't it?

Harper looked up at Lilith, a sudden certainty growing in her chest. "I'll do it."

Lilith's smile grew even wider, and she put her hand on Harper's back, sweeping her other hand before the crowd. "I wanted all of you to see the face of the one who will start our revolution.

Look, and remember well, for her name will be what we chant as we rise to our proper place in the world!"

Lilith nudged Harper forward and they made their way down the aisle between the chairs, banked on both sides with cheering and clapping.

Every single eye glowed violet, the same light that pulsed from Harper's left hand, and all of their left hands, a light in the distinct shape of an 'X'.

The door shut behind Lilith, abruptly cutting the sound of the crowd.

Lilith let out a sigh, but kept her hand on Harper's back.

"It is never easy maintaining that level of energy for that crowd," Lilith said, glancing sideways. Harper let her head nod like a bobble-head toy, numb after the wave of emotion she was just swept under. "You have a unique disposition, Harper, and I need you to use it for me."

Harper's blood. Her Raven blood.

Lilith led Harper down the twisting halls to a part of the basement that appeared abandoned. The dingy walls hung with dust and cobwebs. It was dark and smelled musty. They stopped in front of a wooden door. The boards separated and left gaps in places, showing the beginning stages of rot. It looked as if Harper could kick it once and watch it crumble off the hinges, but Lilith didn't bother even touching it.

She chanted something in a language Harper didn't understand. The door clicked and swung open. It made a sound so like a human sigh that Harper turned, glancing at the dark hall behind them. It was empty.

"Come. We have much to discuss." Lilith's hand tugged Harper inside, and the door shut them in together.

Candles automatically lit, as if on cue, bringing a shadowy, dancing orange glow to the room. It looked similar to Violet's room, though more crowded and with less apparent order. The cabinet shelves held dozens of jars, dried herbs hung from the rafters, and a large, flat table stood in the center.

The surface was stained with a number of unrecognizable substances, but the darkest splotches looked all too much like blood for her liking. A pentagram circle carved into the table's surface was scored and scratched as if someone had intentionally destroyed it. The marks looked like claw and scorch marks.

Harper moved her eyes away from the table, disturbed. Lilith stopped in front of it, then released Harper's arm and walked toward a vault in the corner of the room.

It was one of those enormous standing vaults with a wheel like a ship's on the front —completely out of place in the room and without any evidence it had aged with the rest of the furniture.

Lilith flipped up a black box cover on the side, revealing a digital keypad. She punched in the numbers swiftly. The vault door opened with a slight hiss, revealing a silver glow from inside. Harper leaned over the table as Lilith bent over, blocking the view. Lilith emerged with a cloth covering her hands, holding a basketball-sized orb. A crystal ball. A legit crystal ball.

"Hurry, grab that stand over there." Lilith pointed her chin toward a square bronze construct with claw-like corners coming up on each side. Harper rushed over and snatched it, putting it down on the table. Lilith carefully maneuvered the ball, tipping it into the holder with a clunk. She shook the cloth off her hands, leaving it next to the orb, and they stared into it together. It glowed so brightly, Harper couldn't tell if mist floated inside or not, but either way it was impressive.

Harper laughed nervously. "This isn't a joke, is it? I mean, I'm *actually* seeing this. You haven't constructed an elaborate ruse with electricity and special effects as a new-comer hazing?"

"It is surreal, isn't it? Standing in front of something so powerful, so unworldly. It's okay to be afraid." Lilith bared her perfect white teeth.

"I'm not." The words fell flat in the air, and by Lilith's smile Harper knew the witch wasn't fooled.

Lilith gazed lovingly down at the orb, like a parent at a young child. "I only wish I could touch it, to experience its power for myself."

"Why can't you?" Harper asked.

Lilith's eyes darted up, then back at the ball. "It's made of a particular kind of material. I've waited a long time to find some-one who could activate it, someone who would be in alignment with all we've worked to accomplish. It's taken years. I thought it might be your brother, but he was not interested in helping others. Too afraid. You are different, though, aren't you?"

The accusation of Harper's brother as a coward put a cold dart through her stomach. Harper didn't like to hear anyone thinking poorly of him. But at the same time, Lilith spoke the truth. Quinn always was a man for himself. He brought Harper along, sure, but now that he was free from that responsibility, did he enjoy not being bogged down with his younger sister's needs?

Harper rubbed her lips together, eyes absorbing the white light of the orb. She lifted a trembling hand toward it. Lilith replaced the cloth, covering its brilliance and casting the room back into near-darkness with only sputtering candles for light.

"Let's save that for another time. I wouldn't want you to activate it without understanding its purpose. There are strong forces at work beneath its surface. You would be wise to not touch it lightly."

Harper put her hands behind her back. "What is it called?"

"A Beryllium Orb." Lilith turned her back to Harper, wrapping the orb in the cloth and returning it to the vault.

"So...it's not just a crystal ball?"

Lilith's high-pitched laugh bounced off the ceiling. "Oh no, dear. It is much more than that. You can ask it anything, anything in the world, and the answer will come. But there is also a price." She replaced the orb and closed the vault, the automatic lock clicking with finality. Brushing off her hands, she came back to the table, leaning forward with her eyes locked on Harper's.

"What sort of price?" Harper asked, her tongue feeling swollen in her mouth. Witches and magic items weren't things she dabbled with for a reason. There was always a price for magic. Her wings never betrayed her in that way.

"Once you touch it, you will not be the same, though I can't tell how it will affect you. It's different for each person who encounters it. If the price is higher than you are willing to pay, it'll be too late. You must be prepared for your entire life to change."

"I want my life to change," Harper blurted. "I've been hunted and persecuted for the whole of it. It couldn't get worse."

Lilith's eyebrows raised. "Spunky. And naive. Don't underestimate the orb. It has a way of demanding an equal exchange. Which is why the wording of your question is essential. Asking for a life to be given or taken, for example, is among the most powerful and most costly of questions. You wouldn't need to go so far in this. Think simple, like asking for their powers to be removed."

"Whose powers?"

Lilith gave Harper a sly smile, as if they were two girls planning a prank at summer camp, rather than two grown paranormals in a secret room planning a coup. "The Petrovs', of course! In order for freedom to come to those in this camp, they must be removed from their positions. They've been corrupt for years. You've seen evidence of their influence here."

"If their powers are removed, they will still lead the camp, won't they?"

"You think two mere humans could manage all of the paranormals within these walls? There is a reason witches and enchanters run every Naturalization camp in existence. Humans need us to maintain order. Like a zoo, and we're the zookeepers," Lilith spat the last words as if they left a bad taste in her mouth.

"What will happen after I activate it?"

"You make your request. Your request will be granted, and the price exacted. And I will ensure you are released from the camp, free to find your brother." Lilith beamed, reaching for Harper's hands. Her fingers felt like ice.

There was one question Lilith hadn't answered yet. "Why me and Quinn? Why not one of your other..." Followers? Harper wasn't sure what to call them.

Lilith's eyes glittered. "Because you are Raven born. Others would be burned to a husk, emptied with the price that the orb demands. But you have the power in your blood. The orb won't harm you. Your kind is not easy to find. Not just one touched by Raven himself, but one touched by any creator deity. You have one foot in this world and one foot in the Eternal Source."

Harper had never heard of the Eternal Source. Lilith made it sound like a power or another dimension. The spot between Harper's shoulder blades burned, rather than itched, as if it were confirming what Lilith said about Harper's heritage. Why hadn't this power manifested earlier in her life when she needed it? Not that she would have known how to use it.

Touching the orb would change her. It would change her whole life. In exchange, she could gain freedom for this camp and perhaps other camps across the U.S. Maybe even across the world. Harper couldn't bring herself to hope that Lillith would succeed in freeing all paranormals, but as she said, it was a start. And Harper found that she wanted to be part of it. A chance to make a real difference.

A headache formed at the back of Harper's skull—most likely a side effect of too much excitement and too little sleep.

"You don't have to come to a conclusion tonight." Lilith waved her hand in a dismissing fashion. "I hope you'll say that you'll do it, of course, but the decision is yours. I have dreamed of this day for many years. I yearn to start a new era for our kind. Can you imagine?"

Harper couldn't, not fully, but a glimmer of Lilith's vision formed at the edge of her mind. "I'd like some time," Harper said honestly. Time to see if Tyson had met Quinn. Time to let the words sink in, to decide if she wanted this. What question could she ask the orb? Was there a way to control the price that was exacted?

"Of course." Lilith inclined her head. She moved around the table toward the door, opening it with the same incantation as before.

Harper followed, passing her as she stepped into the hall.

Lilith spoke again from behind her. "Oh, Harper, one last thing—when you decide, come to this doorway and speak my name three times. I will hear you."

With that, the door closed between them.

CHAPTER FIFTEEN
HARPER

THE ALARM CLOCK BLARED at 7:00 a.m. Harper climbed out of bed and fumbled her way toward the table where it sat, hitting the button that would turn it off.

The night before was a blur—a cheering crowd, a glowing orb, something about questions. It all blended together, fighting for her attention to process it in the light of morning. She sat on the edge of her bed, staring at the floor. Stirrings downstairs indicated breakfast was being prepared. She remembered why her alarm clock was set. She was on the roster to help with breakfast.

Harper picked the jeans from off the floor where she left them last night. They were a bit rumpled, but they'd do. Her shirt needed changing, though. She rummaged through a drawer in the tiny cubby-like dresser next to her bed and pulled out a racerback tank top. She grabbed a jacket from the closet near-by—an olive green canvas thing in a cuter style than she usually cared to wear and pulled it over the blank tank. She brushed through her hair, fluffing it a bit to make it look like she tried, then headed downstairs.

Fletcher greeted Harper in the kitchen, wearing an apron while flipping pancakes and turning sausages on five massive griddles.

"You made breakfast yesterday." She failed to suppress a yawn.

Fletcher grinned and handed Harper an apron. "Your help is sick today. Or at least he claims to be. I decided to fill in, rather than leave our breakfast at your mercy."

"Thanks," Harper said dryly, accepting the apron he offered.

"You can start the eggs." He nodded toward two woks on the stove. A literal crate of eggs sat next to it.

"Do I fry them or what?"

"Scramble. It's a lot easier." He frowned as he flipped a pancake and it fell awkwardly on the edge of the griddle, batter slipping onto the counter.

"Glad to see you're not perfect." Harper cracked eggs into a giant glass measuring cup, two eggs at a time, one in each hand. It was a trick she learned at a foster home she once lived in. The father in that home could crack two in each hand at a time. Harper's hands were too small for such a feat, so she stuck with what she could manage.

The woks heated up quickly, and Harper whisked what seemed like a gallon of eggs before pouring some into each.

Fletcher came up behind Harper, whistling as if amazed. "You sure can wield a spatula."

"Yeah, well, you learn a few things in foster care when you get sick of eating cold cereal all the time and have eleven kids to cook for."

"We have over forty 'kids,'" Fletcher pointed out.

Harper laughed. "Hey, your pancakes are burning." Fletcher ran back to his griddle and flipped a few. They were perfect golden brown circles. He made a show of rolling his eyes at her.

The darkness of last night gradually lifted and despite the drizzling gray morning, Harper could see through the bay windows behind the main table.

Residents filtered into the kitchen. They still chattered about yesterday's news, and how today was a day off from classes. No wonder everyone was in a good mood. Even the vamps looked happy, though maybe because it was overcast and they could go outside for once.

They started serving, piling up plates as they were handed across the counter. Harper laughed at the jokes tossed between Fletcher and the other residents.

Ian smiled and asked how her morning had been as he came through and got a stack of pancakes.

Kamri followed close behind, winking and gesturing for a couple extra sausages, which Harper gladly tossed onto her plate.

You're the best, Kamri mouthed, grinning ear to ear and making her way to the breakfast nook where several other werewolves were stuffing their mouths. Some had already been through for seconds.

The eggs ran out, and Harper cracked and cooked more, then ripped open another package of sausages. She was starving, and watching everyone else eat was torture.

"Be sure to set something aside for us." Harper curled her shoulders up at the tickling sensation Fletcher's voice made in her ear, but she smiled.

He set two plates on the counter, pancakes already loaded, and Harper added eggs and sausage. The activity in the kitchen died down as residents finished their food and headed out to enjoy their single day of freedom.

Fletcher switched off the griddles, pulling the last few pancakes off the heated surfaces and plating them for someone else to eat. He untied his apron.

"You want that off?" he asked, gesturing. Harper untied the string one-handed, but she was still pushing a few last eggs around a wok and couldn't get it off her head. Fletcher took it for her and tossed the aprons through a small laundry chute in the wall. She turned off the burner and slid the wok onto a cooler side of the stove, then grabbed their plates.

Fletcher joined Harper at the breakfast nook, now abandoned by the werewolves. It smelled like wet dog, and her nose wrinkled.

"I think some of our furrier friends were outside last night." Fletcher laughed, handing Harper a fork and snagging one of the plates with his other hand. Harper reached the syrup pitcher before he did and poured it onto her pancakes.

"No butter? Heathen!" He made a mock-horrified face, and Harper laughed. He carefully spread butter to the edge of each pancake before adding syrup. Somehow, the mundanity of sitting down and eating breakfast gave Harper permission to relax in a way she hadn't in years.

"So, what are you doing with your grand day off?" Harper set her fork down.

Fletcher's cheerful expression wavered. He cleared his throat and looked at his plate. "I guess I can't blame you for not remembering. Or knowing. Did I tell you?" He laughed anxiously, looking back up but not at her. His fork pushed food around his plate. "I leave for my operation tonight."

Harper's mouth opened in a silent O. "You mean...it's your last day as...with..."

"My wings, yeah. You can say it. I've gotten used to the idea. I promised myself if I had any doubts I wouldn't go through with it, so I've taken my time making sure this is what I want. So don't feel sorry for me."

Harper looked back at her plate, picked up her fork, and scooped a bite into her mouth. Not out of hunger, but to keep from saying something she'd regret. Fletcher put his fork down and stretched his arms, then placed them behind his head, leaning back into the diner-style bench they sat on.

"The last day. It's a big deal. What would you do?"

His question caught Harper off guard, and she nearly choked on her food. "I-I haven't thought about it."

"I didn't expect you had. That's why I asked you. I wondered what you would say before anyone has had a chance to influence you."

Harper licked her lips, glancing over to him, then at the opposite wall. "I would fly."

"The whole day?"

"Yeah. I haven't had many chances. Always monitored by non-paranormal foster parents and teachers, no space to just...be what I am. It's what I've loved most since coming here." Harper realized the words were true as she said them.

She'd grown used to transforming without fear of getting caught for the first time in her life. That kind of freedom...it would be worth fighting for. Without the strings of Naturalization attached. Would Lilith's plan enable a future where that would be possible? No hiding, no limits, just...freedom.

"That look in your eyes, I wish I knew what it meant."

Harper jumped. "What look?"

"The one you just had, as if you were thinking about something wonderful."

"I was dreaming of an impossible world." She gazed across the valley below, noting the gleaming ribbon of water winding between patches of forest.

Fletcher laughed, but not in a mocking way. "You seem like that type. I knew I would like you from the first day I saw you in Mr. Petrov's class."

Harper stared at him. He'd been looking at...at her? She didn't think he'd even noticed her. Certainly not the way she noticed him and his impressive wings.

"Care for a race?" Fletcher asked.

Harper grinned, then stood to take her plate to the sink. Fletcher grabbed it from her, then leaped over the table and landed gracefully on the other side, taking the dishes to the large sinks where two other residents washed up.

They walked toward the front door together. Fletcher's eyes lingered on Harper, and her face heated. She took a deep breath. *It's just flying, Harper.*

Fletcher let out a nervous, breathy laugh. What did he have to be nervous about?

"Can I ask you a personal, possibly offensive question?" he asked.

"Sure."

"What...species are you? If you know? And you don't have to tell me, if you don't want to." He rushed to the end.

"No one has ever asked me that before." Harper stopped before the door. Fletcher reached across her to open it, gesturing for her to go first. "Thanks."

"Sure thing. You...you were saying?" He stood on the porch, making no move toward the stairs.

Harper frowned. "I only know what my older brother told me. He said our parents were from Alaska, from a raven clan that may or may not still exist."

"Not crow?"

"No."

"Good. Crow are too mischievous for me. Raven, that's like, noble. Are you descended from *the* Raven? You know, the one that some native legends say created man? He's essentially God, but cooler because he's a bird."

Harper burst out with a loud laugh. "No way!"

"Yes way!" Fletcher jammed his hands in his pockets, rocking on his heels. "I can't believe you don't know that. Get a library card. Do an internet search sometime. Better yet, go to Alaska, find a tribe leader and ask about it. You'll love it."

"Well, if I ever get out of here, you should come with me."

His smile widened, and Harper's heart galloped in her chest. "Absolutely. Road trip with a Raven daughter, how could I say no to that?"

Harper rolled her eyes. "Are we doing this or not?"

"Let's go." Fletcher grabbed her hand in his, engulfing it in warmth. He pulled her toward the stairs and they both leapt off, then ran down the gravel driveway together.

Harper released Fletcher's hand and shrugged off her jacket, letting it fall into the dirt. Her wings unfurled in a single, swift motion. Fletcher's eyes lit up, but his face fell when he glanced down at his shirt, which was a human civilian style with no holes in the back for him to shift out of.

"Here, let me." Harper went around him, gripping his shirt at the back. The fabric resisted, then gave in to her supernatural strength, tearing apart. She spread the hole out, stretching it across his back and making an opening wide enough to reveal his shoulder blades.

Fletcher shifted, feathers erupting from his back in a flurry of blue. Harper ducked out of the way, laughing to see the gorgeous colors fanned out in front of her.

Passing him, Harper broke into a run, flapping her wings and lifting off into the air. She heard footsteps, then wingbeats, and Fletcher shot past. She chased his laughter and his blue wings, wings that matched the sky except for the strips of white and black here and there. Blue Jay. Harper had never before seen a being as wonderful as he was.

Fletcher did a spiral in the air, gliding on his back for just a moment before flipping back over, wings spread. Harper caught up, a warm updraft catching her wings and letting her glide along beside him.

"Where's your favorite place to fly here?" she asked.

"There's some cliffs on the north side," Fletcher replied. "Want me to show you?"

Harper grinned and Fletcher banked sharply, leading her north.

It was a day like she'd never had before, spent entirely in bird form, flying over trees and diving between rock formations. They made up games as they went, throwing rocks at targets chosen as they flew, calling out challenges to show off different moves.

Together, they owned the sky.

They stopped in at the cabin to grab lunch, breathless and laughing, hardly noticing the others, as if a bubble surrounded just the two of them, keeping out every worry, everything wrong with society and the world. The conversation with Lilith the night before hung in the back of Harper's mind, but every time it tried to come forward, she shoved it away. Time would come for those thoughts later. With Fletcher, all she had was now.

She tried not to think about that too much, either, and Fletcher didn't bring it up again, but as the day wore on, his demeanor changed. His chatter slowed, allowing Harper to lead the conversation. She wasn't much of a talker, however, so eventually all conversation between them died.

They flew over the cabin for the upteenth time, passing the dueling field where white circles were swallowed in the long, reaching shadows of the trees. The sun dipped into the horizon. Fletcher held his course heading north, rather than turning back to the cabin to end the flight. They soared in silence, which wasn't so bad, but Harper kept glancing over, wondering what he was thinking.

"Up ahead."

Harper followed his gaze. The largest cliff in the area loomed ahead, lit up in a brilliant orange. She banked with Fletcher, soaring toward the top of the cliff, where they both landed. Harper shook out her legs, which felt jelly-like after a full day of flying. Fletcher walked to the edge and sat, tucking his wings against his back.

Harper sat down next to him, letting her feet dangle over the side of the cliff. Even with her wings the height made her feel heady. She sensed something change in Fletcher; a feeling of permission.

She cleared her throat, the words she'd resisted all day surfacing at last. "Are you afraid?"

"Terrified."

"Then why..." Harper trailed off. She didn't want to say the words out loud.

He looked out across the horizon. "I guess because I'm more afraid of the life I lived before. Living in fear of getting caught, possibly tortured or captured and shown off as a freak. The people of today aren't much better at acclimating to the strange and inexplicable than their ancestors were."

It made sense...sort of. Harper had been teased and beaten her whole life just because she was a strange, skinny foster kid. What would have happened if they'd known what she truly was?

"Do your parents know?"

"They're waiting for me back home." Fletcher looked toward his feet. "They both naturalized. My older sister, too. They say it's better to wait for the procedure until your body has matured. Something about younger children going into shock making it too dangerous.

"Anyway, my parents met in a camp like this. They were almost forbidden to marry, but by that time my mom was pregnant with my sister and it was too late. The government scrambled to tag us both and created a set of restrictions. We lived super rural, couldn't go to public school, took all of the precautions that could be taken."

"So you've grown up your whole life knowing that your parents' fate ...would be your own?" It was hard enough for Harper to imagine having her own parents at home, but to have them know what would happen and do nothing to stop it, encourage it, even...It was unfathomable.

"I knew about Naturalization from the time I could walk and talk. They were very upfront about it, didn't try to hide it or anything. They encouraged me to choose for myself. I didn't have much choice, though. I was tagged, so I couldn't escape. I would be choosing between euthanization or the surgery." Fletcher's eyes hardened as he watched the light of the sun falling behind the horizon. Harper wasn't prepared when he turned that gaze to her. "I would rather live my life than throw it away."

You shouldn't have to choose. Harper bit her tongue. She didn't want his last night to be tainted with her weak attempts to convince him to choose differently, impossibly, between two horrible choices.

"So, you'll get to see your family when it's over?"

He nodded. "I'll come back here and take some time to get my balance, let things normalize. They'll pick me up in a few days." His shoulders relaxed and a kind of peacefulness passed over his face.

Harper leaned back on her arms, staring at the orange and yellow sky. Fletcher's hand covered hers and warmth flooded up her arm.

She looked at him with wide eyes.

"Thank you. For this. For not freaking out or avoiding me. I...I really appreciate it," he said. "I don't think that it comes along too often that you find someone who understands you without saying anything."

Harper stared into his soft, blue eyes with nothing to say. It had been wonderful. Almost blissful. Well, except for this last part, and what waited for him when they returned to reality.

She wanted it to last forever.

Fletcher leaned in, hesitating inches away from Harper's face, as if asking permission. Harper was afraid to move, so she closed her eyes. Fletcher's lips pressed warmly against hers. The edges of their wings brushed against each other. It was the briefest of moments that somehow stretched into eternity until he drew away.

Harper opened her eyes. Fletcher stared at the sunset, as if nothing happened. Her heart pounded. How could he look so calm? Harper tried to decide whether she liked the kiss or if the strange galloping rhythm and the rush of warmth in her chest meant she was coming down with something, when Fletcher turned and gave her an unexpected, goofy grin.

"Race you back to the cabin?"

Harper touched her lips, then jerked her fingers away. "Yeah. Let's do it."

Fletcher climbed to his feet and helped Harper up from the cliff edge. They backed up together, holding hands, then ran and leapt into the air, separating at the last moment. Harper caught herself right away and pushed the air beneath her wings, flapping hard and fast. Fletcher fell below her in a dive before his brilliant blue wings tilted and brought him up again.

It was a solid tie when they landed, sending a spray of gravel into the air as they skidded, laughing breathlessly from the flight. Fletcher's cheeks were pink when he grabbed Harper's waist and spun her around, wings flapping. He set her down.

"I had a great time tonight, Harper. Thank you, again."

"You're welcome," Harper said, finding her tongue. His head tilted toward hers, and she wondered if he was going to kiss her again.

The crunch of car tires on gravel interrupted them and Fletcher jerked away. He stepped back, wings shrinking fast. He clasped his arms behind him and ducked his head.

"Who is it?" Harper asked.

"James. He said he would take me."

"Are you okay with that?"

Fletcher glanced at his feet. "Yeah. I've known him most of my life. He's friends with my father. I would rather my parents drive me, but he says it's not allowed. No family until afterward."

Harper reached out to take his hand, surprising both of them. He looked at her. She squeezed his hand. "It'll be alright. Just think about how it will feel to see them again at the end of the week."

Fletcher's face split into his characteristic grin, then he released her hand and pulled her in for a crushing hug. She somehow managed to keep it together until he climbed into the car, closed the passenger door, and waved through the windshield. She waved back as the car drove away.

When she saw him again, he'd be wingless.

Flightless.

Damaged.

Harper raked her fingers through her hair, wanting to tear it out. She shouldn't think of him that way. He would be wholly human. Nothing less. Nothing more.

And the world would lose something incredible. Something beautiful.

She clenched her fists against the tightness in her chest, but it was futile. Tears flowed down her cheeks, hot and fast. She watched the car until it pulled onto the road and disappeared, flashing silver amongst the trees in the last bit of sunlight.

CHAPTER SIXTEEN

TYSON

THE INSISTENT BEEPING WOKE Tyson with a start. It wasn't the alarm tone he was used to, and that confused him until he picked up the singing device and swiped up. A calendar reminder glowed on the screen.

FLETCHER REFORMATION

Tyson bolted from the bed, sheets tangling around his legs and sending him hopping around on one leg. The *ulu* knife thumped to the floor, landing beneath the bed.

He managed to get free from the sheets and grab the knife, wrapping it back in the velvety black cloth. It was probably the skin of some animal from Alaska. Seal, maybe? Tyson placed it on his dresser, noticing the bandages on his finger. A cut like he received yesterday should have felt sore, but he didn't feel anything. Was the cut worse than he thought? Had he severed a nerve, or something?

Tyson headed to the bathroom and peeled back the bandages, holding his breath. A thin, white line marked his skin where the cut had been, covered in dried blood. It looked like a scar, but that was impossible.

He rinsed the finger under water, carefully wiping away the dried blood. He kept expecting the wound to reopen, but the skin was sealed tight by that scar. Trembling, he dried his hands and brushed his teeth, trying not to think about what had healed him: *magic.*

Instead, his thoughts went back to Fletcher as he grabbed some fresh clothes and started changing. Fletcher left last night for the operation, making today a critical day. Everyone close to him would need to meet with Tyson, whether they wanted to or not. Evaluating their state of mind was an essential part of the success of the program.

He froze mid-pant leg. He was back to evaluating them, like nothing that happened yesterday made any impact. Could he go back and act as if he wasn't helping Harper, as if the records of Reya's unjustified death meant nothing?

Tyson slid his other leg into his pants and zipped them up. If he didn't show up and do his job, he'd be letting down more than a few people, especially Tom, who was due back from his conference. His own quandary could wait for one day.

The cell phone rang, and a quick glance showed Tom's name on the screen, as if summoned by Tyson's thoughts. He picked it up on the third ring, swiping to answer.

"Good morning, Tom. How was your trip?"

"I'm back, that's all that matters. Why aren't you here?" Tom's rough, low voice crackled through the line, thanks to the patchy service at Camp Silver Lake.

"I got stuck there over the weekend and they let me come home and get a couple days off to make up."

"Well, I hope you're headed in today."

"Of course. I'm getting ready now." Tyson grabbed his keys and wallet and shoved them into his pockets, then checked for his lanyard. All he had left was to get his clothes from the dryer and pack them, since he'd be at camp the rest of the week.

Tom snorted. "I've arranged for Violet to bring you in via portal. Don't want you to miss his arrival."

Tyson groaned inwardly and checked the time. 6:15 a.m. "He's not back yet?"

"On his way. Surgery took longer than expected, but he's made it through. Bring your A-game, this is a big deal."

"I know, Tom." Tyson's heart clenched. He thought of the frost-tipped kid that Fletcher used to be. He was still frost-tipped, but much less a kid now. And he was coming back from the biggest surgery of his life today.

"Five minutes." Tom's end of the line fell silent. Tom had always been that way. Not one for goodbyes. The fact that he was back brought some relief. Tyson wouldn't have to check up on everyone by himself.

Fletcher would spend the next few days at Camp Silver Lake, say goodbye to the other residents, and they could make sure everything was alright. Then his family would pick him up. Tyson grinned at that. Fletcher had looked forward to going home to his family ever since he arrived at the camp.

Most of all, Tyson felt relief that Fletcher had pushed through, and that Harper's arrival didn't throw him. Everything he'd worked to accomplish with this internship and this program would pay off with Fletcher's successful Naturalization. Regardless of the past, things were different now.

Clothes packed, Tyson rushed back upstairs and opened his fridge. Nothing that could be prepared quickly except cereal, and he'd had that for dinner. Fortunately, he could eat at the camp. Breakfast hadn't started there yet.

Tyson ran back into his room to grab the charging cord. He took it out of the wall and as he turned, his eyes landed on the *ulu* knife on the dresser. Some feeling urged him to take it, and he did, carrying it to the living room and zipping the package into his backpack along with the phone cord.

A silvery blue portal bloomed in Tyson's living room, obscuring the window Quinn broke through. He slung his backpack over one shoulder, took a calming breath, and stepped through.

His feet crunched on gravel outside the cabin. Gravel? They had brought him outside. Why?

Violet and James stood together beside Lilith on the front drive of the cabin. Beyond them, on the porch, Tom watched with his hands in his pockets.

The first drops of rain fell from the overcast sky. Tyson's throat clenched at the sight of them. He managed a smile. "This is quite the welcoming party."

"Where is she?" Violet demanded, stepping toward him with clenched fists.

Tyson feigned bewilderment. "Who?" After all, they could be talking about anyone.

Lilith held up her hands, as if approaching a wild animal rather than a reasonable human being. "Tyson, we know Becca was at your apartment. The Supernatural Task Force contacted us this morning after they left your place. If there's anything you know..."

She played her part well. Just another concerned camp leader. Tyson wiped his clammy hands on his jeans. "I don't know where she is. Or Quinn. They didn't leave a forwarding address."

"Do you think she'll try to contact you again?" James asked, holding Violet's arms, whether for comfort or restraint, Tyson couldn't be sure.

James held a relaxed stance, his glasses glinting in the early morning light. But he was far from relaxed. He shifted his weight subtly from one leg to the other, tension bringing his eyebrows together.

"She...might." It wasn't an outright lie, but witches were perceptive, and Tom's instincts were uncanny. His blue eyes pierced Tyson from the porch. Tyson met his eyes deliberately to avoid garnering his suspicion. Becca said she would call, but Tyson didn't know when or where or how. She would have ditched her cell phone after their last encounter with law enforcement.

Lilith glanced at Violet and James, then back to Tyson. "Until we hear word of their capture, we'll have to keep you sequestered, Mr. Miller. For the safety of the residents."

"What?" Tyson exploded. "That could be anywhere from days to months! Today Fletcher comes back from his Reformation, and it's critical I'm available for the residents to process anything they might be feeling."

If they didn't want Tyson there, why have him come back to the camp today? Tyson narrowed his eyes. They didn't just want him away from the residents, they wanted him within their grasp. He couldn't run if they held him here. Not that he would have run, he told himself.

"We have Tom, as you see. He's very capable," James said.

Tyson took a step forward. "I've been working with some of the residents exclusively. They won't respond to Tom as well. He'll back me up on that. I just want to help."

"You mean Harper," Violet said. Not a question, but a statement. "She won't be your problem much longer. A special forces team is gathering as we speak to take her to their high security facility."

Tyson's mouth gaped open. "You're sending her away. You've given up on Harper."

Violet stiffened. "As leader of this camp I determine who is compatible. It is my home, Miller. It has been since you were in diapers. You don't tell me what to do with it."

As an intern, maybe not. When Tyson got that promotion, however...

Tyson froze at the gleam in Violet's eyes. If they suspected him this much, and if Violet and James had decided to send Harper away based on the information he gave them, then that meant...

"You gave your word. Two signatures," Tyson growled.

Violet didn't even flinch. "I don't know what you're talking about." Her voice slid through Tyson like ice.

"It's for the best, Tyson." Tom held out a hand, like he expected Tyson to lose his temper and fly at him in a rage.

Tyson heard a car in the distance. Could it be Fletcher?

"You guys know me." Tyson kept his voice level and calm, though he felt anything but. "I've been here two years. I'm not going to do anything stupid."

"No, you aren't," Tom said. His words had a discomfiting finality to them.

"They're threatening to lock down the camps," James added. "No one in or out, and Supernatural Task Forces would patrol the borders and manage anyone who tried anything suspicious. If an escape attempt was made, all of our protocols and procedures would be put under a magnifying glass, scrutinized, criticized, and changed. The residents could lose every freedom they currently have, and then some. Releasing our highest risk residents keeps the others safe, and it keeps the camp running."

The warlock's words hung in the air.

Behind Tyson, car tires rolled up on the gravel drive. They all faced the black Mazda. A man dressed in grey scrubs got out of the passenger side and opened the back door. Fletcher's blond head appeared, hair uncharacteristically mussed. He eased himself out of the car, every movement causing his face to crease in pain. His bandages were hidden beneath a green t-shirt.

Tyson dropped his backpack in the gravel and surged forward. No one stopped him as he met the orderly helping Fletcher and offered his arm. Fletcher smiled in appreciation. Tyson took on his full weight, the bandages rubbing beneath his arm. Tyson adjusted his hold, careful to stay away from Fletcher's wounds.

"Thanks," Fletcher said to the orderly, who climbed back in the passenger side without a word. Tyson couldn't make out the driver's face. Gravel sprayed from beneath the car tires as Fletcher and Tyson walked toward the lodge steps. No one said anything, but they did fall in line behind them.

Tyson took the first step slowly, but Fletcher grunted and halted.

"You okay?" Tyson's shoulders tensed, preparing to take on more of his weight if he collapsed.

"Yeah." He managed a smile, of all things. Tom's face creased with concern, and he watched the two of them carefully. Tyson avoided Tom's gaze. Whose side was he on? Did Tom think Tyson should be locked up simply for his association with Becca?

They got up to the front door, which Tom opened, and wound their way past the staircase and toward the kitchen. Ahead, someone made a hushing sound. There was a tense feeling in the air that Tyson didn't understand until they rounded the corner.

A cheer erupted. Every person in the room stood, clapping and whooping. As far as Tyson could tell, most of the residents of the camp were there. Not all of them were cheering, and more than a few were crying, but all of them looked at Fletcher with love and admiration.

Fletcher ducked his head, pushing off Tyson's support and straightening. His smile was more of a grimace of pain, but he put on a brave face for everyone else.

Someone brought him a chair and he sat down. Tyson stepped back and people surrounded Fletcher, congratulating and encouraging him.

Tom stood next to Tyson at the fringe of the room. "The high will get him through the pain, but be prepared for two days from now. That's when it will hit him, when he's alone and vulnerable."

"So we make sure he's not alone."

"Easier said than done, son. Are you going to watch him twenty four-seven?" Tom crossed his arms over his chest. "We have to ease him into it, get him to talk about all of his feelings, before his family picks him up. Otherwise, well, that's when we lose them eighty percent of the time."

"We won't lose him. Fletcher is solid. He wanted this."

Tom snorted. "He thought he wanted this. You can't predict how they'll take it once it's happened."

Fair enough. Tyson hated that it had to be said, but Tom knew his stuff. He literally wrote the book on Paranormal Psychology and a whole slew of academic papers on the effects of traumatic events like this. It was what made Tyson want this internship in the first place. He wanted to learn from the best.

"Does this mean you'll let me keep an eye on him?"

Tom took his time answering. "Yes. But you'll be watched closely. Don't do anything funny."

Tyson stuck his hands in his pockets, noting the individuals that hung back as Fletcher was fawned over. He knew many of them didn't agree with the action Fletcher had taken, but it said something about their character that they showed up to support him this morning. Tyson's eyes landed on Harper, hovering at the back near Ian and Kamri, practically a shadow on the wall. Her gaze lifted to meet Tyson's, and he could see that she'd been crying.

Someone had to warn her that Aberration Management was coming to collect her. Violet had been vague about when. Would they be here today or tomorrow? Should he try to contact Becca and Quinn and tell them they had to come now?

Tyson wove through the crowd around Fletcher, toward Harper. He was afraid she'd run, that she wouldn't let him talk to her, but she didn't move. He was only a few people away when his phone rang.

He didn't dare check the screen. The Petrovs should have insisted on taking his phone, but no doubt there was too much going on since Fletcher had arrived for them to think of it. A lucky break. If he checked it now, he risked them noticing and correcting their error.

Tyson glanced around the room. Violet's and James' backs were to him as they retreated down the hall toward the stairs. Lilith stood next to Tom with a pleased smile plastered on her flawless face.

He let the phone go to voicemail as he reached Harper.

"Hey," Tyson said, a bit breathless from forcing his way through the throng. It was only about twenty people, but they were packed around Fletcher like sardines. Harper bit her lip, rubbing her own arms with her hands, hunching over like a humpback. She wasn't okay, so Tyson didn't ask the obvious.

"Would you like to talk about anything?"

She shook her head no.

Tyson had the urge to hug her, but decided against it. Earning as much trust as he had, if he had any, had been hard enough. He could lose it all the moment he touched her without asking first, and asking if she needed a hug seemed...awkward. Not to mention the new level of scrutiny he was under.

Tyson's pocket buzzed again. Harper heard it and frowned at him. If it was Becca, he couldn't answer it in here, and he couldn't tell Harper who it was either, not without knowing no one could overhear.

The phone rang a fourth time. Tyson leaned over. "I know you don't want to talk about this," he gestured toward Fletcher's group of admirers, which was starting to thin. "But maybe there's something else you'd like to discuss? In the office?" He raised his eyebrows. Inside, he groaned. "Meet me in the office in five minutes."

Tyson was terrible at being subtle. She raised her eyebrows back at him, clearly unimpressed with his attempt. Tyson didn't wait for her to reply, but put his hands in his pockets and headed to the office, nodding at Tom and Lilith as he passed them.

The clock was ticking past six minutes later when Harper knocked on the door. Tyson rushed to open it, nearly having a heart attack when, for a split second, he realized it might not be her, but there she was, twisting a lock of hair around one of her fingers.

Tyson ushered her inside and shut the door. "Have a seat."

Harper crossed her arms. "You don't actually expect me to sit and have a heart-to-heart with you."

"No. I have a call to make that you might be interested in." He picked up his phone and dialed back the number that had called four times in the past ten minutes, praying it wasn't a telemarketer or something equally useless. Harper would really think he was an idiot then.

"Tyson. Thank God. Why didn't you pick up the first time?" Becca's irritated voice came through the line. The reception in the office wasn't great, so Tyson plugged his ear and moved toward the window. Harper unfurled her wings, knocking a pencil holder off the desk. She ignored the pointed look Tyson gave her, preening through her feathers with her fingers.

"Hey. You're lucky they haven't confiscated my phone and put me under lock and key. They were waiting for me when I got here. They heard about yesterday morning."

"Oh, God. I'm sorry, Tyson. They suspect you?" She said something muffled, and Tyson assumed she was talking to Quinn.

"Yeah. I mean, we're cousins. You show up at my place and evade capture, and they know I didn't report it, so yes, they suspect me. Fortunately, they need me today."

Harper glared at that, her feathers fluffing up in an irritated way. His turn to ignore her.

"Well, we got bigger fish to fry. We haven't quite shaken the Stiffs that found us at your place. We need to get out of the state. We're headed your way. Can you have Harper ready to leave?"

"Uh…"

It was the perfect storm. With what happened to Fletcher, security would be tighter than usual, everyone on edge. But once Aberration Management arrived, Harper wouldn't stand a chance of escape, and that could happen any time in the next 48 hours.

Tyson swallowed, glancing at Harper out of the corner of his eye. She did the same thing at that moment, and their eyes met. They both looked away quickly.

Who is it? Harper mouthed, moving toward Tyson. She still didn't know who was on the phone, but she'd probably guessed by now.

Tyson mouthed *Becca* back at her. Her eyebrows came together, then relaxed.

Quinn? She asked silently. Good. She realized that he didn't want to say their names out loud.

"She wants to talk to *him*."

A brief second later, Quinn's voice came over the phone. "Harper?"

"Just a sec." Tyson handed the phone toward Harper. She looked at it with wide, hungry eyes, then snatched it out of his hand.

"Qu-" she stopped herself, swallowing before saying his name. Her feathers trembled with her body, making them rustle. "Hey."

She bit her lip and closed her eyes. To Tyson's shock, a tear fell down her cheek. He wished he could hear Quinn's side. He leaned across the desk and passed her a box of tissues. She grabbed one and crumpled it in her hand, pressing her lips together like she didn't want to melt down in front of Tyson.

"I can't leave yet."

Tyson blinked rapidly, and his stomach clenched. He tried to gesture, cutting a hand across his throat.

She dabbed her eyes with a tissue, missing or ignoring his signal. "Yeah, no. Just...a friend needs me." Pause. "It's not like that! Jerk." A wide smile spread across her face, more genuine than any Tyson had seen her make. It chased the darkness from her face. As quickly as it came, it left, and her expression sobered.

"It's too late for him." Harper looked down, hand pressing into the desk's surface. She tossed the tissue ball and it rolled onto the floor.

Tyson picked it up without a word. It made sense now; Quinn must have asked about Fletcher, about taking him with them. Fletcher would never go.

"How long?" It was a question, and she looked at Tyson.

He shook his head and tried to mouth "Aberration Management" and mime getting locked up, but Harper just looked confused. Sighing, he lifted two fingers. Fletcher's family would be here in two days.

"Can you wait until then? What should I look for?" She paused. "Uh-huh. Yeah." She licked her lips. "West side? Okay." She paused again, then nodded. "Yeah, I can do that. Stay safe until then." She handed the phone toward Tyson, giving him a "what the hell?" glare.

Tyson took the phone. "Hello?"

"Hey, me again." Becca. "I assumed you wouldn't want to know the plan."

Tyson swallowed. Now was the time to tell Becca that Aberration Management was coming for Harper.

Becca must have taken his silence as agreement, because she launched into another response before he could reply. "Just help Harper get supplies—some non-perishables, toiletries, you know. Unless that's too much?"

Tyson made a strangled sound. Everything was moving too fast. He looked at Harper, sitting in the office chair, lazily spinning back and forth, wings practically wrapped around her like a cocoon. "No, I think I can do that."

"You're the best. Take care of yourself." There was a pregnant pause. Tyson could tell what she was thinking, so he spoke and their words overlapped each other.

"Don't worry about me."

"Sure you don't want to come?" Becca laughed. "I don't know how you do what you do, spending all your time in that place, day after day. I know I couldn't do it. I'm glad someone does."

"Thanks. I guess." Another silence. "I suppose I won't be seeing you for a while?"

"Unless you change your mind. Or we show up on the news." Her laugh came off forced this time.

"Don't show up on the news," Tyson replied firmly.

"You got it."

The line went silent. Tyson dropped his arm, phone still in his hand, and looked at Harper. Why hadn't he said anything? His tongue still felt tied in his mouth, heavy and useless. He closed his eyes.

Harper tented her hands, fingertips touching as she put her feet on the desk. "How *do* you do it?" Her eyes found Tyson's, a little red from being rubbed. "Watch the oppressed accept oppression, begging at the feet of government officials for scraps of freedom? How do you sleep at night?"

Her barbed tone sank under his skin. "I slept fine last night," Tyson snapped. "Can you get your feet off my desk?"

She removed them, shrugging. "Just wondering. You humans are so emotional, it's surprising to meet one that isn't. Is that why you're so good at this? You just don't feel?"

Tyson gritted his teeth. "I feel plenty, Harper. What do you want?"

"I want justice," she hissed, standing up out of the chair and sending it sliding backwards. She jabbed her finger toward

Tyson's face. "Justice for Fletcher's wings, for his parents and sister, and for every other paranormal that has had to sacrifice themselves for your comfort."

"Oh, so we're doing this now?" Tyson gestured between them. "Because I can put on my shrink hat. Harper, you know what's wrong with you?"

He rushed headlong into the angry words, unable to stop them. "You're selfish. You want the world to bow to you, like you're something special. Well, you know what? You're not. You're another homeless foster-care product, thinking all your anger is justified because of a tragic past. You don't see that other people want to help you, that they might care about you. You just see you."

Air huffed through him. Harper gaped, then sat up straight, expression hardening. She spun and strode toward the door.

Tyson deflated, the fury fleeing as he watched her leaving.

"Harper, wait."

Her hand twisted the doorknob. Tyson crossed the room in three strides and touched her arm above the elbow. She glared down at his hand.

If she never talked to him again, this was important.

"Aberration Management is on their way. Violet called and told them about your unique abilities. They'll take you to a higher security base. If they come before Becca and Quinn get here…" Tyson swallowed. What could he advise her to do?

Harper jerked her arm out from beneath his touch. "I can take care of myself." She ducked her head, avoiding eye contact, then pulled open the door, thrusting past him. Her right wing pushed him back from the doorway, and he stumbled, catching his hip on the desk. Had she done it on purpose? After what he'd said, he couldn't fault her. He wouldn't be surprised if she didn't speak to him at all for the next two days. And then it wouldn't matter anymore. One way or another, she'd be gone.

Tyson rubbed his sore hip. He'd only known Harper for a week. Less. But his heart still clenched at the thought of her leaving.

A knock came on the door. Tyson answered it to find Anita, one of the witches, her lip trembling as she entered. The first of a continuous line of residents needing advice, council, but mostly comfort today while they processed this victory of Fletcher's.

The kind of victory that didn't feel like a victory to everyone here. And, for the first time since he arrived at Camp Silver Lake, Tyson was among them.

CHAPTER SEVENTEEN

HARPER

HARPER DITCHED CLASSES UNTIL lunch, still furious with Tyson. It seemed like a day when classes should have been cancelled, but they must have wanted to carry on as if nothing had happened.

There were more people than usual littering the halls, and no one seemed to care much about classes, though a few sticklers took up desks, and a small crowd dueled outside with Zeke. Harper wandered through the cabin, avoiding people.

Tyson's office door remained shut, though she'd seen several people go in there. He should have told Becca about Aberration Management being after Harper. Quinn was coming to get her out in two days, and it might be too late by then.

When Aberration Management showed up, could Harper fly away? Join the rogues in the forest? Would Lilith help her?

Thoughts swirled restlessly in Harper's mind. Thinking about it made her livid all over again, and the strong emotions made her hungry. She stalked toward the kitchen.

It was lunchtime. The kitchen was still alive with chatter. It looked like Fletcher hadn't gotten away from his crowd of the morbidly curious. He sat upright, but his smile flagged. He winced when he shifted in his chair. He put on a brave show for them. The wounded warrior.

Harper got her food and skirted around the edge of the gathered circle, finding a seat apart so she could listen in.

The conversation had progressed from the polite congratulations of this morning to more in-depth questions with a smaller crowd. He answered questions about the procedure. Did it hurt? Were you scared? How did they do it? He took each one so calmly, one would think it had happened to someone else.

At one point, Harper glanced up as someone departed from the crowd to grab food, leaving an opening where she saw directly to Fletcher. He met her gaze and their eyes locked. His sadness was so deep Harper was afraid she might drown in it. In that moment, she glimpsed the extent of his injured soul, and then the gap closed, tightening the circle and blocking her view of Fletcher.

Harper left her plate on the table, still mostly full. She wasn't hungry anymore. She headed for the forest, planning to stick close to the cabin but needing some time alone. Wind ruffled her hair as she tromped through the grass. Her restless mind flickered between Fletcher and her conversations with Tyson and Lilith.

When Harper had heard Quinn's voice on the phone, she'd realized that she didn't need Lilith's plan anymore. She could leave the camp without ever touching the orb. But with Aberration Management coming for her, well, that changed things. Could the orb be her emergency plan?

She thought of Fletcher, and Ian and Kamri, and all those awaiting Naturalization like it was the only option. With Lilith in charge, things would change faster than they did with Violet. Lilith would be willing to take the necessary risks.

Was Harper willing to risk the price the orb would exact to save them and herself?

Harper kicked at a rock and watched it bounce into the brush on the left side of the path. In the past, she'd kept to herself. She had bided her time with Quinn, waiting for their chance to escape foster care and find their parents together. Could she be more than that? Could she effect change for everyone in this cursed camp?

Harper stopped walking, staring at the surrounding trees.

She could leave. Do nothing but show up at the edge of the warded barrier around the camp and wait for Becca and Quinn to arrive with the device that would interrupt the magical frequency and break her out of here, hoping Aberration Management didn't show up first. No need to use the orb, and she'd be in the clear.

On the other hand, she could ask the orb where her parents were, use it for herself. Or she could get Violet and James out of their corrupt position of leadership and free the people that she would leave behind.

Harper walked forward again, moving a little deeper into the forest now. A rock jutting into the path drew her eye and she made her way toward it. She perched on the hard, cool surface, rubbing her hands along it.

"Can I sit here?"

Fletcher's voice.

Harper closed her eyes. She couldn't talk to him about this, and she didn't want to talk to him about anything else. But that wasn't fair; she had told Quinn she wanted to be here for Fletcher. Her friend. Perhaps, in another lifetime, something more. But that future was eradicated the moment he'd gone through with the Reformation.

Fletcher sat down cross-legged with obvious effort and pain, adjacent to her spot on the grass. His fingers picked at the green blades, tugging a few from the ground and rubbing them between his fingers.

"I've been looking for you." The sun wavered across his hair where it broke through the canopy overhead. Was it just yesterday they had flown over it together?

"I've been around."

"Oh, right." His expression deflated. "I thought you might...want to talk."

"I'm not much of a talker."

"You talked plenty yesterday."

That was different. You were whole, then. I could pretend things were normal.

Harper said nothing, glancing down at her fingers tracing the orange algae on the rock's surface.

Fletcher let out a long sigh. "I was afraid this would happen. You know, they warned me. They said some of my friends would get it and be happy for me, and that others...well, some of my friends have reacted the opposite." He looked at her, then out across the field. "Some of them won't even talk to me."

"Okay!" Harper stood up. "I get it. You're upset because you think I'm upset. Well, you're right, I am. What happened to you is wrong. The fact that you had no other choice, other than giving up your life, was wrong. We shouldn't have to choose death or compliance. It's abuse of the worst kind."

Her arms gestured wildly at the forest around them. "This place isn't some day camp for people who are different. It's a prison. The walls and chains might be invisible, but they're there. You can't convince me this is all good and right and wonderful just because it's better than being hunted down and killed. We shouldn't be comparing it with the past, but with what we deserve."

Harper had a thick, uncomfortable feeling in her chest as she stared at Fletcher. His face was so still, so calm, far more terrifying than if he argued his side with equal passion. His eyes seemed hollow when he finally responded.

"You're right." A laugh escaped him, a harsh, cold kind of laugh she never expected to hear from someone as kind and cheerful as him. "You're right about all of it, Harper."

"I am?"

He climbed to his feet, tossing the wilted grass from his hand. "I walked into that room with confidence nothing could shake. I was nervous, nothing more. And then they asked me to shift. I complied. As soon as my wings came out and I saw the looks of fascination and shock on the doctors' and nurses' faces, I knew I was making a mistake. I wanted to walk straight out of that room and demand that James take me home. But I knew that I couldn't come home, come here, to leave that place, without going through with the surgery." He paused, breathing heavily. He looked down at his hands, then back to Harper. "They had a man in another room with the drugs for euthanization prepared for me. I either left there without my wings and went through with Naturalization, or I didn't leave at all." He swallowed, and his eyes took on the strain of someone trying not to cry.

Euthanization. Lethal injection. What could Harper say to that?

She held her face passive, but the emotion welled up inside of her, threatening to burst out in a hail of tears and rage. Her shoulder blades itched fiercely, her wings desperate to stretch and prove that they were there, that she was still whole, even if Fletcher wasn't. But that would be cruel, to make him see her with wings outstretched, as if she were taunting him.

Harper's hand reached out automatically and touched his arm. "I'm sorry," she murmured.

He scoffed, kicking at the ground with his foot. "You don't have to be. I made the choice, after all."

"The choice sucked."

"Yeah, I guess it did." He sounded unconvinced, like he didn't want to believe it.

Harper wanted to comfort him. "At least you'll see your family soon." It was a desperate stab, and she was certain it had failed. "You can start life over. Completely new."

"Yeah," he said again. His eyes didn't light up like they did the last time they had talked about his family. "I talked with my dad on the phone. He says they're excited to see me." He choked on the words, and this time the tears escaped from his eyes, falling down his cheeks. His hand came up to his mouth, and he sniffed, then wiped his nose on his sleeve.

"He said he's proud of me. Mom too." His voice was broken, and from the look of things, so was his heart.

"It's okay to be hurt." The words came out of nowhere, but they felt right to say. "You're going through something unimaginable right now. No one should expect more of you than to let you grieve your wings."

Fletcher held his breath the way people do when they were keeping a dam of emotion beneath the surface. He managed it for a moment before the sobs broke free, and his entire face crumpled into an expression of such despair Harper could hardly stand to see it. He moved forward and practically fell into her. She leaned back, grasping him in her arms. His face pressed into her shoulder. Her hands gently patted his quivering back.

The bandages beneath his shirt criss-crossed and wrapped his shoulder blades where his wings used to release each time he extended them. Harper's eyes filled. She sniffed, keeping quiet so she didn't distract from Fletcher's grieving.

No one had ever cried on her like this before; no one ever trusted her enough to bare their soul to her. No one had ever cared like Fletcher cared. It wasn't right that this happened to him.

If Harper had any say in it, no one else would go through what he had again.

Harper's legs trembled, and she wondered how much longer she could take Fletcher's weight. As if sensing her concern, he straightened. He smiled such a broken smile that she wanted to look away, but she knew that would be hurtful, so she offered a smile back as if everything was all right.

"I knew you were the only one who could understand," he said. "Everyone else thinks this is the greatest thing in the world. I want it to be that way for them, so they will make the right choice when their time comes, but damn, it's hard." Fletcher's eyes filled up again, but the tears held this time.

"You should have thought about that before you allowed them to mutilate you." The harsh male voice penetrated the trees. Fletcher and Harper looked up at the same time and saw a man standing before them, his pose perfectly at ease, his expression intense. His bald head glinted with sunlight. It was one of the rogues from before—the werewolf that attacked Tyson. Clearly, her death song hadn't been as fatal as she presumed.

Harper jumped to her feet, wings flaring out of her back. She did it without thinking. Fletcher stood too. Seeing her wings might not have been the best thing for him, but if they were going to escape, Harper needed them. Her fists clenched at her sides.

"Here for an encore?" Harper's voice sounded tougher than she felt. She didn't know how that song had worked before, but she was certain she could do it again. Despite the fact that her chest felt cracked open like an egg after oozing so much emotion. She tried to pull her grit together, ready for this to turn into a fight, but the bald man only chuckled.

"Your pretty tune might have put me to sleep, songbird, but I came prepared this time." He turned his head, neon green foam earbuds jammed into his ears. The fact that he put them in prior to approaching meant he intended to encounter Harper. As soon as she had that thought, she relaxed. They'd been watching her. If they wanted her dead, they would have struck while she was vulnerable with Fletcher a few minutes ago. They waited, waited until the right moment so they could talk.

"You want something," Harper said.

Fletcher made a strangled sound, and his eyes widened as he looked between Harper and the rogue.

"I have a message to deliver," the man said, jutting his chin out. "If you have need of any assistance in two days' time, you know where to find us."

"Why should I trust you?"

"We have no quarrel with you. You were defending someone you thought was innocent. If you do this thing..." He shrugged as his voice trailed off.

"I won't need your services," Harper stated calmly with a sideways look at Fletcher, hoping the bald werewolf picked up on the need for discretion.

Fletcher wouldn't understand the value of Lilith's plan, not the way he worshipped Violet and James and the whole system of Naturalization. Even after what they had done to him.

The man's intense stare fixed on Harper. "You will. When you do, use this sign." He reached a fist up to the nearest tree and tapped out a rhythm. He did it twice. "We will come." At that, the forest blurred. When the trees stopped swirling Harper panted to keep from retching.

"What was *that* about?" Fletcher asked, looking at Harper in bewilderment. His face was pale and sweaty, maybe with the same sick feeling she had. "It was like he knew you."

Harper shook her head. "I don't even know his name. We met once, and I kicked his ass."

He watched her carefully. "So you don't know what he wanted? You're not trying to escape again, are you?"

"Nope." The bald-faced lie rolled off Harper's tongue smooth as butter. Fletcher wasn't a fool, he was just giving her a chance to tell the truth. He tried one more time.

"What's happening in two days?"

"You go home." She softened her voice and gave him a small, sad smile. Her gut twisted with guilt at the redirection, but she ignored it. It was for his good. He was leaving, too. He didn't need the burden of knowing what she was going to do.

He tilted his head, but let her change the subject. "Yeah, I guess I do."

Awkwardness filled the air between them. It seemed as if a lifetime had passed since their kiss on the cliff. Harper scuffed her boot on the ground, and her feathers brushed her arms.

My wings. She shifted quickly, before looking at Fletcher. That pinched look was back on his face.

He covered it up with words. "Hungry? I think dinner must be ready. Nothing makes me hungrier than crying. Except maybe being terrified out of my mind by strangers in forests."

Harper nodded, still mute and uncertain. They walked together toward the cabin. It was as if their entire conversation, his meltdown, her freakout, the rogue offering his help...none of it ever happened. They got inside and the hall was empty. Everyone was in the kitchen, eating.

Fletcher's hand reached toward Harper's, covering it with his warmth. She didn't pull away. He needed the comfort, and it was a small thing she could offer him. They were still holding hands when they entered the kitchen. Harper wondered if he caught the looks shot their way, subtle glances, little whispers of gossip.

Food, friends, and laughter. Nothing was wrong, but a dark undercurrent flowed beneath the conversation, and Harper wondered if anyone else felt it.

Ian glanced up once, moving his long black bangs to one side, and his sea-green eyes spoke a sorrow she connected with instantly. Her food tasted bland, but she pushed through the meal and emptied her plate, doing her best to stay in the conversation happening around her.

It was movie night again, apparently. Fletcher dragged Harper to the common room and debated heartily over which movie to watch. Nothing sad, he insisted, and everyone agreed because they knew what he'd been through, and they all liked him. Some of them couldn't seem to take their eyes off of him.

It made Harper sick to her stomach, but she stayed to help Fletcher so he knew that someone was here who understood that there was more beneath the surface. Someone who saw him in his pain and could sit in it with him and not be frightened away. She could be that person for him. So, she crossed her arms over her stomach and sat on a couch beside him.

He fell asleep at some point, head coming to rest on Harper's shoulder. She let herself be in the moment, pretending she was a normal young woman with a normal young man, watching a movie with some friends. And the illusion actually lasted until the credits rolled and people started leaving the room. Harper was left with Fletcher's head on her shoulder and his arm around her neck weighing her down.

She tried to push his arm off, to no avail. She nudged his ribs with her elbow.

"Fletcher," she whispered.

He grunted and moved closer. Harper considered fighting her way out of his embrace, but decided against it. Someone passed her a blanket from a stack near the wall, and she took it, adjusting until she was in a more comfortable reclined position. Someone else turned off the TV screen.

A little light from the moon outside filtered through the windows. It was nice and warm, curled into Fletcher's side on the couch. Listening to the heavy breathing of those sleeping around her, Harper finally relaxed enough to drift to sleep.

She stirred around dawn as the room brightened but refused to wake up fully. Some residents stirred in rooms overhead, and promising sounds came from the kitchen. People started walking through the common room to reach the kitchen, some of them trying to be quiet, others without any regard for those sleeping on the floor and chairs.

It was then Harper noticed Fletcher was missing. The blanket they shared lay rumpled on the ground, but the couch beside her was empty.

He'd cooked breakfast two days in a row, an extra day to help her out, so he couldn't be in charge of that. Laundry happened on Saturdays. She couldn't think of any reason he would be gone, unless he just wanted to be alone. Or maybe he woke up and decided to sleep in his bed. Harper let herself relax. That had to be it.

Harper was convinced she would see Fletcher at breakfast, but her cereal went soggy and her appetite disappeared as her eyes wandered the room looking for him. It had been a long day and a late night. Perhaps he slept in. But past breakfast time?

She took a guess at his favorite cereal and poured him a bowl before the pantry locked, guarding it at the table amidst stares from the other residents who came through for breakfast. When the bell rang for class, she knew something had to be wrong.

Harper wished she knew where his room was. Beckett was his roommate, though, so if she could find him...She ran down the hall, glancing in classrooms, ducking to avoid Mr. Petrov catching her skipping class. She went outside, looking around the garage where she first met the one-legged werewolf, but it was empty. She headed around the back and found the dueling fields full, Zeke instructing a class gathered around him.

Beckett stood at the back, balanced on one leg, arms folded. Harper came toward him, trying not to draw attention. Zeke saw her, of course, and gave her a disapproving look, but didn't stop his animated explanation of the tools a Hunter used to track paranormals. Beckett turned around before Harper reached him, his grin dissolving with worry when he saw her haunted expression.

"Harper. What's going on?"

"I can't find Fletcher."

Beckett considered. "He is supposed to meet with Tyson this morning. Have you checked with him?"

Harper bit her lip. She *really* didn't want to talk to Tyson. "He never came to breakfast." Zeke shot another look their way, the kind that told Harper she'd better get lost if she didn't want an earful. "I'm worried about him."

Beckett's eyebrows creased. "Me too. He wasn't in bed last night, but I assumed he slept on the couch."

"He did. I thought he went to bed, though. The couch was empty this morning."

"Do you two want a demonstration? I can certainly make this subject more exciting, since it doesn't seem to be holding your attention," Zeke warned. His dreadlocks swung across his face as he glared at the two of them.

Beckett looked at Zeke and cleared his throat. "Harper is concerned about Fletcher, Alpha. Permission to start a search party to make sure he's okay?"

Harper held her breath. She didn't want to get Fletcher in trouble if he was doing something that might damage his perfect Naturalization record, but his safety was more important to her, especially after their conversation yesterday. He seemed fine last night, but...

Zeke considered them, then nodded. "Let's make sure we know where he is, and that he isn't alone. You two are dismissed. Let me know what you find."

Beckett nudged Harper. "Come with me. You can fly, I can run. Where do you think he might be?"

She shrugged. She truly had no idea.

"I'll round up some of the pack, then. We can search in several directions, starting inside. I'll check with Tyson. Take to the air and see how much ground you can cover. We'll meet back here in an hour, hopefully with Fletcher."

"All right. Thank you, Beckett." She watched him transform, a stomach-churning and yet fascinating sight, then he bounded off toward the cabin on three legs.

Harper stretched her wings out and flapped them a few times, feeling their strength. She hadn't used them much since her flight with Fletcher, so they seemed a bit stiff, but otherwise ready to go. She ran and let the wind catch them, taking her higher until she was far enough above the tree line to see for miles. She started in a circle, looping around the camp grounds.

He wasn't on the porch or anywhere near the cabin. She widened her loop, her heightened vision seeing clearly between trees, looking to catch a glimpse of someone sitting, or perhaps walking.

Harper spotted the werewolves from Beckett and Zeke's pack—about a dozen sprinting in each direction. They must not have found him in the cabin. Despite her anxiety, she felt relieved that she wasn't doing this alone.

An hour later, trees blurred in her vision. She was dizzy from flying in circles and forced herself to land on a branch near the top of a tall pine to rest. Fletcher was nowhere to be seen.

A howl carried through the forest, and then a string of howls was taken up. Harper's skin went cold at that eerie, sad sound. Did it mean they had found him?

She headed back to meet Beckett where they had previously agreed, just outside the cabin in the back. Beckett wasn't there. A few of the other werewolves were, some in their shifted forms, others changed back into human form. They stopped talking when Harper landed. She recognized Kamri and waved.

Kamri's face looked somber. "Hey, Harper."

"Did they find him?"

"It sounds like it. Though Zeke isn't saying much else."

"Zeke?" Wasn't he teaching?

"He joined the hunt a while ago. That was his howl we heard first." She sat cross-legged on the ground, one of her pack members resting its wolf head on her knee. She picked at a blade of grass in her hands until it became stubble, then dropped it and picked another, starting the process over. Her eyes looked toward the tree line.

Harper followed her gaze, waiting impatiently for any sight of them. It took a long time. What would Fletcher be doing so far out? If she had the direction right, he had gone nearly as far as…as far as…

Two wolves appeared through the trees, running fast. Harper recognized Beckett's grey-brown form and Zeke's black one. They were both regular-sized werewolves, not giants like Keith. They trotted up to the group, tongues lolling, sides heaving.

Zeke immediately transformed. His face was impassive, but there was something in his eyes…

"We found his body." His mouth kept moving, but Harper couldn't follow what he said. It didn't make sense. She stared at Zeke, who asked her a question, but she couldn't react because her mind hadn't caught up yet.

Kamri shook her shoulder. "Harper? Are you okay? I'm so sorry."

"What did he say?" Harper asked, finally finding her tongue.

Kamri blinked back tears, her voice breaking. "He jumped off a cliff on the north side of camp. They found his body at the bottom."

They found his body at the bottom of a cliff.

His cliff.

Harper walked away, ignoring Kamri and Zeke both calling after her. Inside, she passed Ian, who didn't know what had happened, so he smiled and said hello. Harper ignored him.

She couldn't think, couldn't process, couldn't do anything but walk. Her legs moved automatically up the stairs and down the hall to her room and locked the door. Sitting on her bed, she waited for her world to crumble.

Nothing happened. The alarm clock's digital numbers clicked forward a minute at a time, and Harper waited for the hurricane of emotion to hit her.

Fletcher was dead. But she hadn't seen his body yet, so how could it be true?

Harper ignored knocks on the door. Someone fetched a key and opened it. To her surprise, it was Ian.

"Can I come in?"

Harper said nothing. He stepped through the doorway, but kept his distance.

"They've retrieved his body. You...you probably don't want to see it, though. But if you want to say goodbye or..."

She stood abruptly and pushed past him into the hall. He followed her into the basement to an empty room with a table holding a shrouded body. The sight of blood staining the sheets released the wave waiting to crash down inside of her.

Harper sprinted from the room, bolted up the stairs and out the front door and took off into the sky.

There was no comfort in the wind or the sun. Still, Harper didn't return until nightfall, body spent, spirit spent. She couldn't go back to her room, couldn't stop thinking about that body in the basement. She curled up on the couch where she last saw Fletcher alive and cried.

Tyson's voice hovered over her, asking if she needed to talk.

"Go away!" She screamed in his face like a harpy, wings beating threateningly until he backed off and left her alone.

Fletcher's parents arrived the next day expecting to see their son alive, leaving instead with the empty shell that remained. Harper watched them from her bedroom window on the second floor, the body draped across the back seat of the car, wrapped in layers of white sheets. His father half-carried his mother as she leaned on him, sobbing. Did she realize that it was her fault? Or did she care that the only reason Fletcher even considered that horrid operation was because he had no choice other than the one his family forced him into?

Sorrow gave way to anger, boiling in Harper's heart. At least her parents didn't give into the Naturalization nonsense. They couldn't have been like Fletcher's parents, cowardly turning their babies in to be tagged by the government and followed until they came of age to be maimed and tossed back to society like a hooked fish. Could they?

Harper narrowed her eyes, fingers tapping the windowsill. What if the reason she didn't remember receiving a tracking chip during the warding, the reason she couldn't feel it in her back, was because it was somewhere else, placed there when she was a baby?

Harper scratched her arms, working on a non-existent itch, feeling the emotion rise inside and wanting to maintain clarity, to finish this thought process, to...

Hello. What was that?

Her fingertips glided over the spot again and caught on a small bump just beneath the skin at the crook of her arm. She rubbed at it, wondering if it could be a tight muscle.

It felt like a large, fat grain of rice the length of her pinky nail, and it didn't seem like muscle. No, something harder. Plastic or metal, maybe. Excitement rose in her. Harper searched the room, looking for something sharp, something she could dig into her arm with and pry the horrid thing out of her. Then she could escape with Quinn, and they couldn't track her. She didn't have to go through what Fletcher did. Her story would end differently.

Downstairs the doorbell rang, and Harper froze. What was she thinking? They'd know if she took it out now, and it wouldn't do her any good to be stuck here, warded against escaping.

But there was something she could do to change that. She could remove Violet and James from leadership over the camp. Put someone who truly cared about what happened to paranormals in charge, someone who would fight for the government to change the limits placed on them, to stop hunting and killing them if they didn't comply.

Prevent what happened to Fletcher from happening to someone else. Lilith had given Harper the chance to be the force that initiated change. For once in Harper's life, she wasn't powerless.

She'd been a victim of the system all her life, and she wasn't going to wait another moment for that to change.

CHAPTER EIGHTEEN

TYSON

TOM STOOD ACROSS FROM Tyson, leaning on the desk between them. The office Tyson used was technically Tom's, but there was no evidence of that. No pictures of his family, no personal paraphernalia. Half a dozen copies of his book sat on a shelf, and there was a plant next to them.

Just the day before, Fletcher sat in a chair in the exact same place that Tom now stood. A smile on his face despite the pain. How had things gotten where they were now?

Tyson tapped his finger rhythmically on the hard surface, unable to look at Tom.

"Hey, snap out of it." Tom snapped in front of Tyson's face. "Listen, I've been where you are. Too many times to count."

Tyson blinked. "Really?"

"Yes. My book gives the impression that I've only ever seen success, but that's because the sponsor of the study buried the suicide numbers. They're there if you look closely. This isn't that uncommon."

Tyson's stomach clenched. Hearing him say it didn't make it hurt less. Each breath Tyson drew felt more shallow than the last. "Fletcher was my first real case, you know? You gave him to me because he was a shoe-in for Naturalization. He just needed a nudge to stay on track. If I couldn't help him..." Tyson swallowed. "What am I doing here?"

Tom came around to Tyson's side of the desk. He clapped a hand on Tyson's shoulder, letting it rest there like a weight. "I ask myself the same thing every day. Kids like Fletcher kept me here. Watching them enter society is rewarding, but also devastating. I know what they have to give up to get there. No one is talking about after Naturalization, how these kids—adults too—are dying. I presented it at this conference. Blew the place up. No one wants to face reality. We're killing more than we're saving."

"Then what's the point?" Tyson choked on the words. This was all he had dreamed of for the past several years, to be part of the change.

"Sometimes we're called to do things in our lives, and the journey we embark on is not the journey we end up taking." Tom patted Tyson's shoulder again. "Give yourself time, son. This is no small thing." Silence passed between them. "Was there any indication of what he was planning? In your professional opinion?"

Tyson didn't feel like a professional. He felt like a fraud. He ran his fingers through his hair, then flattened it. Fletcher had met with Tyson in the morning after classes started.

"How are you feeling?" Tyson asked. He watched Fletcher's body language carefully, noticing the way his eyes flickered away, the wince as he moved. He was in a lot of pain.

"The painkillers help some, but it's going to take time, isn't it?" He shrugged, the nonchalant gesture causing him to suck air between his teeth.

"*Do you want to talk about the procedure? Anything about your experience?*"

"*It...it wasn't anything like I expected.*"

"*Were you awake?*"

He shook his head. "*No, they put me under. I had to make the change first, you know? Climbing onto that table with my wings out felt so...wrong. Then I woke up alone and there was just pain.*"

"*That must have been frightening.*" *Tyson made a note on Fletcher's chart. It was harder than Tyson expected to hear Fletcher talk about it. Tyson kept seeing his blue, black, and white feathers in his mind's eye. Stretched out, ready for surgery. Tyson shuddered and finished taking the notes he started.*

"*They...they had to sedate me, at first. It just hurt so much. I didn't feel like myself.*"

"*Do you feel like yourself now?*"

Fletcher screwed his face up. Tyson waited while he breathed through the wave of pain. "*More than yesterday. Seeing my friends helps.*"

"*How is it being back?*"

Fletcher's face contorted with amusement. "*It's strange, you know, being a celebrity for something so...morbid. People are curious. They want to know. It's hard to say it so many times. Relive it.*" *He chuckled dryly.* "*I just want to sleep.*"

"*Then sleep. Do whatever you feel like doing. You don't owe them anything.*" *Fletcher fell silent and closed his eyes.* "*Do you regret it?*" *Tyson asked.* "*You don't have to know, yet. Anything you feel is valid.*"

A moment passed, then another, and then Tyson caught a slight nod of Fletcher's chin. His face trembled, and he pulled his lips in. His shoulders began to shake.

"*Hey, it's okay to cry.*"

Tyson pulled himself out of the memory, looking up at Tom through damp eyes. "He was hurting. It was...normal. Expected. No one left him alone the entire day. Harper spent some time with him." What did she say to him? Could it have pushed him so far? It didn't seem like they had fought. Their relationship had apparently developed since Tyson saw them two days ago. When Tyson peeked in on the movie night, looking for Fletcher, he found him leaning his head on Harper as if they were just a normal couple out on a date. How close were they? Did he tell Harper he felt like ending his life?

Tyson would have to speak with Harper, though she wouldn't like it.

Tom walked back to the other side of the desk and leaned against a cabinet on the wall. "Tell me about Harper. Bird shifter, right?"

Tyson scrubbed at his eyes. He didn't want to talk about her. But if he didn't, Tom would know something was up. "Yeah. Like her brother, Quinn."

"Ah. Yes. Stubborn like him, too? Could she have influenced Fletcher?"

Tyson shrugged. "She seemed supportive. Even though she didn't like the choice he made."

Tom's eyes analyzed Tyson's face exactly the way Tyson examined Fletcher's yesterday. "You're worried about her."

"Of course I am. They were friends. Harper was a reluctant capture. She has a violent history, tried to escape on her first day. No doubt she's planning to again, after this. I'm not sure she'll ever accept Naturalization."

"Sometimes they surprise you."

Tyson had nothing to say to that.

Tom sighed, running a hand through his thinning grey hair. "You know, Tyson, this is a difficult time, and I hate that I have to do this now, but I think it will be easier coming from me.

"This was a test. The conference was the ideal opportunity to see how you would do on your own, and I'm afraid we don't like what we've seen happen the past few days."

A lump lodged in Tyson's throat. He tried to swallow past it. "A test?"

Tom nudged a pencil across the desk. "You're a good counselor, Tyson, just not good enough for the pressure of this work. After hearing of the events of the past few days, I'm pushing back my retirement. I'll be here for a couple years, maybe longer, to help smooth this over and train a new replacement."

Tom's sympathetic gaze passed right through Tyson. *A new replacement.* "I-I can do better, Tom. I can."

"Once you've gotten too close, and my information says you're..." He trailed off and held up two intertwined fingers.

Tyson shook his head. "No. Nothing like that. I've had to work more with the latest resident, that's all. I've remained professional." As soon as the words left Tyson's mouth, he knew they were a lie.

His cheeks burned as he scrambled to save his shredded future. "Give me a chance to prove it. This career is all I have wanted my whole life. I just want to make a difference."

Harper's face appeared in Tyson's mind, her characteristic scowl chastising him for the second lie. Tyson couldn't even be honest with himself anymore. What sort of difference did he want to make? Was this it?

"Consider this your two-weeks' notice. You'll get an official letter in the mail in a day or two, but I didn't want you to find out that way. You're a good kid, Tyson. Heart's in the right place, but you're just not the right person for this job." Tom's tone made it clear the conversation was done.

Tyson blinked, then raised a trembling hand. "Thanks for everything, Tom."

"Sure, Tyson. It's been a real pleasure. Count on me for a recommendation, whatever you need."

Tyson snorted. "Better you than Violet."

Tom's smile was more of a grimace. "Oh, one last thing. Your lanyard," he gestured.

Tyson reached up and touched the hard plastic. "But I'm still employed. Two weeks, you said."

"Certain privileges are revoked upon termination, for the safety of the residents. You understand."

Tyson did, but it sucked. He looped the lanyard over his head and handed it to Tom. He took it from Tyson, tapping the card on his palm and looking as if he'd like to say more, but instead he opened the office door and stepped into the hall.

"Hey!" Tom barked.

Tyson glanced up as Harper barreled into Tom. She mumbled an apology and darted around him, not glancing toward the office at all. Where was she going? Her shoulders hunched, Tyson couldn't see her face to notice whether or not she'd been crying. She pivoted at the staircase and headed down before she disappeared from view.

There was one person here who definitely needed Tyson's help. He squared his shoulders and stood, glancing around to make sure he hadn't left any important papers out for others to see, then turned toward the door.

A figure blocked Tyson's way, hair loose and ragged, clothing rumpled, eyes red-rimmed. Violet.

"V-Violet. I didn't expect you. How can I help?" Tyson might have just been fired, but as long as he was here, he was still a counselor at Camp Silver Lake.

She bared her teeth. "What did you *do*?"

"Excuse me?"

"He was ready for Reformation. You evaluated him, said he was mentally and emotionally fit for the operation. How could you have miscalculated like this?" Violet stalked into the room, clenched fists swinging at her side.

Was it what Tom had said? Tyson didn't want to accept that answer. He leaned on the desk for support. "No one can predict how the Reformation will go. I had every positive indication that Fletcher would be fine. He checked every box. That's why we have them come back to camp after, to see how they're doing before we send them out into the world. He had family coming. How could I possibly know he felt that badly about it?"

Violet's eyes widened. "It's your job to know!" Her voice rose to the level of a shriek, and she surged forward. "Do you understand what this means? What they'll do? We'll be lucky to get an evaluation before they shut us down."

"If it helps any, I've been fired." Tyson shot back.

She froze, then a smile spread across her face and she cackled. The cackle devolved into tears. This wasn't the first time Tyson had a sobbing witch in his office—not his office, he reminded himself— but this was his first time facing a sobbing superior.

The mad laughter ceased abruptly. "You don't understand anything, do you?" Violet's voice dropped to a guttural low. "They are about to pass new legislation to go hand-in-hand with the distance extension for Naturalized citizens. They want camps to be run stricter, candidates screened better. They're changing some of the Naturalization criteria. We only have six months to determine compatibility, for one. Everything is being given more weight, escape attempts, acts of violence, compliance…"

Her gaze drifted off toward one wall, then snapped back to Tyson. "Suicides show a camp's ineffectiveness. We will be assigned an evaluator, who will stay on for weeks, possibly months, nitpicking everything. I've heard of them going to work in other camps. They're leeches. They clamp on and don't let go until you're ruined."

"But this camp is one of the best in the country. If it were shut down…"

"Exactly," she hissed. "Now you see. Now that it's too late."

Tyson raised his hands defensively. "I couldn't have done anything more with Fletcher." *I'm a failure.* The thought latched onto his brain. *Fletcher deserved better.*

"Tell that to his family." Violet's finger jutted toward the door where Fletcher's parents had left half an hour ago, sobbing as they followed their son's lifeless body to their car.

"We're all hurting, Violet." As the words left Tyson's mouth he realized they were the wrong thing to say.

Violet let out a sudden howl, an inhuman sound of grief and rage, and leapt for him. Tyson's fingers scrabbled under the desk's surface to find the safety button, and he slapped it. The wards activated, but they didn't touch Violet.

Of course. Her lanyard swung from her neck. Tyson's had left with Tom.

Violet's hands closed around his throat, coated in glowing green light. The wards lit the room in an emerald glow. Her grip tightened, and Tyson's vision pulsed. That green light would be the last thing he saw. He choked and gurgled, helpless to stop her.

A knock on the door. She must have closed it when she came in, though Tyson didn't remember seeing it. Violet's face contorted, thumbs pressing into his windpipe to crush it. Dark blobs formed in front of his eyes. His head throbbed. Any moment he would lose consciousness and never regain it. The knock came again, and someone jiggled the handle.

"Agh!" Violet released Tyson with a sound of disgust and wheeled around, hair flying about her face. She stalked toward the door and flung it open. "What?" she snapped.

Tyson gasped, still frozen. His eyes strained at the corners to glimpse two men in suits standing in the doorway wearing black sunglasses. Typical government Hunters by all appearances.

"We're here to speak with Violet or James Petrov about the aberration."

Aberration. Harper. This was the management team that had come for Harper. The Raven born.

Violet grabbed the door handle, and her hand glowed again briefly. The lock mechanism clicked. "No one will be able to open this until I return," she hissed. "We can continue our conversation when I'm finished." She shut the door.

Tyson swallowed past the soreness in his throat. His ears rang in the silent room, and his thoughts spun. Violet had always been prone to irritation, but he'd never known her to be violent. Had Fletcher's death sent her off the deep end or was it the mounting pressure from the government?

His phone buzzed in his pocket. His fingers twitched. Fortunately, the faintly lit wards on the floor had started fading. They weren't designed to last long, only a few minutes were typically needed for help to arrive. James and Lilith should have felt the wards triggered, too. Would one of them come to Tyson's aid, or did they hate him as much as Violet apparently did? Who else blamed him for Fletcher's death and the demise of Camp Silver Lake?

Tyson's phone stopped ringing, and he was left in silence. The paralysis drained gradually, allowing him to move his wrists and flex his hands. When he could bend at the elbow, he angled his arm to reach into his pocket and slid his phone out, but his fingers fumbled and it fell to the floor, face-down.

Tyson focused his breathing, feeling the minutes tick by. Harper was who-knew-where now. What would she want in the basement? Time alone? Dread trickled into his heart. The pool. She wouldn't kill herself. Not with Quinn coming for her.

Would she?

A tingling sensation in his feet and shoulders told him the warding was lifting in those areas. A moment later, he wiggled his toes. The paralysis bled away faster until his hips were the only area locked in place. He sighed, placing his hands on the table as the muscles slowly released. His jello legs gave way, and he stood trembling against the desk, then bent down to pick up his phone.

The missed call was from Becca. Tyson recognized the number she used last time. He punched redial and held the phone up to his ear, wincing at the muscle cramps in his legs and arms as he moved them.

"Hello?" She sounded breathless.

"Are you running?"

"Yes."

"Should I call back later?"

"No! I need to talk to you. Is there any way we can bump this operation to today?"

"Sure, why not. We're having a wake this afternoon. Aberration Management just arrived for Harper. Might as well join the party," Tyson muttered, rolling his shoulder opposite the arm holding the phone, pushing through the stiffness.

"Who died?"

"Fletcher." The line fell silent. Tyson swallowed past the emotion welling up. "It's a mess. We're all a mess. His Reformation appointment went well, but he didn't tolerate the procedure as well as we thought he would."

Shouting in the background on the other line drew Tyson's attention, and Becca took a moment to respond. Was she being chased? He almost missed it when she finally said something. "That doesn't sound like Fletcher."

"I know. I know. We just can't predict..."

"Are you certain no one else could be involved?" She still sounded breathless, but the shouts were gone, as well as any noises that indicated she was outside.

Trying to figure out where she was, Tyson's mind took a moment to catch up to what she implied. "You think Fletcher was *murdered*? Why would anyone do that?"

"Who would profit from it?"

"Violet says they're going to shut down the camp. It can't be her. She's furious. She locked me in my office and..." He couldn't bring himself to say it. *Tried to kill me.*

Could she have murdered Fletcher, after all? Maybe she had well and truly snapped. Harper was right, after all. Violet needed to be evaluated as soon as possible. Tyson might not have made the cut as a camp counselor, but he could still recognize a psychotic break when he saw one.

"She's been under review for violent behavior before," Becca said quietly.

Tyson thought back to Reya's file. After years of running this camp, doing everything she could to please the government and keep it as safe as possible for those who survived the older Naturalization procedures...Had it become too much?

"How did I not know this? How does everyone know everything before I do?"

"You're just the intern. But that's not critical right now. We need to get you out. Wake or no wake, it sounds like you need us to break you out before Violet gets back. And Harper's probably not doing so great, either."

"I don't know. I haven't talked to her." Too busy being locked up.

"Can you get a message to her? Never mind, you're locked in. We're close, so it shouldn't be long. Just have to gather some things. Expect us in half an hour."

"What are you going to—" Becca hung up before Tyson finished. He set the phone down and swung his arms, praying half an hour would get them there before Violet returned.

Could Violet really be a killer? Reya came to mind, her sweet face, framed with red hair. Violet ran the camp when it happened, when they killed her. She could have been the one to pull the trigger, so to speak. Or at least order it.

She had proved she would do damn near anything to keep this camp running in the past, but murder?

Tyson tapped his mental resources, trying to come up with someone else with motive. Unless Tom harbored some secret anger no one knew about, it couldn't be him. James was Violet's husband and could be in on it with her, though it was a stretch. They both loved Fletcher. They were supportive of his Naturalization, and they had no reason to want the camp shut down. Lilith...

Could she have aspirations for leadership of the coven, of the camp itself? She had been here a long time, always happy to go along with whatever others wanted, never putting up a fuss, quiet and likeable...

Tyson swallowed. The profile his mind was generating of Lilith Adiel. If Lilith created enough chaos, the camp would fall apart, giving her the perfect opportunity to put her plans into motion, whatever those plans were.

Fletcher's death had put everyone into a state of grief. No one would be watching for something to happen.

Harper. What part did she play in all of this?

Tyson's feet pricked with pins and needles but finally released. He ran to the door. He knew it was useless, but he had to try anyway. As soon as his flesh contacted the metal doorknob, an acid-like substance burned into his skin. He yelled and stumbled back, holding his red, blistered hand.

The office chair hit the back of his legs, and he slumped into it, staring at his burned skin. It throbbed, the skin red and shiny-looking. Tyson bit back tears, breathing deep against the pain, and stared at the door. How would Quinn and Becca get through *that*?

He didn't have a first-aid kit in the office, so he had nothing for the burns. Just hand sanitizer, and he knew that wouldn't do any good. His eyes landed on the long, spiked leaves of the plant next to Tom's books. *Aloe vera.* That was the stuff they used on sunburns, right?

He grabbed the plant from the shelf and set it on the desk. He pinched the thick arm of the plant, his nail piercing the waxy flesh. Some juice stuff squirted out, and the inside of the leaf glistened green. He needed to cut it open.

Tyson's eyes landed on his back pack. The *ulu* knife was inside. He rummaged through until he found the dark, velvety package, and he unwrapped it on the desk. Bone and blade gleamed in the bright electric lights of his office. He picked it up in one hand, holding his breath.

Besides feeling awkward holding it in his non-dominant hand, nothing happened. No strange dreams, no ice, no northern lights. Tyson sliced at the plant and the end came cleanly off. That knife was *sharp*.

The inside of the plant gleamed, slightly translucent. He set the knife down and squeezed just below where he cut. A chunk of the plant's insides fell out, plopping to the desk. He scooped it up and rubbed it into the burns on his left hand. It felt soothing, so he kept rubbing, squeezing the plant to get more. The gel created a tacky barrier on his skin.

Tyson eyed the plant. He was getting broken out of here soon, and it would be wise to bring something for the burns. He picked up the whole plant and placed it in the top of his backpack. There was no way it would fit.

He cut one of the stalks off and slid it into a side pocket. The *ulu* knife followed, after Tyson did his best to clean the blade with a tissue from the desk. He wished he had some bandaging, but wasn't willing to sacrifice his spare shirt to the cause. The burns weren't that serious.

A thunder clap, or a gunshot, sounded outside. Tyson ran to the window blinds and peeked out between them, but saw nothing. If that was Becca and Quinn, they were at the border of the camp, too far away for him to see from there. He had maybe ten minutes.

He glanced around the office. Like Tom, he hadn't done much to the place. There was nothing personal, except the picture of Tyson's sister and her kids. After a moment, he opened the back of the frame and slipped the picture into his backpack, then slung the strap over his shoulder, being careful of his injured hand. The last thing he did was log out of everything on his account, cleared the internet cache, and shut down the computer.

Tyson stood ready by the door. Any moment, either Violet or Becca would come through. He bounced impatiently from one leg to the other. Did he hear shouting outside, or was he imagining things? He resisted the urge to look through the office window again. He needed to be ready to run.

The front door, just outside the office, banged open. Muffled voices outside. Tyson leaned toward the door, then thought better of it and stepped back.

"Tyson? You in there?" Becca's voice came through the door.

"Yeah."

"Step back. And cover your ears." Tyson heard an electronic whirring sound and slapped his hands over his ears just before it went off. That same gun shot sound was deafening in close proximity, and his ears rang despite covering them. Becca opened the door without getting burned like Tyson did. Her device must have disrupted the warding. Becca returned the device to a bag swinging at her side and smiled, tucking her hair behind her ear.

"Hey, cuz,"

"Hey," Tyson replied, stepping through.

Quinn nodded in Tyson's direction. "You ever blown a joint like this?"

Tyson rolled his eyes. "No."

"Well, time to run. Most everyone is outside that we could see. It's all gone to hell. The rogues are attacking. It's the only way we got through to you, with all the chaos. Where's Harper?" Becca said it all in one breath.

"She headed downstairs, last I saw." Tyson shifted his backpack strap, uneasy at the thought of rogues invading the camp. Too much was happening at once. His run-in was the last he ever wanted to see of them. "What's the plan to get out past everyone once we're outside?"

"Run like hell." Quinn spoke up from behind Becca, still tall, dark, and brooding.

They were both familiar with the cabin, but they let Tyson lead the way as they all ran down the stairs. It took Tyson's eyes a moment to adjust to the darkness. Water lapped against the pool on the other side of the basement, otherwise the air was silent.

"Which way?" Becca hissed, coming to a stop behind him.

"What are we looking for?" Quinn asked after a minute. Vague shapes appeared in Tyson's vision, but it wasn't enough to make out the features of his companions.

"I'm not sure." Tyson didn't get to talk to Harper, so he didn't know why she would be down here. Would she have gone to the pool? He didn't think so, but…A sensation nudged him in the opposite direction, down a maze of hallways he knew held unused classrooms and the staff shower room.

The sensation alerted his mind as if he'd heard a quiet sound, except he was certain he hadn't heard anything. He motioned for Becca and Quinn to follow.

When Tyson rounded the second corner, a soft light emanated from an open door. Rushing down the hall, he peered into the room.

Harper's face was illuminated by a magnificent glowing ball, almost like a bowling ball, but something about the luminescent object felt distinctly other-worldly. Her hands hovered over the surface.

Tyson stepped fully into the doorway, letting that silver light wash over him. Whatever she was about to do, it felt wrong. Fear twisted in his gut.

"Harper, don't—"

A flash of light cut off Tyson's words as Harper brought her hands down on the orb. She glanced up, saw him, recognized him.

Tyson's head screamed with pain, and Quinn and Becca both doubled over, hands clasping their heads. Tyson faced Harper, taking a vast amount of effort to perform the simple task. Her short hair flew behind her in an invisible wind, and silver light shone through her open eyes and mouth, casting her skin in negative darks and lights like a setting on a camera.

Tyson's muscles wouldn't obey him. He shuffled at a snail's pace to get to Harper, fighting an invisible force. Lines on the floor glowed faintly, and he recognized a giant pentagram shape sketched onto the concrete. A pentagram that protected Harper and the orb, preventing him from getting closer.

Harper, what the hell did you do?

CHAPTER NINETEEN

HARPER

"LILITH. LILITH. LILITH." HARPER felt like an idiot chanting the name in the dark hallway, but Lilith had said that was the way to contact her.

She'd stood there for at least fifteen minutes, and that was after getting lost in the tangle of hallways in the basement. She jumped at every sound from upstairs.

A whisper sounded behind Harper, and the hairs on the back of her neck rose. She turned, but saw nothing. A shadow flickered in the corner of her eye, near the ceiling.

Her gaze darted around until it landed on a mass of curling, pale smoke to her right. The smoke billowed, then settled over the invisible figure of a woman who gradually became solid.

Lilith.

The witch smiled. "I am pleased, Harper. You will be praised by many for this."

Harper didn't care for praise, she wanted justice. Lilith unlocked the door and let Harper through. The same shelves, strewn with lit candles, and the pentagram on the floor. Everything looked the same as Harper had seen before. Even the orb, to her shock, waited on the table.

"You knew I would come?" Harper's skin tingled, and the center of her chest went cold at the thought.

"Harper, you and I are people of similar convictions. I knew you would come because it's what I would do." Lilith smiled again, her words pricking a warning in Harper's heart. Harper brushed the sensation away, stepping toward the orb.

"Do you know what you will say?" Lilith asked.

Harper swallowed, eyeing the orb. "I think so." She stood before it. "Lilith, how will this change me?"

No answer. The hallway stood empty. Lilith wasn't going to stay, to make sure Harper didn't mess this up?

Harper stared at the orb's surface, taking deep, shuddering breaths. It was now or never. Sooner or later, someone would come looking for Harper and try to stop her from what she was about to do.

Her trembling fingers moved toward the orb's innocently glinting surface, fingertips sliding across the smooth dome. It was warm.

"Harper, don't—"

Harper's head shot up, and she caught a blurred glimpse of Tyson before the world collapsed on itself.

Tyson stood, a reaching, gape-mouthed ghost, unable to come through the door. The orb bled to gunmetal grey beneath Harpers' fingers, and the whole room beamed with white light. Furniture and items on shelves became a wispy grey. The pentagram on the floor lit up like a Christmas tree, pulsing in rainbow colors along the thickly drawn lines. Her hands remained glued to the Beryllium Orb, quivering with the vibrations that came off it.

Harper King.

A graveled voice whispered in Harper's ear, tickling her eardrum. She shuddered, unable to move a finger to rub away the itch. She opened her mouth, but no sound came out. Her vocal chords were seized, but the words came through as thought. *What are you?*

I am Creator of the past, I am Author of the future. What have you brought for me?

A request. The words sounded hollow in Harper's head. She ignored the voice of her conscience telling her to let go of the orb. She had to do this. For Fletcher. She steadied herself, focusing on the orb in her grip.

Name your request.

Harper breathed deeply, but her lungs locked up, unable to draw the air all the way in. She took another quivering breath before projecting her thoughts. *I want the powers of James and Violet Petrov removed permanently.*

Righteous anger curled within Harper, like a snake waiting to strike. Her thoughts seethed at the memory of what they did to Fletcher. How many deaths like his were they responsible for?

Black tendrils of the orb reached into her mind, searching for their faces. Harper gritted her teeth at each memory that flashed up from the day she arrived at camp. She tried to clench her fists, but her hands remained glued to the orb's gleaming surface. The smoky tendrils wrapped themselves around the memories, clinging to the folds of her mind like sticker weeds.

A price must be paid, Harper King.

Harper breathed in. If the price only affected her, she would pay it without question.

I'm willing to pay.

Ahead, two figures joined Tyson in the doorway, gesturing to Harper and down the hall, talking in slow motion. A woman and a man. Harper's eyes lingered on the blurred grey lines of the man's form.

Quinn.

He was here. Harper tried to open her mouth to shout, but she couldn't convince the muscles around her mouth to move. The orb reached toward her memories of her brother.

Not him. You can't take him from me. Harper couldn't move to shriek and throw herself to the floor to beg like she wanted to.

He won't be dead to everyone. Only you. The voice in the orb said.

Harper cried out and struggled to break the connection of her hands on the orb, but she couldn't. Having named her desire, she was forced to accept the price the orb had chosen. This was what Lilith had meant. *Forever changed.*

The intelligence within the orb began with Harper's very earliest memories, blurred images from infancy that she never would have been able to summon consciously. It was the sweetest torture she could ever experience, seeing each moment relived as it was stricken forever from her mind. Her sense of Quinn narrowed, her feelings weakened. Quinn existed on two planes, in her mind's eye at age eight, and in front of her at twenty-four. Her brother. What would happen when she forgot him entirely?

Harper yanked again at her hands, desperate to get away, to keep the orb from taking everything from her. Her limbs quivered with the effort. She yelled internally, pulling with all of her paranormal strength, muscles burning.

Her right hand twitched, and the orb flickered back to crystal for a brief moment.

No! The orb's voice shrieked in Harper's mind. It increased its efforts, slicing through memories without giving her a chance to live through them.

Quinn sheltering her while a foster parent yelled in the background. Quinn teaching her to fly. Quinn raising fists to a playground bully. Quinn hard-knuckling her head. The last day Harper saw him, his seventeenth birthday, saying goodbye with her arms wrapped around his waist and her head on his chest.

She'd heard he got sent to juvie only a few days later and wondered if she would ever see him again. She promised herself that she would. She wouldn't lose that chance now.

Harper redoubled her efforts, eyes and muscles bulging. Her left hand quivered. The tendrils reached for the last memories of Quinn, greedy and hungry. They flickered.

You. Can't. Have. Him! With an internal scream, Harper yanked her hands away from the glassy surface of the Beryllium orb and clenched her fists at last. The grey light disappeared, and her vision of the room tunneled. Her legs collapsed. Harper breathed heavily, her head ringing and her eyes screwed shut against the pain.

The forms at the door rushed toward Harper. Tyson reached for her, but her eyes went to the other faces beside him, searching. Nameless faces. She'd lost something. If only she could remember what.

"Harper, wake up!"

Harper murmured and stirred, eyelids blinking open. She was on the floor of the pentagram room in the basement, the orb glinting, dark and innocent from the table above. She shook her head, pushing concerned hands away and standing on her own. She tore her eyes away from the orb, glancing toward the person crouching next to her. Earnest brown eyes gazed at her, framed with long black hair. He had a beautiful face.

"God, Harper, I thought you were..." The man swallowed. Harper squinted, and her head ached.

Do I know him?

"We need to get out of here. Grab her and let's get going." A female voice. Harper tipped her head back and blinked at the blonde woman with hair to her waist and delicate features. Harper had never seen the woman before.

"I'm sorry, who are you?" Her voice slurred, like she'd been drinking. Another face dipped into view. Finally, someone she recognized. "Tyson."

"At least we know she hasn't got amnesia," Tyson said, glancing at the others.

"There they are," a man barked. Their heads all jerked toward the doorway where two men in black suits stood shoulder to shoulder, blocking the only exit. From the floor, Harper couldn't see more than their legs and torsos. She moved to stand, but the man with the black hair crouched next to her put a hand on her shoulder, holding her down. Harper was pissed he touched her but glad for the intervention. Her head spun and throbbed at the same time, and she wasn't entirely certain she wouldn't have fallen down immediately.

"Who are you?" The man stood and addressed the two intruders, moving around the table. He gestured for the woman and Tyson to stay back, but the woman ignored him and came to stand next to Tyson. The men didn't respond. They advanced, their hands pulling something from their suit coats.

Guns.

Well, one looked like a gun. The other seemed like some sort of electronic reading device. It beeped like a metal detector as the one suit scanned the room. He gestured at Tyson's two companions, the dark-haired man and the blonde woman.

"There's two of them."

"The witch called about one," the other suit said.

"I'm not picky. Readings this high? We take both." The first suit shrugged.

Harper scoffed. No one would take anyone if she had anything to say about it. Now, if she could only stand...She pushed off from the floor with her hands, but her arms wobbled alarmingly, still weak as jello.

She heard a click and froze. A crackling sound filled the air.

Tyson's companions yelled and their limbs jerked as they fell stiffly to the ground, wires coming off the guns stuck into their backs. Not guns. Tasers.

"Hey! What are you doing?" Tyson ran around the table and right at one of the suits, but he threw a punch and Tyson was thrust back against the wall. He crumpled to the ground.

They weren't wearing Stiff uniforms, Harper realized. This was a whole different faction. Aberration Management? She frowned, trying to remember what Tyson had said earlier in the office.

Tyson groaned, breaking her train of thought. He needed her help. Harper managed to turn over onto hands and knees, shaking the spinning sensation out of her head. She reached a hand up to the table and used it to prop herself up in a kneeling position, legs still shaking.

The suits each slung a body over a shoulder. The woman woke up and beat at the suit holding her, shrieking.

All Harper could do was watch them leave. They didn't even notice she was there as she gasped with the effort of keeping herself in a kneeling position, held up by the table. They disappeared into the hallway.

Harper yelled in frustration, slamming a fist down on the table, enraged at the loss of Tyson's companions, even though she still wasn't sure who they were. The reaction seemed extreme. Maybe she wasn't thinking right.

Harper's yell woke Tyson, and he sat up, moaning. When he looked up, there was a bruise forming over his eye and half his cheek.

"You all right?" Harper called out. She dropped her grip on the table and let herself fall back to the floor. Given a moment longer, she would surely be able to stand. She'd have to. They needed to get out of there and make certain Lilith let Harper go as promised, now that the orb had done its work.

"Yeah. Man alive, that hurt." He touched his cheekbone gingerly, prodding at his bruising skin, then stood. He crossed the room to Harper's side.

"I can't believe they didn't take you."

"They were here for me, weren't they?"

"Yeah. But why did they take...and Becca instead?" Tyson leaned his head to one side, as if it hurt. Then he looked at Harper strangely. "You seem to be doing really well for what just happened."

What exactly happened? Harper wasn't sure. She gestured to her legs. "Except for not being able to stand."

Tyson frowned. "Yeah, that. But I meant..."

"Was that Becca? And...?" Harper trailed off, unable to think of the man's name. Odd. She was sure Tyson had told her at some point.

"I'm so sorry, Harper."

Harper gave him a perplexed look. Maybe he was worried about his cousin. "Look, it's all right. We can go after them."

"We don't know where they're being taken." Tyson spread his hands, then ran one through his hair. Some of the sweaty brown strands stood straight up. He didn't notice, putting his hands on his hips and glancing around the room. "Are you going to tell me what you just did here?"

"Just removed the undeserving from their position of power."

"Violet and James?"

Harper looked to the orb. What had she done? She wouldn't know until she got upstairs. Tyson's mouth gaped open, and then he clamped it shut.

"We should go." Harper reached a hand up toward Tyson. Shock stood out stark on his face, but he clasped her hand and pulled her up so fast their bodies met. Harper tried to move away, to test the strength of her legs, but he held tight, her face inches away from his.

"What if you killed them?" His blue eyes searched Harper's with an intensity she hadn't seen in him before. It took her a moment to realize who he meant.

Harper broke the gaze and jerked herself from his grasp, stepping back. Her legs held, though shakily. She couldn't look at him. Her face and hands both heated. She pushed her shoulders back and walked around the table, away from the orb, crossing the dulled pentagram drawn onto the floor.

Tyson followed after a moment, not speaking. Was he angry or relieved? Hell, Harper didn't know what she was feeling either. Her emotions swirled beneath the surface, confusion and anger and curiosity and relief all rolled into one.

She stepped into the hall. The walls reverberated with a drawn-out howl. Claws scrabbled for purchase on the carpet around the corner, reminding Harper of the time Keith shifted to werewolf and attacked her. She didn't have to see anything to know that a pack was on their trail. She swung her head toward Tyson.

"Run!"

"How did they find us?"

"I don't know!" Harper stumbled into a clumsy sprint. She resisted looking back, afraid to see the black wolf that could be leading the pack. Zeke.

The wolf pack barked and howled. They had caught their scent. Harper pumped her arms and put on more speed. Tyson fell behind, unable to maintain the supernatural pace. A corner loomed. Harper rounded it with too much momentum and slammed into the wall. Her body twisted and her head rang.

A wolf entered the end of the hall. It wasn't Zeke or any of the werewolves Harper recognized.

A dead end met them at the back of a long hall filled with doors, doors that led to nothing but empty rooms. Harper jiggled the handles as she passed anyway. They stopped against the far wall, looking up at a narrow window, a bit high off the ground.

Harper took a deep breath and set her gaze on the window.

"Are you going to break through?" Tyson stood behind her, panting.

Harper backed up to get a running start, taking a deep breath through her nose.

Tyson made a strangled sound, but Harper ignored him, launching toward the window at a full sprint.

Her wings erupted from her back in a flurry of midnight feathers and filled the hall. She pumped them once and used them to flip her body so her legs struck the window first. The glass shattered.

Harper flared her wings out to catch herself as she dropped, landing in a crouch. She shifted back to human form faster than she'd ever done before. Wings gone, she jumped for the window ledge and dragged herself up, glass crunching beneath her hands as she wiggled through the narrow space. Hopefully Tyson's shoulders could fit.

She reoriented to face the window and backed up. Tyson sprinted for the opening, arms and legs pumping. He halted and threw his backpack off his shoulders.

"Catch!" he yelled.

Harper leaned forward and grabbed the strap just before it fell.

Tyson jumped and his fingers gripped the ledge. They slipped and he fell with a grunt. He had no room to get a running start; the wolves were ten feet away.

Harper reached her hands out and he jumped straight up, grabbing her wrists. Her paranormal strength burned through her muscles, and he landed on the damp grass beside her.

A wolf leapt up into the opening, snarling, eyes red-rimmed. Its paws scrabbled on the sill but found no purchase, and it fell to the floor below. Four of them prowled beneath the window, taking up a frustrated howl. Their wolf forms were too awkward to navigate the narrow space.

Or so Harper hoped.

"We made it," Tyson said, glancing down at his body. "Well, mostly."

Harper looked and realized he had a shoe missing. "We'll find you new ones. Come on."

She spread her wings and extended her hand, criss-crossed with red cut-lines from the glass.

"Where are we going?"

Harper pointed toward the sky. "Out of reach."

CHAPTER TWENTY

HARPER

HARPER'S HAND HOVERED IN the air, and for a heart-stopping moment she thought Tyson might not take it.

Her breath seized in her chest. It was okay. She was used to being alone.

He finally slapped his palm into hers. Harper yanked him closer and swept her arm under his knees. He gripped her neck reflexively, yelping at the sudden movement. Harper ran forward, flapping her wings, and lifted off. They rose above the cabin. Every stroke was harder than usual, and she breathed hard, focusing on coordinating her muscles to stay airborne.

The dueling field below was in chaos—rogues and camp residents engaged each other in snarling, bloody battles. Harper scanned the ground, searching for anyone she recognized, but it was impossible with how fast everyone moved.

A streak of silver shot across the field from a window in the lodge, hissing and smoking as it split and struck two dark-haired figures fighting back-to-back against the rogues.

The two living, fighting people became two bodies.

Harper's heart froze as she recognized them.

Violet and James Petrov lay in a black ring on the ground, silver fire sparking from the center.

Dead.

But who had killed them? Had the orb...?

I'll take care of the rest. Lilith's voice echoed in Harper's head. She closed her eyes against the scene.

"Harper!" Tyson yelled, pointing up. She looked to the sky as the shimmering green wards became visible and collapsed towards the ground, making a sound like a knife slicing through the air.

Harper tilted her wings, steering them towards the edge of the camp, still some miles out.

James and Violet were dead. And Harper as good as killed them.

The thought repeated with every beat of her wings as she flew out over the forest, past the cliff where Fletcher kissed her, beyond the border of the camp.

The now-invisible inked spells on her skin held no power to hold her within camp boundaries. She was free.

Harper's arms ached—more from the position she held Tyson in than from fatigue. His weight made her top-heavy, and her wings strained to hold the odd position as she flew. She'd have to touch down soon, but she didn't want to risk getting caught. If she could leave the camp, so could the rogues. So could everyone else. Would they take the opportunity and run to freedom?

Harper's left wing faltered with the next downbeat, and she tipped dangerously to one side. Tyson gripped her neck tighter and let out a strained sound.

"I have to go down." The wind carried Harper's words behind her. Tyson's arms tightened again and he nearly choked her. She angled her wings into a shallow dive, the extra weight making her fall faster than she would have liked. She could see a bit of a clearing in the forest below, and she aimed toward it. She had to dodge a few trees, getting whipped in the face by the branches they fell past.

Harper's knees buckled as she crashed, rolling on top of Tyson. They scrambled to free themselves from the tangle of arms, legs, and the backpack, but eventually they got sorted out, sitting a few feet away from each other, panting.

Tyson wouldn't make eye contact. Or maybe he was just in shock after everything he saw back there. Harper stared blankly forward, her mind struggling to process. He moved first, taking off his remaining shoe and tossing it to the ground.

"Do you have a knife on you?" Harper asked, coming out of her stupor. The look Tyson gave her was part terror, part suspicion. She rolled her eyes and reached out her hand. "It's important."

He hesitated, then swung his backpack to the ground, unzipped the bag, and dug around until he took out a large package. He unwrapped it to reveal a curved knife unlike anything she'd seen before. Harper's eyes widened.

"What is that thing?"

"It's an Inuit *ulu* knife. A gift from my grandmother."

"I think I would like your grandmother," Harper said. Tyson moved closer, holding the knife in a nervous grip that he kept adjusting like he'd never held it before. "You can give it to me, I know what I need to do."

Tyson licked his lips. "I don't think I can. It's...it's something from my ancestors. I can't just give it to anyone."

"Fine. Cut here." Harper gestured toward the spot on the inside of her arm near the crook of her elbow where she felt the raised bump. "Just a shallow slice."

Tyson looked at her like she'd grown a second head. "No way, Harper."

"I'm not asking you to kill anyone, just cut me! Just a little. Unless you want an army to come down on us at any moment. There's a tracker just beneath the skin. It's small, and I think I can get it out and destroy it. If I don't, we might as well sit here and wait until they find us." Harper stared at Tyson, hoping her serious expression drove home the importance of what she said, and that he didn't suddenly change his mind about helping her.

"Where do I need to cut?" he asked, coming closer and kneeling next to her arm.

Harper put her finger just above the hard bump in her arm. "Cut below here. Start small, I don't have any bandages."

His hand shook when he lifted the knife.

"Take a breath," Harper reminded him. He set the tip of the *ulu* knife against her skin and cut in a swift, short motion. Blood welled up instantly and she pressed down hard on either side like popping a pimple. She bit her lip against the pain but couldn't keep from yelling, startling birds from the trees. Something moved, and in a spurt of blood, a sleek metal object, like a rice grain-sized bullet, slid from her arm and fell into the dirt on the ground.

The blood continued seeping out of the cut. "Something to stop this, quick."

"You didn't think of that before?" Tyson said, voice pitched higher than normal. He crawled back to the backpack and produced a handkerchief from nowhere, like a magician. Harper snatched it and pressed the cloth against the wound.

"Tie it around," Harper commanded. Tyson grabbed either end of the fabric and threaded it under her arm, pulling. "Tighter. Not tourniquet tight, just tighter."

He did a decent job, but Harper held her opposite hand on it to apply extra pressure.

"You don't happen to have a first aid kit, do you?"

"Not *that* prepared," Tyson said. He stared at the drying blood where it streaked down Harper's arm.

"We'll need to smash it." Harper's voice jarred Tyson from his trance, and he walked around the clearing until he returned with two rocks in hand. He set the flatter one down and picked up the bloody metal object between two fingers. It rolled down the rock a few times before he got it to balance.

"Do you want to?" He gestured at the tracking device.

Harper lifted her still-bleeding arm.

"Oh, right." He picked up the other rock, adjusting his grip, then brought it down hard. The rocks clacked together and there was a promising crunch sound. Tyson lifted the top rock. It looked more like a squashed bug than a surveillance device.

Harper released her grip on her arm and held her uninjured hand out toward Tyson. He stared at it as if it was a snake that might bite him.

"We need to get away from this spot. Otherwise, they'll see the last transmitted location and come here." Harper wasn't entirely sure who "they" were. With James and Violet dead, Lilith would take over the camp, and she wouldn't send anyone after them, would she? The wolf pack could still be hunting them. If Lilith withheld the truth about what the orb would do, Harper wouldn't put it past the witch to decide she needed Harper for something else.

"Oh, right." He said again, clasping her hand and pulling her up. They locked eyes. Harper tried not to look away.

"Is that the result you wanted?" Tyson finally asked.

"I don't want to talk about it."

"You need to talk about it, and I need to know." He jabbed a finger into his chest.

"Why do you need to know? Why is it so important that you know everything about the way everyone thinks? It didn't help Fletcher, and I don't believe for a second that you care that much about me. So, why?"

He looked stunned, his eyes wide and breath heaving. His fingers flexed, and he glanced around the clearing, avoiding Harper. She must have struck a nerve. The back of her throat started aching, and she swallowed repeatedly. She didn't need anyone digging around in her feelings, least of all him.

He breathed in deeply, then blew the air out in a rush. "Okay. You don't want to talk about it." He paused, then cleared his throat. "We should figure out our next step. Aberration Management has Becca and...How can we get them back?"

"Who?" Harper asked, confused. She recognized the first name as his cousin. The second came out of Tyson's mouth all garbled in her mind. Harper shook her head.

"Becca and...You know? The whole reason you busted out of camp."

Harper had busted out of camp to find her parents. Her parents had never been at the camp. She didn't know what Tyson was talking about.

She gave Tyson an odd look, who stared right back until he gave up and knelt down to pick up the *ulu* knife on the ground next to his backpack. As soon as his fingers brushed the bone handle his eyes rolled back into his head and his body convulsed.

"Tyson? Tyson!" Despite everything Harper just said about not caring, she ran to his side. Could she touch him? His limbs seemed locked up, and his eyelids flickered like he was asleep.

Harper nudged his shoulder, and he gasped. She shrieked, falling onto her backside. His eyes opened. Light faded from his irises as they returned to normal dilation.

"What the hell, Tyson?"

He looked from the knife to Harper. "I think I know where to find Becca and…"

That name again. It sent the strangest clenching sensation down Harper's spine in a wave, and she shivered. "How?"

"The knife apparently gives me visions. Recent development." One he wasn't a fan of, based on his strained expression. He slid the curved blade into a velvety black pouch and zipped the pack. "I've had a few. Visions, I mean. Some of them are strange, like I'm another person in another land. I see the Northern Lights."

"Is that what you saw? Becca and…?" That name she couldn't hear pestered the back of her mind. Why couldn't she remember it. "You saw them? There?"

He clicked his tongue. "I saw a raven cawing on a rock, and a serpent coiled beneath it. I don't know what that means. But I also saw mountains standing like an open gate to this wilderness…I have a strong feeling that north is the direction we need to go."

Harper studied his face. "You don't like it."

He nodded, jaw tightening. "It's new. Frightening."

Harper couldn't keep the stupid grin off her face. "*That's* why you helped me! You're one of us, now. They wouldn't want you working for the camp, they would want you *in* the camp if you were found out! Hell. Do you have any witch blood?"

Tyson clenched his fists, then released them, flexing his fingers. "It's strange that I never knew before. I mean, shouldn't there have been a sign earlier, in my childhood?"

"There might have been. You just weren't looking. Or maybe it's something that was meant to wake up later when the right conditions were met. That knife is strange. Have you had it all this time?"

He considered, then shook his head. "Aberration Management is supposed to be based in an isolated, unknown location. Maybe Montana?"

Back to talking about Becca and the other guy. Harper eyed him, but let it go. If he wanted to tell her how he got his supernatural abilities, he would. She took the edge of one wing in her hand, plucking at a fluffy down feather that stuck out from beneath the larger ones.

If Tyson's cousin was headed to another state, how could Harper and Tyson get to them? Harper could fly, but not while carrying Tyson. Not without resting frequently, and that would make them vulnerable to capture.

The wheels in Harper's head turned and, glancing at Tyson, she could tell he did the same, though whether they were thinking along the same lines or not she couldn't tell. She wasn't a mind reader.

A boot scraped the rock behind them, and they pivoted to face a familiar bald man.

"You again," Harper stood, wings flaring. A protective urge surged in her, and when Tyson tried to stand next to her, her wing flicked into him, knocking him back a step.

The man held up his hands. "Just a messenger this time." He reached out with an envelope, handing it to Harper. He shook it when she didn't immediately take it. "Come on, it won't bite." He grinned, front teeth baring literal vampiric fangs.

Harper snatched the envelope and ripped open the flap. Tyson ducked under her wing and peered at the folded paper with her. There was a plastic credit card inside with a pink sticky note.

Cheers.

A single word on the sticky note. No name. Harper flipped the credit card over, searching, but it was one of those generic, pre-loaded cards.

"Is this from Lilith?"

The man shrugged, shoving his hands into his pockets. "It's yours. And I'm supposed to tell you that if you ever need help, you're welcome here. Just show up at the boundary and we'll let you in."

Let them in? "Wait, does that mean she's closing up the camp again? I thought she said they would be free."

"They are free. Free from the tyranny of those two you offed. Listen, you have what you need. Get outta here before the Stiffs swarm the place. There's been a murder, or didn't you hear?" He gave a wicked grin, and his body blurred. One moment he stood in front of them, the next he was a smeared line zipping among the trees. Super speed. Harper would feel more envious if she weren't so confused.

"She *paid* you?"

"I-I wasn't expecting this." Harper held the card daintily, staring at it. "Wonder how much is on it?"

"Harper!" Tyson's voice rose in pitch. "You can't accept that. It's blood money."

"It's not a bribe if I didn't know she would give it to me. That's not why I did it," Harper snapped back.

"Then why did you?" He crossed his arms over his chest.

Harper ignored him, shoving the card into the back pocket of her jeans. "Come on. We don't have time for this." She walked ahead a few feet, expecting him to follow. When he didn't, she spun around. A few drops of rain pricked her skin.

Tyson gave her a critical gaze. "You know she probably has a plan. She won't stop with a single camp."

He was right. Lilith had said that her coven sisters outside of Camp Silver Lake were doing the same. Did they have orbs, too, or was there only one? Harper kept silent, turning back toward the tree line. Her hand throbbed, a deep thrumming ache from the palm. She flipped it over, staring at the glowing purple 'X' on her palm.

"You all right?" Tyson asked, walking up beside her. Harper closed her hand in a tight fist to hide the mark.

"Yeah," she lied. Her feet moved forward of their own accord. "Listen, whatever Lilith's planning, it's not our problem anymore. We need to focus on finding your cousin." And what's-his-name. *Damn it.* Why couldn't she remember his name? Her spine trembled oddly at the thought of Becca's companion.

"Yeah. Maybe you're right." Tyson squinted, looking forward with one hand gripping his backpack, the other dangling by its thumb from his pocket. If it weren't for Harper's wings and Tyson's missing shoes, anyone looking at them might think they were two hikers out for the day. A couple enjoying nature together.

Harper buried the thought as memories of Fletcher crashed down on her. His earnest smile. His brilliant wings. A kiss on a cliff.

No, Tyson and Harper were not a couple. Not human, not paranormal. Just a couple of lost souls waiting for their turn to die.

**Keep reading for an excerpt of Wings of Rebellion book 2:
Serpent Cursed!**

EXCERPT FROM SERPENT CURSED: WINGS OF REBELLION BOOK 2

TYSON

A WEEK AGO, IF someone told Tyson he'd be hitchhiking with a wanted murderer and potential demi-god, he would have laughed in their face. And yet there he stood, thumb up as he squinted in the sun on the side of the road in Nowhere, Oregon.

He sweated up a storm, the moisture mixing with the grime of several days of hitchhiking.

"That one will stop," Harper muttered, angling her head and pasting on a wide smile. "Keep your thumb out."

He obliged, straightening his wilting arm. "Why the crazed look?"

Her smile faltered a bit before firming back up. "Looking human and friendly gets better results. Don't want to look too grim or they'll drive by. Our appearance is bad enough without making them think we're homeless. Smile."

Tyson took a breath in and stretched his mouth in a passable smile. Hunger and heat wore on him, having hiked through the woods for a few hours before reaching the road without any water.

The RV coming up the winding road gave a honk and passed. Tyson dropped his arm and groaned, dejected. Harper swatted his arm. "Stand up!"

Behind them, the bus-like RV had slowed and pulled off the road, parking in the grassy gravel strip next to the pavement. It was cream with strips of faded pink and green color wrapping around the outside, and it looked pretty beat up. Harper headed toward it, gesturing for Tyson to follow.

A woman stepped out from the side of the RV, letting the little white door slam behind her.

"Oh, you poor dears!" She spread her thick arms wide as if she would run and embrace them. Tyson really hoped she wouldn't. Obvious sweat marks stained her blue flannel shirt around her armpits.

Who wore flannel in the summer?

Tyson glanced at Harper, who had a sheepish smile so out of place on her usually scowling face that he actually did a double-take. She had to be acting, right?

"Thank goodness you stopped," Harper said. "We've been hiking all day trying to catch a ride." She elbowed Tyson.

"Yes, thank you." What else was he supposed to say?

The woman beamed. "Well, my mother taught me to never pass by someone in need." She walked up to them and put a hand on each of their shoulders, looking back and forth between them and tsking in a motherly way. "My, my. You look like you've been through the wringer. Let's get you inside before we get some liquid sunshine." Her chin jerked to the right and

Tyson followed the gesture, noticing a bank of darker clouds. The morning's overcast skies had cleared up for a few hours, but apparently, mother nature was back for more.

"I'm Wendy, and my husband's Fred." Wendy gestured toward the RV door. "He's driving, you'll meet him in a moment. Who did you say you were?"

"T—"

"Trevor and Jessie," Harper cut in, flashing Tyson a glare.

Right. Fugitives. Tyson clamped his mouth shut and let her take over. Harper had more experience with this sort of thing, no need to get it more mixed up than it had to be. He tried to focus on the story she fed the woman so he could recall the details later.

"You know, we were just on a hike as part of our honeymoon, and we got robbed, if you can believe that! Right on the trail. Thank goodness we were together, and that they weren't violent. They took our keys and our car with most of our belongings."

Wendy's hand dropped from the RV's door handle. "On your honeymoon? Bless you!" She pressed her hand to her chest and teared up. "I'm so glad we stopped. Fred!" she hollered suddenly. Tyson jumped. He gripped the straps of his backpack as the woman flung the RV door open and stormed up the steps. She gestured for them to follow her inside.

"Can you believe these poor dears!" she said as Tyson and Harper climbed the stairs, the RV swaying a bit with the movement. Wendy shook her head. "And you didn't want to stop. They're on their honeymoon!"

"Don't see why we have to ruin it." Fred grumbled the words, but his eyes twinkled. Tyson liked Fred instantly. Fred had a similar squat, wrinkled face as his wife and a mop of grey hair.

Wendy brushed her wispy brown hair out of her eyes, chest still heaving from her charge into the RV. "Where can we take you two? You'll want to report this. Police station?"

"No!" Tyson and Harper blurted together.

"We mean, no thank you," Harper said, glaring in Tyson's direction.

Tyson gave her a desperate "Now what?" look. Harper bit her lip, which somehow changed from suspicious into cute.

Wendy and Fred stared at them.

Tyson waited for Harper to say something, but instead she turned and burrowed her forehead into his shoulder, acting too upset to talk. Tyson patted her shoulder awkwardly. He cleared his throat. "We don't want our entire trip to be ruined by this. If you could get us to the next town, we'll find a hotel and make a call from there. Unless you have a cellphone?"

He winced as he said the words. If they did have one, he'd have to pretend to make a call. Harper's hand gripped his forearm, fingernails digging in.

Wendy frowned. "Oh no, dear. Sorry, but we don't believe in that kind of gadgetry. We'll be happy to take you to the next town, though. It's a few hours." She waved toward the table in the cramped kitchen area. "You just get yourselves settled on those benches and Fred and I will consult the map."

Harper sniffed and turned her head to smile at Wendy. Rubbing her face on Tyson's shoulder had given her a reddened face, almost like she had, in fact, started crying. Tyson didn't know whether to admire or be concerned at her skill.

Harper tugged on his arm, pulling him toward the back of the RV. "Come on, sweetheart." She growled the last word with a fierceness that Tyson thought would surely blow their cover, but Wendy only laughed and exclaimed about young love. Fred grumbled under his breath.

Harper sat on the vinyl seat, pulling down a table folded against the wall. Tyson moved to sit next to her, but she slapped a hand on the vacant spot and gave him a strained smile.

"Tired, pumpkin?" Tyson said sarcastically. He took the opposite bench, clasping his fingers on the table and leaned in. "You make us look like we had an arranged marriage. Would it kill you to act like you like me?"

"It might," Harper replied. "Look, I got us a ride, okay? If I'd left it up to you we would still be wandering in the woods."

Tyson watched her face. There were streaks of dirt on her cheeks and dark circles under her eyes. Her short black hair was tousled. Her hands trembled. Tyson reached out and placed his hand on top of hers to offer a bit of empathy. Harper stared at their hands, rigid. After a moment, she slid her hand out from under his and put it in her lap. She focused on the road moving past the window outside.

"When we get to the next town I can check for any paranormal contacts there." Harper leaned on the table and it tilted alarmingly. She quickly sat back.

"You know that many?" Tyson's behind slid a little as the RV served lanes. He eyed the seatbelt buckle dangling next to him. Something about the way it hung told him it was broken.

"No, but I know how to look for them. We need a ride that can get us over the state line."

"And all the way to Alaska," Tyson finished.

Harper glanced at him. "How sure are you that we need to go there?"

Tyson poked at the chipping surface of the table. "Not at all, to be honest. These... visions. They're confusing, more than anything. I don't know why I'm having them, except they started when I got that knife from my Nana."

Harper closed her eyes. "Remind me again what you saw, exactly?"

Tyson thought the images would have faded, but as he spoke they showed up clearly in his mind's eye. "A raven on a rock, cawing. A serpent coiled beneath it. A mountain standing like an open gate to a wilderness. And just the feeling that it's north."

Harper tapped her finger on the table. "Raven, serpent, and a mountain passage?" She frowned. "Do you think the raven could represent my people? And the snake…danger? Or a threat?"

"Are you dears hungry?" Wendy called from the front. She lumbered toward the small kitchen and wrestled with the door of a small fridge. It looked to have plastic clips holding it shut, but they refused to budge. She finally gave up, red-faced and sweatier than before, and pulled open a cupboard with a jerk. After a moment of rummaging, she pulled out a jar of peanut butter and a slightly squashed loaf of bread.

"No jam, I'm afraid. And the honey's out." She plunked the two items on the table and opened them, placing the bread on napkins she fished out of the cupboard above Tyson's head. She then started going at them with a table knife she had pulled out of a drawer without even having to turn around. "At least you won't starve on my watch." She chuckled.

In such close proximity, the faint stench Tyson had noticed upon entering the RV intensified. A cloyingly-sweet smell, like rotting fruit, clung to the inside of his nostrils, thick and pungent. He choked down a new wave each time Wendy's flabby arms moved. He put a hand beneath his nose and tried not to gag.

Harper's entire face went white when the woman shifted close to her. She wiped at her nose, then dropped her hand and smiled at Wendy with clenched teeth, who smiled back and plunked a chunky-peanut butter sandwich down. A few quick strokes and she had another one. She slid them in front of her guests.

"Now, I know we have some bottled sweet tea somewhere. I'll rustle it up and be right back." Wendy's smile stretched across her face, and she stood there with her hands folded in front of her, as if waiting for something.

Tyson managed to gasp out a strained, "Thank you."

Harper nodded, her lips drawn in a thin smile. Wendy picked up her own sandwich and took a bite, then lumbered to the cupboards above the sofa near the front of the RV in search of sweet tea.

Harper released her breath. "In the name of all... how can a woman smell so bad?" She stage-whispered at Tyson.

Tyson shushed her. It didn't seem like either of their hosts had heard her over the rumble of the engine, but he didn't want to take any chances. "That's rude. You know, they might not have a shower. And if they're only around each other all the time, well, they're probably used to it." He prodded the sandwich in front of him. "Do you think this is safe to eat?"

"She ate some. So probably. Honestly, I'm too hungry to care." Harper took a huge bite of her sandwich, locking her mouth up with the gummy peanut butter. It didn't stop her from talking, but Tyson couldn't understand a word.

"What?" he asked, taking a more reasonable bite out of his sandwich.

Harper scraped the roof of her mouth with her finger, making little choking noises.

Very attractive. Tyson wanted to roll his eyes, but he withheld the urge.

"Nothing human has that smell, Tyson." Harper set her sandwich down. She steepled her fingers and pointed them at him. "Can you think of any magical creatures that might? We need to figure out what we just walked into."

"For the record, hitchhiking was your idea," he pointed out after he finished chewing.

"And your idea was...?" Harper cocked her head.

Tyson took another bite of sandwich in response.

"Ah, lovers' quarrels," Wendy said. Both Tyson and Harper jumped as the woman appeared at their tableside again. She held two glass bottles of iced tea in her hands. "They're warm, but better than nothing. Enjoy!" She folded her hands again.

"Thank you." Tyson reached for a bottle.

Wendy stared, unblinking, at Harper, who froze mid-bite and glanced at the woman out of the corner of her eye. "Oh, of course. Thank you." Wendy turned without comment and walked toward the front of the RV, sitting next to Fred. Harper eyed her sandwich again. "Well, that was weird."

"Weird for her to insist on manners? First you think body odor is cause for alarm, now this? You're paranoid." Tyson managed to untwist the bottle and took a chug of the tepid, sicky sweet drink. It was barely tolerable, but better than choking down a dry peanut butter sandwich.

"Something isn't right about her," Harper whispered loudly. "They're too dumpy to be vampires, werewolves would be weird, but I guess believable. I don't believe for a second she's a witch, there's nothing to indicate that."

"Maybe it's just her. The man might not be anything peculiar."

"Do you enjoy disagreeing with me?" Harper glared at Tyson. "I'm starting to think that's all our conversations ever are."

Tyson took another sip of his drink. "No, I think you jump to conclusions too fast, that you act rashly. Take some time to think about the things we know for sure. Decide whether you will act and how. Slow down, before someone ends up dead."

Harper blinked at him.

"Just a suggestion," he added lamely.

Harper placed her hands on the table, palms down. Tyson's skin prickled at the dead-calm in her eyes. "You're saying I acted 'rashly' when I used the orb?"

No point hiding it. "Yes. You did. You could have waited an hour. Becca and Quinn would have arrived and taken you from the camp, and you would have been none the wiser."

"And I would have left everyone else to continue on as they had. Trapped and brainwashed into believing in your damned system like Fletcher. Look where that got him." The RV filled with silence. Her voice had escalated at the end, and there was no doubt Wendy and Fred had heard, but to their credit the older couple kept their eyes forward and didn't say anything.

Tyson closed his eyes. Fletcher had been his first solo client at Camp Silver Lake. Did Harper think she was the only one grieving his death? He dropped his voice, hoping Harper and her temper would get the hint. "I knew Fletcher for two years. You knew him for a week. Don't pretend you're hurting more than I am."

Harper's entire body tensed like a spring ready to release. She took a fierce bite of her sandwich and chewed viciously, folding her arms and staring out the window. She didn't look back at Tyson, not even a glance. Bite, chew, stare.

Tyson focused on his own food, but his appetite was gone. He finished, more out of desire to not appear rude to Wendy's hospitality, and he drank the too-sweet tea. By the time he finished, Harper's rock hard exterior had mellowed slightly, her shoulders relaxed, her face screwing up with each sip of her tea. He didn't try to break their silence.

After a few miles of passing scenery, Harper reached a hand across to him and leaned in. "Don't think I've forgiven you," she said, "but we're being watched, and we need to look like we're making up." She pasted on a smile so endearing Tyson nearly choked. He let her take his hand and she rubbed small circles with her thumb. He leaned in, and Harper kissed him, then sat back on the bench.

It was just a simple peck on his cheek, but Tyson felt Wendy's eyes boring into the back of his head. She coughed a little.

"No need to be awkward around us, dears. We expect to see a bit of kissing. It's the best way to make up." Her tone increased in pitch, clearly angling for Tyson to respond somehow. If he was reading her correctly, a peck on the cheek wouldn't do it.

Tyson leaned across the table and ran his fingers through Harper's hair, feeling the new growth like fuzz at the base of her neck. His thumb stroked her cheek. It felt awkward right after an argument, the air still heated between them.

Harper cocked an eyebrow, either in a warning or confusion, he wasn't quite sure.

Tyson swallowed. He leaned all the way across the table, bringing her head toward his, and pressed his lips against hers.

The soft kiss lingered. Harper's palm rested on his left cheek, the side facing the window, and she flicked him.

The sharp sting of her fingernail broke the spell and Tyson sat back down. Harper smiled that fake, sweet smile.

The reality hit Tyson like a ton of bricks. His cheeks flushed. What had he been thinking? He cleared his throat. Harper gave him a look halfway between murderous and admiring.

"Didn't know you had that in you," she muttered as she picked up her tea and took a swallow. Her fingers tapped on the table, and her head darted from side to side, jittery and nervous.

"A lot of things about me would surprise you." Tyson put his hand over her fingers to hide them from the couple at the front. "It wouldn't do for us to get kicked out now. We need this ride."

"Not sure it's worth the trouble," Harper said shortly. She pulled her hand from under his and stood, making her way to the front of the moving RV to start a conversation with Wendy, who seemed all-too happy to oblige.

Maybe it was for the best. He needed a moment to think. Everything was happening too fast for him to make clear decisions. He should never have left Camp Silver Lake. He could have told authorities he wasn't involved in the deaths of Violet and James. But after Violet attacked him and sold Harper out, could he have stayed even if they had lived?

One thing for certain, things would not improve with Lilith in control. That witch had put Harper up to using the orb. She had known it would incapacitate the leaders of the camp, and she had been the one who used magic to bring them down from the window of the lodge. What would Lilith do with the remaining camp residents? Would she give them more freedom, as she had implied to Harper? Or were her plans more nefarious?

And would Tyson ever return to find out?

A deep grinding sound interrupted Tyson's thought process. The RV veered to the shoulder and jerked to a halt. Fred shouted curses as he wrenched at the gear shift, turned off the key, and tried turning the engine back over. It shuddered twice, then died with a depressed hissing sound.

Fred slapped the wheel. "Come on, you overgrown four wheeler. Not now!"

Wendy patted his shoulder. "There now, Fred. Bessie isn't what she used to be. We knew this was coming." She turned to Harper. "I'm just sorry we've gotten you two all mixed up in it." Her look of sympathy melted into a strange smile. "Luckily, we have more than enough room for you to spend the night. We're still an hour or so out of town, but we can enjoy supper and games while Fred gives Bessie a look around inside." Wendy tilted her head at Harper, who gave her a nervous smile.

Harper jabbed her thumb over her shoulder. "It's still light out. We don't want to get in your way. I'm sure we can find someone else to take us to town. You've been more than kind."

Wendy's smile widened further. She glanced over her shoulder at Tyson. "Your man will agree with me. You were lucky we picked you up and not someone with worse intentions. I insist that you stay and enjoy our hospitality. My mama wouldn't stand to hear otherwise, and I won't either."

Tyson swallowed. Wendy's persistence made him uncomfortable, but some women couldn't seem to help being nosy. Was there such a thing as being too nice? Tyson nodded to Harper, who gave him a wide-eyed, panicked expression, but he just folded his arms and smiled reassuringly. Unless Harper could give him a good reason not to trust the over-endearing Wendy and her husband Fred, it looked like they could be staying the night in Bessie the RV.

∽

Continue the story in book 2: Serpent Cursed, available on Amazon and in Kindle Unlimited now!

SPECIAL THANKS

Deep gratitude to the numerous people who watched my kids so I could make this book happen. Special thanks to Vanessa, Lynette, Rachel W., Annalise, Aerin, Dana, and Karen for the time they gave me.

Thanks to my mom for bouncing ideas and talking book marketing even though it's not your jam. You help me stay sane.

A million thanks to my writing group, the Brambles Girls, for the hours they've spent reading, critiquing, answering my questions, settling my fears, and helping me become a better writer and person. You're all beautiful, and you deserve to have all of your dreams come true. Thank you for helping me with mine. Thank you, Melissa, for being my book doctor. You're magical.

Of course, this would all be just a dream if it weren't for the support of my husband. Tyler, you inspire me, put up with me, encourage me, and love me. You're everything I could hope for and more.

Bree Moore lives in Iowa with her husband, seven children, and two cats. When she's not busy homeschooling or folding laundry, she sneaks off to write more fantasy.

Bree writes urban and epic fantasy to explore different worlds with amazing creatures and magic systems. She enjoys giving her readers a story that is both entertaining and emotional, with a healthy dose of romance. When she's not writing, Bree can be found foraging for edible plants, watching fantasy shows and movies, or hanging out with her husband and kids.

Published works include: *The Shadowed Minds* series, the *Lost Souls* series, and *Shadows of Camelot* series. She's currently working on *The Plague King Chronicles*.

Visit www.authorbreemoore.com for a FREE fantasy book!

tiktok.com/@breenovels

instagram.com/breenovels

<u>Shadows of Camelot</u>
The Lady's Last Song
The Queen's Quiet End

<u>Shadowed Minds Series</u>
Prequel: Thief of Lies
Thief of Magic
Thief of Aether
Thief of Bones

<u>Wings of Rebellion Series</u>
Prequel: Raven Blood
Raven Born
Serpent Cursed
Coven Bound
Serpent Turned
Siren Called
Rebel Sworn

<u>The Plague King Chronicles</u>
The Keeper of the Well
The Quill and the Vial
The Arrow and the Ivy
<u>Of Dusk and Dawn Collection</u>
Sacrifice for the Standing Stones
Vows Beneath the Frozen Stars

www.ingramcontent.com/pod-product-compliance
Lightning Source LLC
Chambersburg PA
CBHW020332120726
47904CB00002B/382